PILLARS OF SIX

KELLY ST. CLARE

PILLARS OF SIX

Dynami Sea

N

W   E

S

Exosian Realm

Life is never stagnant for those who continually grow.

ONE

Ebba sat across the bay, watching as her fathers readied *Felicity* for sailing. It was early morning, but she hadn't slept.

Her fathers had argued all night as she lay wide awake in her hut. Eventually, she got sick of listening and walked around the inlet of their hidden Zol sanctuary to sit in silence.

Tears dripped onto her knees, and Sally, her companion through the night, made a sad whirring sound, hugging her face. "Why does he have to leave, Sal?" she asked, sniffing hard.

Sally hugged her harder. Slightly too hard, if the honest truth be told. The wind sprite was fiercely strong. Her strength didn't really make sense with her being so tiny, but she also glowed, so the why behind her super strength had been thrown into the pile labeled *magic*, along with all the other strange things Ebba had encountered.

Somewhere in the midst of all those strange encounters, their crew made a promise to Cosmo. And a promise was a promise. That was why the pirates of *Felicity* didn't make them very often.

They'd offered to drop Cosmo at Kentro, so he could make

his way back to the mainland. Yesterday, the Exosian took them up on the offer.

Cosmo leaving didn't feel right; he belonged here. "Sal, am I only thinkin' o' myself?" Ebba asked. Sally knew Cosmo's father was King Montcroix. Ebba had to tell someone after the truth was revealed, or her guts would've burst out.

"I just think he'll be happier here," Ebba continued. "King Montcroix be evil, everyone is knowin' that. He won't help Cosmo, but *I* can help Cosmo get used to havin' one arm. I just need more time."

Sally pulled back and shrugged. The glowing wind sprite flew over to her bottle of brandy and took a swig. The magical creature had started on grog, but recently moved to stronger stuff. Sally lowered the bottle and shrugged again, pouting her lips.

Ebba screwed up her face, trying to decipher the message. There was a bit of a language barrier between them. Which was why Ebba had told her the truth about Cosmo.

"Mistress Fairisles," someone called softly.

She jumped but recognizing Cosmo's voice, remained staring across the turquoise inlet at *Felicity*.

"We'll be leaving soon. Your fathers sent me to get you."

She didn't budge. "I ain't goin'. Tell them I'll wait here. The voyage be foolish. *Malice* is after the *purgium* and the *dynami*. Ye're puttin' everyone in danger." Ebba latched on to Locks' argument from the night before.

Truthfully, Ebba didn't even really care about the healing and power cylinders falling into the hands of *Malice*'s crew, but she did care about losing her innards in a forced exchange.

Cosmo neared her, hovering a few paces away. "If it wasn't so important to me, I wouldn't ask. You know I wouldn't."

"Aye, well I thought I knew ye, *Prince Caspian*, but I didn't. So how do I know what ye would and wouldn't do?"

Sally took another swig of brandy, eyes darting between them.

He scratched his jaw, saying quietly, "I deserved that."

The mainlander had changed since losing his arm.

He didn't ask so many questions anymore. He went off by himself for long walks around Zol, the cliff-bordered inlet that was their secret sanctuary. Some days, he just slept, and sometimes a whole three days passed without him looking at her with that intense look he used to always hold in his amber eyes.

She missed her friend, even if he was a *prince* friend.

Ebba didn't know what the rules on being friends with a prince were. She'd been raised by pirates and lived with pirates. Despite being of tribal descent, Ebba might still be a pirate herself. She didn't know what to do with his royal confession. On one hand, she had to be nice to him because he'd lost an arm. On the other hand, he'd lied to their crew about being the son of their enemy, King Montcroix—hunter of pirates and sovereign of the navy that patrolled the Caspian Sea.

Ebba supposed their crew probably would've marooned Cosmo if he'd admitted it from the start. . . .

The result of all this thinking—which was far more thinking than she liked to do, as a rule—was that she still didn't know what to do with the information. So, she'd kept calling him Cosmo and decided to pretend he wasn't the prince of Exosia and that half of the ocean wasn't renamed at his birth. Her fathers would kill him if they found out, and Ebba couldn't trust herself to keep saying Cosmo if she started thinking of him as Caspian in her skull.

"I hope you'll reconsider, Mistress Fairisles." Cosmo finally broke the silence again. "I'd like to spend as much time with you as possible before we dock at Kentro."

Guilt stirred her insides. The trip to Kentro was eight days with a good wind. If she was honest with herself, the thought of taking a small trip out of this inlet was appealing. Deep down, she wanted to see as much of Cosmo as she could, too.

"Why are ye leavin'?" she asked, silently adding *me* on the end.

He heard it anyway. Cosmo sucked in a breath. "You think I'm leaving you?" He closed the gap and wrapped his arm around her shoulders. His hold was light, but warmth seeped into her skin. After what they'd been through on Pleo, the action felt natural.

"It's because of you that I don't wish to leave," he said. "What made you think that?"

She shrugged.

"Is it the . . . situation with your fathers?"

'Situation' was a polite way of saying her fathers had lied to her for nearly eighteen years about their merciless pasts and her origins. "Aye, I be supposin' so. Things've been strange-like since that all happened. I don't want to forget and pretend it away this time. I ain't even sure I could. Everythin' feels off-kilter."

Ebba scowled at the water lapping gently onto the white sand shore.

Caspian nodded. "If it helps, I know your fathers are struggling too. I caught Barrels reading a book yesterday with the title, *How to Raise a Child at Sea.*"

She scrunched her nose, and pushed back her black dreadlocks. "Why do they need that? They already raised me."

A smile softened his face. Russet curls framed his high forehead and square jaw, and in that moment, a hint of boyishness entered the quirk of his lips, and a familiar light sparked in his amber eyes. Ebba's heart squeezed. She didn't know how to make him like he used to be—alive, interested, and passionate. Peg-leg said trying was pointless and that Cosmo was changed now, but that he'd get better in time. Ebba didn't like the thought of Cosmo changing if that change was for the worse. Though maybe not altering was impossible with everything he'd gone through.

What she'd put him through.

Ebba was the one who'd held the *purgium* over the black taint spreading to his heart. The *purgium* had demanded a sacrifice. Cosmo didn't have an arm, and it was her fault. Her fault he so rarely smiled anymore.

He watched her, the quirk on his lips fading. "I believe, Mistress Fairisles, it's because you've never given your fathers trouble before."

"I hid a wind sprite in the hold because I wanted a pet."

"Yes, but that's normal. Kind of. Well, if the pet was a kitten and not an alcoholic. Your fathers' struggle has more to do with what happened on Pleo. I guess the same struggle as yours: how do you move forward from here?"

"Aye, ye're likely right." Caspian was soft and pretty distant of late, but he had a whole bunch of mangoes in his skull-basket. Ebba did want to move forward.

From her first memories, life had been just her and her six fathers. Seven pirates sailing the navy-free part of the Caspian Sea in their ship, *Felicity*. She'd assumed one of them was her real father, but asking which one had always seemed pointless because Ebba loved them all the same.

The issue wasn't just that they'd lied to her about who they'd been, and who she was. The issue was that Ebba had always been a pirate. She'd thought that she'd always *be* a pirate —that she'd die a pirate. Now, her place on *Felicity* didn't seem as secure. The sense that everything before the revelation was a pretty lie kept nagging at her.

Ebba was born to the tribe, but raised as a pirate. What did that make her?

She certainly hadn't belonged with the Pai Marie. They

were wise and all, but they had a warped idea of how to survive. *Things weren't simple any longer.* That wouldn't bother Ebba so much if she could handle it in the normal way, by pretending. And the inability to pretend made her feel even *less* like a pirate because a pirate wasn't supposed to care about the why.

Ebba sighed heavily, realizing her anger at Cosmo for leaving was really not about the prince at all. When it came to the prince, all she felt was sadness that he'd soon be gone and that she'd lose her only friend. And sadness that he was still hurting in his heart after losing his arm.

Cosmo had changed. The pirates of *Felicity* had changed. Seemed like they'd both need to deal with that.

"Tell me why ye're leavin', Caspi— Cosmopian? I mean, Cosmo," she blurted.

"Exactly what I said, Mistress Fairisles. I have things I need to fix. Life as a pirate, illuminating as it has proven to be, has also been fraught with danger, and I worry that if I do not see my father now, I may not get a chance." He let his right arm fall, staring vacantly at the limb.

"I also mean to inform my father of *Malice*'s presence in these waters. Pockmark attacked a navy ship, and I must seek retribution for the crew and their families." He paused. "I hope to make the seas safe for your crew once again. Pockmark will hound *Felicity* until the *purgium* and *dynami* are in his hands."

She turned to look at him for the first time. "Why would ye be doin' that?"

He smiled at her. "When your crew took me in after Neos, I was saved from a terrible fate, Mistress Fairisles. I am certain the *Malice* crew would have recognized me. Jagger certainly did. And then there are the dangers your crew recently went through to save me from my tainted wound. I would have been a slave to darkness if not for your actions."

Yet he'd still lost an arm. Ebba startled, though. "Ye think that's why Jagger hates ye? Because he recognized ye?" Jagger had hated Cosmo from the first time he'd seen him.

Cosmo shrugged his right shoulder. "I imagine so. I'm son to the man who is renowned for hunting pirates. That's ample enough reason for hatred. I thank the powers that be daily I fell into the hands of your crew and not theirs. It is a debt I can never fully repay, but I'm going to try." He squared his shoulders. "I'm a prince, and I'm in a position to ensure justice is served. *Malice* cannot fight the entire navy," Cosmo said, intensity returning to his amber eyes. "I won't sit back and do nothing after seeing the things I have."

"I thought ye said yer friends wouldn't be believin' ye about the magic."

His jaw tightened. "No, I don't expect they will. I don't plan to tell them any of that. My father hates pirates; he'll need no more excuse to engage in war with *Malice* after I tell him of what they did to his navy ship and his son."

In that order? Ebba shared a long look with Sally. The sprite shrugged and grimaced, drawing a circle in the sand with her toe.

Nope, no idea what that meant.

Ebba slid off the rock and tilted her head to look up at the prince. He smelled like sandalwood and shoe polish. "Do ye really need to do this, Cosmo? I wish ye would stay. I don't know what I'll do without ye."

He took her hand and laid a gentle kiss on the back of it. "What ye always do." He mocked her with a smile that displayed his dimple again. "Barge through life in your vibrant and unique way."

"Even if I'm pretendin' everything be okay?" she asked, blinking away the burning in her eyes.

A wrinkle appeared between his brows. "Mistress Fairisles, I can see each of your fathers in you. You've picked up traits from them all. You also cope in the only way you know how. You certainly aren't the only person here pretending."

She stared at him with wide eyes, not trusting herself to speak.

"Everything will work out, Mistress Fairisles. You love your fathers, and they love you. You'll reach an understanding simply because you each want to." He kissed her hand again. On the same spot.

Heat filled her cheeks. How long had they been holding hands? She pulled away, resisting the temptation to rub at the hot spot where his lips just were. Flustered, Ebba said, "We have a week until we reach Kentro, Caspian. There be no need for goodbyes just yet."

"No," he agreed, adding, "but we *will* need to say goodbye."

She sniffed hard, leading the way back around the inlet to *Felicity*. "Aye, Cosmo. I know. And if ye need to do this for yerself, I'll try not to fuss."

Ebba hoped she could stick to that when the time came to part ways.

TWO

Ebba sat out on the tip of the bowsprit, holding on to the long wooden beam with her thighs, relishing the feel of the seawater spraying over her face. She let her head fall back, hearing the beads in her hair rattle. She had two dreadlocks filled with beads and another started. The bottom of her dreads tickled underneath her ribs, and Ebba lifted a hand to push her green bandana back into place over her hairline. Her yellowed tunic and slops were soaked from the spray, but the water dripped off her tight black-laced jerkin onto the tops of her thighs. A sheen covered her brown skin from her forehead to the tips of her bare and grubby toes.

Ebba felt a true pull to the sea. Whatever she was now, that remained true.

For as long as she could recall, a pirate life was the only life she'd considered. In the last few months, so many things had happened to weaken that truth her head was spinning. Was Ebba limiting herself by not exploring other facets of herself? The villagers on Neos were slaughtered by Ladon simply because they never left their homes. What if they'd considered a new and different life? Were the limitations she'd created for herself the reason her sense of self shattered so easily on Pleo?

Yet Ebba might be content to return to that single-minded focus, if not for the Earth Mother's words. She'd said Ebba had a fracture in her soul that had to be fixed, or all would fail—whatever that meant. Ebba suspected the crack was due to not knowing who she was anymore. And probably because of how rocky things were with her fathers.

Cosmo was right. She'd learned to pretend from her fathers, but now Ebba was so angry all the time pretending wasn't working. She couldn't go on this way, hurting her fathers and hurting herself in the process. There was only one place to start that she could think of. After Pleo, her fathers had made a promise to tell her everything about their lives prior to raising her.

A promise was a promise, after all.

The desire to ask had eluded her until now. She'd been too furious to listen, and too upset over Cosmo's troubles. But the sea had given her courage. Maybe by listening to their stories, she'd be able to figure out a few things.

The southern part of the Caspian Sea was surprisingly calm today. The black waters were renowned for large swells and chaotic winds, and seeing as there weren't any islands beyond Zol, none of the other numerous pirate ships in the Free Seas, the area not monitored by navy men, ventured this far. Of all the places to drop Cosmo off, the westernmost island, Kentro, was the safest. Neos was overrun by Ladon and his snakes. To go to Maltu again was far too risky, though it was nearly as close to the mainland as Kentro.

So, Kentro it was.

She sighed, tightening her resolve, and on her butt, began to shuffle backward on the beam. She reached down to pat the mermaid figurehead on the way—fierce bad luck to neglect a figurehead.

The cedar wood of the main deck gave a familiar thud when she jumped down off the bulwark. Pillage, the black ship cat, hissed at her.

Ebba hissed back, and the cat slunk into the shadows of the closest barrel.

"Mistress Fairisles?" called Cosmo. He sounded a scant bit harassed.

Cosmo was engaged in a conversation with Locks, the carpenter and sometimes surgeon of their crew. That explained the look of desperation on the prince's face.

She crossed to where they stood under the mast, eavesdropping.

"Her eyes were always too close together for my likin'," Locks was saying. "Her body be ill-propor'tioned, and she gets an evil look sometimes—"

Ebba snorted. Locks was talking about Verity—the soothsayer he 'hated' who rejected him eighteen years before.

"Ye mean when her eyes go black and red lava cracks appear all over her face?" she asked her father.

"Eh?" Locks asked, glancing at her. "Oh, that, too, I s'pose." He took a deep breath to continue, and Cosmo closed his eyes.

She'd save him. Leaning against a barrel, Ebba spoke. "Tell me o' yer past, Locks."

His mouth shut with a click of his back teeth. "Huh?"

"Ye heard me," she said, glaring. "Ye said ye'd tell me everythin' about the bad stuff ye did."

He gulped and took a nervous step back. "I ain't rememberin'. . . ."

No way was he getting out of this. Ebba rounded on him. "Ye promised, Locks. A promise be a promise."

Cosmo crossed to stand beside her, and Locks scowled his way. He darted his blazing emerald eye around the boat, but the rest of her fathers seemed to have made themselves scarce, either during his talk about how much he didn't like Verity, or upon hearing her demand. Wiley buggers.

The waves slapped against the ship in the heavy silence as Ebba stared at her father.

He heaved a great sigh, hooking both hands in his belt. "I thought for sure ye'd start with Barrels."

She *had* planned to start with Barrels, but Locks didn't need to know that. "Out with it. Tell me all the bad stuff."

Locks held out his hands, calloused from rope and tools. "It ain't that easy, lass. I need some time to think o' it all."

"Ye're tryin' to get out o' it." Ebba shook her head and made to turn away. She should've known better.

Cosmo reached out and stopped her. "I believe what your father is trying to say is he would like some time to assemble his thoughts."

Locks nodded, watching her warily. "I've been avoidin' thinkin' o' my past for a long while. I need a scant moment to dredge it up. I want to make sure I'm not missin' anythin' ye might wish to know."

Ebba's anger deflated, but she kept up her glare nevertheless. Locks was a pirate, after all, and he hadn't raised her to be dumb about using emotional blackmail to extort information. "Aye, ye can have until tonight then, but I'll be hearin' yer story afore bed."

His gaze turned inward, and he adjusted the sheets on the mast, unnecessarily. The sails above didn't need any tinkering with, full and happy as they were. "Aye, lass. I hear ye. Tonight it is." He stared at his hands, slowly exhaling, and walked away.

"Thanks for yer help, Cosmo," Ebba said as her father disappeared down into the bilge. "He was tryin' to get out o' it."

They ambled over to the side of the ship, and Cosmo pursed his lips, watching a pod of dolphins springing out of the water beside the ship.

"I didn't get that," he answered her. "He might be afraid of what you'll think of him. How would you feel if someone asked you to talk about everything bad in your past?"

Ebba lifted her brows. "That be easy. Born, stolen, raised by six pirates who weren't my real fathers. Spent most o' my life trading fruit and veg for provisions, dropped at a brothel for a month when I was fifteen. Battled against Ladon, sailed through the siren's nest, got the *dynami* off the selkies, met my family on Pleo, then here."

The prince's lips lifted in a wry smile. "Have I ever told you you're refreshingly straightforward?"

"Ye're callin' me stupid," Ebba shot back, arching a brow. "I ain't afraid to hurt ye just because ye have one arm."

He threw his head back and laughed.

She hadn't heard him laugh in so long; the sound made her smile, too.

"No, Mistress Fairisles, I wasn't calling you stupid. But I thank you for not using kid gloves around me."

". . . Why would ye make gloves out o' children? Is their skin strong-like?"

Cosmo laughed again. "They're made from goat babies, I believe."

Ebba wrinkled her nose and adjusted the black hose tied over her belt. As was habit, she felt to make sure the *purgium* was in place there. The Earth Mother said the healing tube would hurt her fathers really bad if it touched them, or else she'd tie the cylinder to the ship cat, Pillage, for safekeeping. Actually, maybe she should do that with the *dynami*. Grubby had probably stashed it in the kitchen drawer.

"We both know there's far more to your story than that," the prince said.

Well, aye. If she were inclined to speak of her mistakes and regrets, sure. She'd started the whole battle with *Malice*, and she regretted healing Cosmo every time she saw sadness in his amber eyes. There wasn't anything else she could think of.

Ebba looked up to find the prince was watching where her hand rested over the *purgium*. Guilt stabbed her hard and fast. She quickly released it.

"What about ye?" she asked. "Tell me o' yer past."

His expression faltered, and he glanced around, likely checking for her fathers. "Not as uncomplicated as yours, I'm afraid." He glanced at her. "My father doesn't appreciate my fondness for learning and seeing new things. To my memory, we've never really seen eye to eye. And that worsened after my mother's death when my youngest sister was born."

"I'm sorry about yer mother," she said softly.

He threw her a wan smile. "It happens to a lot of people, I'm afraid. Royals aren't exempt from the dangers of childbirth. But thank you."

"He doesn't like to be told he's wrong then?" she asked.

A curious smile ghosted his face. "I gather most kings don't, but no, not that. More that he doesn't desire to look at the truth anymore. There are many criminal things happening that he has no urge to fix—like the corruption I've seen in Governor Da Ville's mansion on Maltu. My father doesn't seem to care about keeping the realm safe at all now. When I mention such problems, he tells me I'm too kind-hearted to rule. Not decisive enough."

Clearing up that corruption would be bad for pirate business.

"Well," Ebba said reasonably, "ye know I think ye're a mite soft, but ye've toughened smart-like in the last while. Ye even have some muscles on ye. Plus, everyone from the mainland be soft. So, ye'd be rulin' people who wouldn't know the di'ference."

Cosmo fixed his amber eyes on her. "I don't feel stronger. I feel like I've learned how dark the world can be, and the truth shook me apart so forcefully I don't know how to assemble the pieces of myself. I feel like half the person I was before—not bodily whole and not mentally whole."

His words shocked her. Ebba swallowed hard, hoping to conceal the tremor in her voice. "I don't know what to say to ye, Caspian. Except ye ain't half a person to me." She blinked quickly and turned to face the ocean. Peg-leg had said she could never cry about Cosmo's arm in front of him. "Ye be hurtin', and I s'pose it wouldn't make sense if ye weren't. Truthfully, I can't imagine what ye're goin' through. But don't let this overrun ye. Ye're stronger than that, and ye'll get stronger each day until ye're even stronger than ye were."

He didn't answer, and Ebba caught sight of his shaking shoulders. Her heart squeezed with the urge to give him comfort, but she hesitated. She hated people making a fuss when she got upset.

. . . But Cosmo wasn't like her.

Ebba took a breath and moved to him. Stepping close to his side, she wrapped her arms around his waist, leaning her head on his firm chest. His tears dripped onto the shoulder of her yellowed tunic, and he rested his chin atop her head, the breath catching in his throat as he sobbed. She held on to him until he calmed, and then stayed still despite hearing her fathers return to the main deck.

"I can't even hold you with two arms," Caspian finally said.

Ebba dropped one arm to her side and hugged him tightly with her right one. "Then I won't either. Things will always be equal with us."

THREE

Ebba watched as Peg-leg limped across the main deck in the steadily dimming light, plates balanced all over his arms. He stopped by Grubby, who took a plate, and then side-stepped Pillage's deliberately extended paw. Spotting the evil bastard of a cat was easier since Ebba tied the *dynami* to his back. The magical cylinder caught at the light, making the feline visible in the shadows—a great hiding spot for the cylinder *and* an alarm system. Two fish in one net, if she did say so herself.

Grubby was the only one who agreed that her idea had merit.

Peg-leg crossed to her, holding out a plate. Fish and baked potato with white sauce.

She beamed. "Thanks, Peg-leg. Hey, do ye know where Sal be?"

"Yer sprite be passed out on one o' the barrels in the hold." His eyes slid to Locks. "I thought ye might like yer fav'rite."

Her fathers were trying to butter her up on Locks' behalf. Fish and baked potatoes with white sauce *was* her favorite. . . .

. . . She accepted.

Ebba took an extra plate for Caspian, who sat beside her in

silence. He'd been that way for most of the afternoon. She balanced the plate on her knees and cut up the potato, passing it to him. He stared at the bite-sized bits of potato for a long moment and sighed, throwing her a small smile, and tucked in.

"Oi, Stubby," Ebba called to the helm. "Where are we stoppin' on Kentro?"

His deep voice carried over the light breeze and hiss of sea spray. "We be headin' to the west end o' Kentro, the bay closest to Selkie's Cove. Grubby said his kin can guard the entrance while we be in there. They'll warn us if *Malice* be about."

Plank carried his dinner and sat next to them on the deck. "We'll hike into the village and find Cosmo passage back to Exosia. I'm assumin' he'll be safe once he gets there."

Caspian snorted in response. "Yes, I'll be fine once on Exosia."

No pirate ventured into the strip of sea between the mainland and Kentro or Maltu. If harm came to Cosmo there, it wouldn't be from *Malice*.

Ebba shoved a mouthful of fish, potato, and sauce in her gob, smiling widely at Grubby as he sat down and again when Barrels came up from the bilge.

"How long until Kentro?" Caspian asked.

Stubby strolled over. "About eight days in this wind, lad."

Eight days. Ebba felt like Cosmo had made real progress today. It was the first time the prince had cried since losing his arm, unless he'd been hiding his tears before now. Still, Ebba felt like he'd moved forward. Now the order of grief dictated that he blamed someone else, yelled a bit, and then he'd be happy. The nightmares and darkness he'd referred to would become a bad memory and then flitter away. It always worked for her.

Locks joined them, with Peg-leg at his side. They sat in a circle in front of the mast, Stubby the only one standing, so he could keep an eye on *Felicity*'s path.

He cleared his throat. "Ebba, ye said ye wanted to hear o' my past."

"Aye," she replied.

"Well, then. I'll tell ye. A promise be a promise as ye said. Though—" He scowled around the circle of her fathers. "I'm not sure why the rest o' ye be here."

No one budged.

"I need to know how much ye say, so I can say the same amount," Stubby said. The rest of her fathers chorused, "Aye."

Ebba licked her plate clean, saying, "There ain't to be any cheatin'. Ye need to tell me as much as I want and answer my questions. Right, Caspian?"

There was silence.

"What did ye just say, little nymph?" Plank said.

Ebba frowned at her plate and licked it again. "I said there ain't to be no cheatin'."

Stubby shifted closer. "Nay, the other part. Ye just called Cosmo 'Caspian.'"

Her eyes widened, and she froze, plate held in the air. "Nay."

"Aye," Peg-leg said, getting to his feet.

Grubby rose also, wringing his hands. "I heard Cosmo, mateys. Let's everyone get along and be happy."

She didn't dare look at Cosmo, who had stiffened beside her. *Shite*; she'd known calling him Caspian in her head would lead to trouble. "It was just a slip o' the tongue," Ebba blurted. "I was thinkin' o' the strip o' the Caspian Sea he'd need to get across. Cosmo across the Caspian Sea. Caspian across the Cosmo Sea. Caspian. . . . See?"

Her six fathers surveyed her with varying degrees of doubt. Barrels and Stubby appeared highly doubtful, the others somewhere between, and Grubby looked to fully believe her lie.

Cosmo rested his hand on her arm. "It's okay, Mistress Fairisles."

She spoke low from the corner of her mouth. "*Shut yer gob. I got this.*"

He shook his head, and her heart fell as he got to his feet and faced her fathers, every one of them now standing.

"Cosmo, *don't*," Ebba hissed in warning, standing too. Her fathers would hurt him. They hated the king with the fiery passion of Davy Jones, and the prince knew where their secret sanctuary was.

He ignored her, meeting the heavy gazes of her fathers. "Months ago, my father sent me on a tour of Maltu in his stead. My first official duty as heir to the throne of Exosia."

Grubby's jaw dropped.

"For safety reasons, my father and his advisors decided that while there, I would masquerade as my servant, Cosmo, and he would take my place."

Stubby took a menacing step closer, and Caspian hurried on. "We left Maltu unharmed, but I. . . ." He glanced at his feet. "I wasn't ready to go back to being a prince. I'd never ventured out of Exosia before that moment, and I wanted to see more. So, I ordered the captain of our ship to sail around the other islands." He closed his eyes. "I thought we would be safe, sailing under my father's name. He'd raised me on stories of how he'd conquered pirates and how they trembled in fear of him."

Peg-leg snorted, and Caspian nodded tightly, saying, "I found out when *Malice* attacked our vessel how incorrect I'd been in my assumptions. This part of the sea is not tightly governed at all. *Malice* killed most of the crew, and left the rest to burn with the ship. If not for the foresight of the captain of *Fortitude,* who demanded I vacate to Neos with my servant for the duration of battle, I would not be here. I don't *deserve* to be here," he admitted. "It was I who ordered them into pirate-ridden waters."

That made pirates sound a bit like lice. And she supposed *Malice* were, but *Felicity* mostly weren't. Ebba heard what he was saying though; that choice to veer off route was the prince's mistake and regret.

Caspian lifted his head again. "Cosmo was hit with a bullet as we went overboard, but he never said anything. He just rowed me around the island where we found Barrels on *Felicity*. I was desperate for help, and at first, seeing how tidy Barrels looked, I mistook *Felicity* for a merchant ship."

Stubby gasped. "Take it back."

"Cosmo died soon after, and I quickly discovered my error in assuming *Felicity* was a merchant ship. However," he said, glancing to where Ebba hovered nearby, still ready to push him overboard in case her fathers attacked, "there was one among you whom I recognized. It was the first pirate I ever met at the governor's dinner. The young tribal woman who laughed all the way through the governor's speech and didn't give a care in the world who knew she was a pirate. She hadn't seemed like a bad person, nothing like the pirates in my father's stories. Her presence gave me hope."

Ebba tilted her head. That was what he'd first thought of her all those months ago? She supposed, compared to now, she had felt joyful. Or at least confident about her place in the world, even after being beaten up in the alley.

"So, what?" Locks demanded. "Ye lied to us for months on end about who ye were, like a stinkin' coward."

That was rich, coming from them.

Grubby's eyes filled with tears, and Ebba forced down her irony and stepped over to take his hand, squeezing it.

"I did." Caspian tilted his chin. "I wanted to tell you many times, particularly since Pleo." His eyes slid to Peg-leg. "But do you blame me for staying quiet, knowing all pirates detest my father, and that most would use me to their own gain?"

Barrels absently bent to pick up Pillage, stroking the purring cat. He frowned. "No, Prince Caspian, it probably was the smartest course."

"O' course," Plank said, drawing his cutlass, "that doesn't help ye now. A pirate must do what a pirate must do."

His eyes widened, but Caspian held his ground. "I will accept any treatment you deem fit. I've betrayed your trust."

"Nay," Ebba cried out as her fathers closed in around him. "Just maroon him. Ye can't kill him. I'll never forgive ye."

Stubby snickered.

She paused where she'd been about to shove Plank away.

Peg-leg wheezed and thumped his chest.

In seconds, her fathers were falling about the deck in torrents of laughter, tears streaming down their cheeks as they howled and slapped each other's backs. The only one who didn't join in was Grubby, who stood beside her and Caspian with a toothy smile.

"*Any treatment,*" Barrels burst out, his salt-and-pepper hair escaping from its leather thong.

Locks' shoulders shook uncontrollably. "*A pirate must do what a pirate must do.* I nearly lost it when ye said that, Plank."

They held on to one another for support, continuing to howl in booming waves.

"Do ye . . . know what's happenin'?" Ebba asked Caspian, watching her fathers. "Are their mangoes be spillin' out?"

She glanced up at the prince's face and saw his lips were pressed together, his brows furrowed. "I can guess," he replied. Louder, he said, "You have known the truth for some time."

Stubby came over and clapped him on the back. "I ain't never seen a servant stand so straight. Were ye born with a rod up yer nether parts? We could barely keep straight faces when ye told us what ye were. Just a tip for next time, don't be goin' around providin' Latin interpr'tations, lad."

"Ye knew the whole time?" Ebba said, her stomach tightening. "Why didn't ye tell me?"

Plank wrapped an arm around her. "Ye can't keep secrets very well, little nymph."

She felt Caspian's eyes on her, and her cheeks warmed. "Aye, ma ybe."

"I don't understand why you didn't just leave me there," the prince said with a vague wave. "Or worse."

Peg-leg grinned at him, wiping his eyes. "Ye saved us from the gaol, lad. Plus, ye were without help and around our daughter's age. We weren't goin' to leave ye to die. Immediate-like, anyhow. Then we kind o' liked ye."

The prince looked at each of them in turn, blinking slowly. He peered at Ebba last as her fathers began to exchange gold. "I can't believe they knew this entire time," he said, still blinking. "Do you know how terrified I was of them for the first few weeks?"

Aye. "Ye ain't scared o' them any longer?" Ebba asked. "Since when?"

He shrugged. "I'm not sure. It happened gradually, I suppose. I feel . . . foolish now. This whole time I believed myself so clever."

"Aye," she said darkly. "I can't believe they've known for months, and I only found out on Pleo. But I guess they've met Exosians afore." Ebba nudged him. "Sorry for callin' ye Caspian." She was angry at herself for doing so. That was how the whole shite storm with *Malice* had started—she hadn't guarded her tongue.

Sink her, maybe Ebba should start thinking before she spoke. That was a scary thought.

"It's all right," Caspian said. "I was planning to tell them before I left anyway. They're right. You're not the secret-keeping sort. Too . . . free-spirited."

Ebba smiled sheepishly, listening to the clink of coin and her fathers' jubilant talk. Her eyes rested on Locks, who was collecting money from a dazed Grubby. He caught her eye and quickly looked away.

If Locks thought he was getting out of telling her that easily, he had another thing coming.

FOUR

"Where's Locks?" Ebba asked Stubby the next morning after climbing the shrouds to monitor the ocean surrounding *Felicity*. Last night, her talk with Locks had been swept out to sea. She hadn't had the heart to pull their attention back to her questions with the way Caspian's eyes lit up over tales of the last few months when her fathers had pretended not to know who he was.

Today, though. . . .

Stubby swung the wheel to the right. "He be pluggin' up a leak in the hold."

"Thank ye kindly."

Ebba skimmed to the bilge and slid down the ladder. She ran down the cramped passage past Barrels' office, leaping over Pillage's extended paw where he lurked in the shadows like the furred sod he was.

"The *dynami* be shinin' on yer back," she sang over her shoulder.

A deep grinding noise slowed her steps. Ebba turned and peered back through the shadows toward the cat.

Her jaw dropped. *Shite.*

"*Bad Pillage*," she scolded in a low voice, lest the others hear. Trailing back down the passage, she studied the eight gouges in *Felicity's* deck from where Pillage had just scratched. Sharks' teeth, the *dynami* had given him super strength. The gouges were deep—permanent. Stubby would have a fit. Besides that, no cat should have that kind of power; they were all bastards.

Cooing, Ebba crouched before the cat. "Here, Pillage boy. Come here calm-like now."

He paused in the act of licking a furry black paw, regarding her with narrowed eyes.

"Give me the tube back, ye furry rat," she hissed, darting a look at the closed door of Barrels' office. When Stubby found those scratches, he'd hit the roof. She couldn't be anywhere near the scene of the crime.

Ebba lunged for the *dynami*, and Pillage yowled in fright, jumping out of the way and kicking off her shoulder in a bid to escape her clutches. The force of his kick was akin to being kicked by a horse. Pain ripped through her shoulder as she was shoved back from the cat by the power of the *dynami*. She hit the other side of the narrow passage with a loud *thwack* and rolled onto her back with a hearty groan.

"Ouch," she wheezed, massaging the spot where he'd connected.

Footsteps sounded from Barrels' office, and Ebba scrambled to her feet, running on tip-toes down the passage. Glancing back, she caught Pillage's eye, the *dynami* still gleaming on his back. *Sodding cur.*

He turned his back on her, tail high in the air as he slunk away.

So tying the cylinder to his back hadn't been the best idea. But this wasn't over.

Entering the hold, Ebba slowed, waiting until Barrels had

opened and closed his door before calling out, "Locks, where are ye?"

She heard a muted thud, cursing, and then the hold fell silent. Ebba sighed loudly, stalking between the barrels and listening hard. "Ye said ye'd tell me, ye spineless jellyfish."

Someone groaned, and Ebba set off after the sound. Her feet slowed as she saw it was only Sally waking up. "How ye doin', Sal? Seen Locks?"

Sally held her arms aloft, and Ebba smiled, picking her up. She placed the wind sprite over her heart underneath the black jerkin she wore.

"I know ye're down here, Locks," Ebba sang out. "If ye don't talk to me, I'll put a slit in yer hammock."

There wasn't an answer.

"I'll throw yer tools overboard." He was down to his last set after she'd tossed his tools in Pleo. There was a small shuffling noise halfway up the hold. She wandered in that direction on quiet feet. Choking on a breath, she screwed up her face and raised her voice, going for the throat. "Why won't ye talk to me? Don't ye love me?"

Locks popped up from behind a barrel, his aghast expression turning to irritation as she smoothed her face into a grin.

"Got ye," she crowed.

He scratched his stubble, emerald eye blazing. "Aye, can't be too mad at ye for that."

Ebba threw a barrel open and cupped grog into her hands, slurping down some of the watered-down rum and nutmeg mixture. She wiped her hands on her slops. "Talk. This is as good as it'll get."

Locks sighed and lowered his head to the barrel to slurp a mouthful. He straightened, casting her a surreptitious peek before leaning back against the inner wall of the hull. "I don't right know where to start, lass. I guess I'll be startin' with my childhood. Ye know I was born on Febribus?"

"Aye," she said warily. He wouldn't be slipping anything past her. She was determined to wring everything out of his gob.

He nodded. "I grew up with just my father, who was a carpenter like me. My mother left my father shortly after I was born, and I'm hardly recallin' her now. Just her laugh. Febribus were different back then— like Kentro, or Maltu. The odd pirate ship would come and go, but the township was small and the people poor. The pirates didn't bother us overmuch."

Febribus was the most notorious pirate island nowadays. Ebba had only been there once, but it was hard to imagine it as a quiet place after what she'd seen. "What was yer father's name?"

"Trent," Locks said with a smile. "Had a different woman on his arm each week, he did. Said Mum leavin' him was the best thing to ever happen."

Ebba wrinkled her nose. That explained a lot. "Did he teach ye to be a carpenter?"

"Aye, he did. But he died afore I was fully taught. There was another carpenter on Febribus who had more experience than I. People started goin' to him. Wasn't long afore the pickings were slim. . . . That was when a pirate ship came into our harbor, looking for a carpenter." He shook his head, staring into the back of the hold. "Seemed too good to be true. And what do I always say about that, Ebba-Viva?"

"If it look too good to be true, it probably is."

"Aye. Well, I was only about yer age then and as stupid as most are. . . ." He trailed off with a hasty glance at her. "Anyway, the quartermaster, Barrels, seemed nice enough—as fancy as they came but a good sort."

Barrels? Ebba jerked but didn't interrupt him again.

"And so, I packed a rucksack and left Febribus on the pirate ship *Eternal* to sail under Captain Cannon, as he were known then."

She'd always assumed Cannon, Pockmark's grandfather, must have captained *Malice*. But she supposed the king's navy ships would have sunk *Eternal* in the final clash in the Battle for the Seas—Cannon was the last pirate left standing against King Montcroix.

"Ye didn't meet Mutinous afore ye agreed to work for him?" she asked.

Locks flinched. "Nay, lass. But I should've. My life would've been a lot di'ferent if I had. I got on board, and the ship set sail immediately." He frowned. "Sumpin' wasn't right about it. The men didn't laugh and joke. If anything, I got the feel one o' them would stab me in the back rather than help me. There were only a handful o' men there who were more friendly-like. I weren't on that ship one hour afore I saw it had been a mistake, and by that time, it was too late. Febribus was a blip in the distance."

Her father fell silent, his face working. Ebba took a breath. "What did ye do on the ship, Locks?"

Locks closed his single eye. "Ye know a carpenter often doubles as the surgeon on a ship."

Ebba nodded, and he continued. "I didn't. Not afore they strapped a man with gangrene in front o' me and told me to cut off his leg with the same saw I'd used on a plank." A shudder ran through him. "I couldn't do it, lass. The sight o' the blood, it made the world spin. I couldn't handle the screamin', the rusty smell."

"Ye do okay with it now," Ebba said, remembering many instances where he'd patched her up.

He smiled tightly. "I was made to conquer it, lass. In horrible ways I don't want yer young ears to hear."

Ebba gritted her teeth against the urge to go along with his comment. "Locks, I want to be hearin' everythin'." How else could she understand why they'd lied to her? How else would she be able to feel able to resume the life they'd all had together before?

He searched her face, his color fading. "Ye're sure, lass?"

"Aye, ye promised me all."

Locks nodded sadly. "That I did. It just, they be my most painful memories. The thing I used to hate, though, the thing that haunts me most, was when Mutinous would rub my face in the blood like I was a dog who'd soiled a rug. He'd drag my face across the deck. It used to take me hours to get all the splinters out."

Ebba froze and stared at the thin scars on his cheeks with new eyes. She'd always thought he must've had bad skin in his youth. "H-he did that to ye? Gave ye the scars on yer face?" *By dragging his face over the deck through another's blood.* She expected cold-blooded murders, theft, lies, betrayal. Not. . . .

"Aye, Ebba. Mutinous' fav'rite tool was ridicule. The crew would watch as he did it, and they'd laugh until they were howlin'. Some o' them laughed because they enjoyed the sight, but the rest only laughed because it weren't them being hum'liated for a change. It's how I lost my eye, too," he added.

Her gaze shifted to his black patch. "Ye told me ye lost it to infection."

He studied her with his emerald eye. Normally, Locks' eye blazed, but right now, the vibrant color was lackluster. "Aye, I didn't want ye to know."

"I wish ye'd just said ye'd tell me when I was older or sumpin'. I feel like a fool for goin' around repeatin' yer lies, even if I knew some o' them were fibs."

He avoided her gaze. "We know. We just wanted you to be proud o' us, lass."

"I was. How could ye think that me knowin' any o' this would change that? Now I can't get past that ye've all been talking behind my back. I don't feel like part o' the crew anymore."

He opened his mouth, but Ebba shook her head. "No, we ain't talkin' o' me; we be talkin' o' ye. Keep goin'."

Locks closed his eye. "I can't tell ye anymore."

"Ye promised."

"I know what I promised," he choked. "But young as ye are, ye can't understand, and I hope ye never have cause to. When ye're forced to do the things I was, that we all were back then, ye lose trust in yerself. Ye wonder if there was always a darkness in ye that was never tested, and ye begin to believe ye failed some big life test because ye ain't the person ye thought." He cut off, chest heaving. "Lass, I never want ye to understand that."

She didn't understand because she was young? Ebba hated when they said that. "I *do* understand," she replied.

Locks shook his head. "Resp'ctfully, ye don't. Ye've been through some right bad stuff in the last two months. But ye've never been broken. And that's what Mutinous did to me . . . to all o' yer fathers."

Heat crept up Ebba's neck. "So ye're not goin' to tell me the rest?"

He surged to his feet. "What do ye want to know? That Mutinous used to capture men and women from the towns we pillaged and had me work on them though they weren't injured? While they screamed for me to stop? While they begged me for the end?"

Ebba blinked, rearing back. She stared at him.

"Do ye want to know that I didn't stop? That I don't know why I didn't or couldn't? That for some reason, after months on that ship, I began to think they deserved it?"

Her breath came fast as her chest tightened. "What are ye sayin'? Ye tortured people and liked it?"

Locks turned away, his shoulders hunched as though he'd

been socked in the gut. "I'm sayin' he broke me, lass. He broke us all. I've never been able to figure out if the cracks he hammered at were already there or if he was makin' them himself. If he made them, wouldn't I have known the di'ference? Wouldn't I have stopped the madness, even if it was meanin' my death?"

She didn't reply, sensing he was speaking to himself.

He shook his head, not turning back. "Nearly fifteen years I sailed on *Eternal*, and now, eighteen years after we all escaped, not a day goes by when I don't remember the first step I took onto that nightmare. Please, lass, I don't want to be sayin' no more."

Why hadn't he gotten over it by now? That was what Ebba struggled to understand. He'd been hurt, horribly so, but the better part of two decades had passed. . . . Ebba was torn up about a lot of things right now, but she knew everything would sort itself out in time, and with a whole heap more thought than she was used to. To her, it seemed as though Locks and her fathers hadn't bothered to try. But she'd also never seen Locks so out of control as now. Not even when he sprouted lies about hating Verity.

"Barrels hired ye," Ebba said, changing the subject. "How could he do that to ye?"

Locks shrugged. "I don't carry a grudge against him. That ship and the people on it had a way o' creepin' inside o' ye. Bad acts became normal acts, and then worse acts became normal, until ye didn't blink an eye at anythin'." His hands trembled.

But how was that possible? Ebba couldn't connect that mindless depravity to her fathers. They weren't evil.

They fell into silence, Ebba's mind working overtime. Pockmark, the captain of *Malice*, was bad, but his grandfather Mutinous sounded one hundred times worse. Her stomach roiled at the thought of anyone dragging someone's face across a bloody deck until they lost an eye.

The heat in her cheeks reached boiling point. "If that man were here," she spat out, "I'd run him through." Not just for Locks, but because she strongly suspected the boom that struck Grubby in the back of the head hadn't been an accident, and she now wondered if Peg-leg's missing leg was even from an unlucky injury.

"He's gone, thank the powers o' oblivion for that. But rest assured, if I saw him again, I hope I'd try to kill him, too. Such a man should never exist in the world, lass."

"But his grandson be black-hearted, too, and ye won't fight him," Ebba said.

Malice and *Felicity* were locked in a battle over the two magic cylinders. The soothsayer had said the war wouldn't end in their lifetime if they sat around and did nothing about it.

Locks' eye blazed across the space between them. "Aye, Pockmark be cruel, but nowhere near as smart as his grandfather. Mutinous had a hold over piratekind that I could never fathom. He had a plan for a plan for a plan."

"Caspian said he's goin' to get his father to hunt Mercer Pockmark down."

"Well, King Montcroix always did hate pirates. And he hates Cannon's line the most, with Mutinous killin' his father and all. Let's hope that be the end o' *Malice* and that slime o' a captain, Pockmark."

Ebba hopped off the barrel, and they both took another long drink, sipping in quiet.

The prince said her fathers' secrecy over their pasts was simply a matter of them not wanting to confess their every mistake to their child. But their avoidance of speaking about anything prior to her arrival in their lives didn't seem so clear cut to her. It was as though they'd been irreversibly damaged by whatever happened to them on Mutinous Cannon's ship, and they now had no desire or strength to fix themselves. Their only effort to heal was to steal her from the tribe and change their ways. Even that effort was drenched in the blood of slaughtered tribespeople and deep-rooted lies. Ebba couldn't correlate what she'd heard with the fathers she knew and loved.

Instead of mending the relationship between them, the conversation with Locks had left an uneasiness deep inside her.

"When did ye meet Verity?" Ebba asked.

His face tightened. He wiped his mouth and answered, "I met her when I was thirty-two. I thought I'd been in love afore that moment, but no one prior even held a light to her, and they haven't since. In the darkness o' what I'd been through, she reached me. Beautiful, fierce woman."

"Is that why ye have so many girlfriends?" she asked.

He shrugged. "I've always had a smidgen o' trouble trustin' women after my mother left. My father didn't help matters, I s'pose, as much as I loved him. Plus, Verity be the only woman I ever thought o' settlin' with, but she told me good and proper what she thought about me."

Ebba pursed her lips, remembering how the soothsayer had paused on the brink of sending a message to Locks. "Didn't ye ever think to try again with her, though? Maybe she's changed her mind."

"I'm afraid I got a bit busy raisin' ye after that," he said, his ears reddening. "And what would I say?"

Ebba shrugged. "Tell her the honest truth-like. Not the pirate version."

Locks blanched. "I ain't so good at that."

Perhaps none of them were. She took two steps and hugged him around the middle, smiling when his arms circled her in return. "Thank ye for tellin' me what ye did."

"Do ye think di'ferent o' me, lass?"

Aye. She didn't understand his festering hurt and why, in eighteen years, he hadn't healed from what Cannon did to him. Yet even pressed against his chest, she could hear the still-raw anguish in his voice and knew she'd never voice her inner musings aloud. "I don't think o' ye any di'ferent, knowin' yer past. It just makes me want to hurt that captain bad. I love ye, Locks."

"I'm sorry we didn't tell ye about yer parents sooner," Locks said over her head, rocking them. "That was wrong o' us. Don't see how ye could love a big pack o' cowards like us, but I'm glad ye do."

Moving up on tip-toe, Ebba kissed his cheek. "Aye, ye should've told me. I won't pretend I ain't in big knots about it, but yer apology be a'preciated."

"Accepted?"

She couldn't accept anything until she sorted her head out. "I reckon there still be five more stories to hear afore I decide on that," she said, hugging him close again.

FIVE

As soon as they passed north of Syraness and were nearing the west end of Kentro, Grubby shucked his tunic and dove overboard.

Ebba leaned against the bulwark with Caspian, watching in amusement as hundreds of seals gathered around her part-selkie father within minutes.

"I've certainly seen things I never thought to see while aboard this ship," Caspian said, staring wistfully out at the joyful gathering of selkies beside *Felicity*.

Aye, the sight of her father in the middle of so many selkies was an oddity, even for a pirate.

Ebba teased, "Ye don't see such things in Exosia?"

Caspian cleared his throat. "Can't say we do."

He glanced over his shoulder, and she tracked his gaze to where Sally was riding Pillage around the deck.

"Hey, where'd the *dynami* go?" she blurted.

"Barrels decided to give Pillage a break from it after finding some gouges outside his office this morning. I believe Grubby has it now. He wanted to show the selkies it was still safe."

Ebba replied hastily, "Gouges, ye say? I guess the tube was givin' him super strength. Best he not have that one."

Caspian regarded her curiously. "Yes, Locks is down there trying to repair the damage. Stubby was too upset."

"Hey," she said suddenly, not liking the knowing gleam in the prince's eyes. "Do you think the rest o' the realm knows magic be back? The wall must be completely down by now; the Earth Mother said it'd only be weeks until magic was returned for good, and more than seven have passed. Won't others have noticed?"

The Earth Mother had told them their crew was on a path they couldn't avoid. She'd said that only *they* could save the realm from the evil immortal power, the pillars of six. Except the Earth Mother neglected to mention just why the crew of *Felicity* had to be the ones to fight the pillars. If the magical woman had given them some solid answers, maybe the members of *Felicity* wouldn't be torn in two over whether to get involved. As it was, Plank, Grubby, and Ebba thought they should figure out why magic was returning, at the very least, while the other four members had outvoted them in favor of returning to their hidden oasis and waiting the storm out. In their eyes, and previously in hers, the looming danger had nothing to do with their ship or crew.

Ebba still wondered why evil immortal power spreading through the realm should be their problem. But after seeing the fear in the Earth Mother's age-old eyes, she'd finally been convinced these six pillars *would* be their problem whether they liked it or not.

Cosmo tipped his head back. "I'm not so sure many people will have noticed. I mean, you saw Ladon at the top of a mountain, the siren in treacherous cliff passages, the selkies in a deep cave, and the sprites after surviving the cliffs—except for Sally."

The Taniwha and the Earth Mother had been in an underground cavern. "I guess the places we've seen magic have been tucked away a scant bit."

"They have," he said with a frown. "But if magic was spotted on Exosia, it might be that much easier to secure my father's agreement to send the navy after *Malice*. You said the Earth Mother warned of a great evil who was trying to attain the root of magic. Maybe he'll help your crew to fight against the pillars of six, too—wherever they are."

With what Caspian had told her of his father, that didn't seem likely. Ebba studied the intensity in his gaze. She hated to think it, but if going back to Exosia would help her friend, if it gave him new purpose, she wanted him to return to the mainland.

"I'll miss ye, but I think ye're makin' the right choice," she said hoarsely, and left to cross the deck to where Stubby and Plank had their heads bent together. They were just gouges, but Ebba should make sure Stubby was all right.

"What are ye talkin' o'?" she asked them.

They both jumped and whirled toward her.

"Nothin' innocent-like, I see," Ebba said drily. She held up a finger as Plank prepared to run away. "Tell me."

Stubby muttered under his breath. His face was twisted into a scowl she knew well. Aye, he was jumping mad about the gouges all right.

". . . Better to maroon him." Stubby bit out.

Ebba's jaw dropped. "Better to maroon who? Ye can't mean Caspian?"

"*Prince* Caspian," Plank said. "And aye, we do. Ye're our first priority, little nymph. King Montcroix be a dangerous man. We like Cosmo." He shook his head. "*Caspian*, but we don't trust him with ye. We don't trust anyone who be havin' the power to harm our child whether that be ac'idental or otherwise."

She planted her feet between her fathers and her friend. "Ye ain't maroonin' him. Not after everythin' he's been through. It'll be the last thread on his hammock. And what happens if he's picked up by someone? Then he'll definitely be after us, *and* he knows where our retirement spot be. Best to believe in goodwill."

Stubby's scowl deepened, and Plank gaped at her briefly before facing him.

"He knows where our spot is," Plank said.

Stubby nodded, crossing his arms. "He has to die."

With Plank, the matter seemed more about the prince. With Stubby, it appeared more about the scratches on the ship and seeking any available outlet to his anger. "What? Nay," Ebba said firmly. "Ye can't do it to him. If ye don't trust him, then trust that I know he won't cause any harm. Do ye trust me?"

They shifted uncomfortably.

"We trust ye, little nymph. But sometimes, being a parent is about doin' things yer child doesn't like."

"Ye won't be keepin' me safe if ye do this," Ebba snapped at them. "Ye'll just be actin' the way Caspian expected ye to when he first happened upon us. Ye knew he was the prince this whole time."

"Aye, but we'd always planned to maroon him," Plank said reasonably.

Her fathers stared at her with wooden expressions. Ebba threw her hands in the air and stormed off to stand beside Caspian again.

She wouldn't be letting him out of her sight until he was safe on a ship to Exosia.

CASPIAN HESITATED. "I'm glad you're coming with us to the village, but I hope it hasn't caused any trouble with your fathers."

Trouble? Aye, it had. She'd raised Davy Jones himself when Locks, Plank, and Stubby told her to stay at the ship with the others.

"Nay, no trouble," Ebba answered.

He smiled. "You don't call jumping off the side of the ship and swimming to shore trouble?"

She grinned at him. "I'm not goin' to miss a chance to spend another couple o' hours with ye." And she'd be keeping an eye on her fathers to make sure there wasn't any funny marooning business.

His face softened, and he drew closer. "You know, whatever has happened in the last three months, I count myself singularly fortunate to have met you, Ebba-Viva Wobbles Fairisles."

Her throat tightened. "Ye, too, Caspian. I ain't sure I'll ever have another friend like ye."

The prince squeezed her hand briefly, dropping it at a warning look from Locks. "I'll miss you. More than you know. Leaving you is the only reason this choice feels wrong." He sighed, his amber eyes moving over her face.

She cleared her throat as her cheeks heated. "Aye, Caspian. I'll miss ye fierce-like."

Ebba turned away and increased her pace to get to the front of their procession as her eyes began to prickle. If she was teary now, what would she be like when it was actually time to say goodbye?

They marched through the low-lying and flowered forests of Kentro. All of the islands were pretty in their own ways, but Kentro was particularly beautiful with its exotic colors—reds streaked with black, mixed among electric blues and any number of purple hues. They'd started out at first light, so they could be back in good time to journey back to Zol. Stubby and Locks would go top up their supplies of food. They all carried large empty rucksacks for the return journey. Plank had come to arrange Caspian's passage. Grubby was back in the water by the ship, making sure *Malice* was far away. And Sally was staying behind to make sure the grog barrels were safe.

The low trees and flowers became patchier, and the dirt path widened into the outskirts of the southern Kentro village. Ebba had only been here a handful of times. There tended to be navy men to spare at the southern harbor, which was why her fathers hadn't wanted her to come.

"This is it?" Caspian asked, walking next to her as the path became a worn road, wide enough for a wagon.

She nodded. "Aye."

Plank broke out of the humming daydream he'd kept up for most of the walk, saying, "Hopefully we can find ye a vessel leavin' this evenin'."

"So eager to be rid of me?" the prince asked with a hint of a smile.

Plank winked at him, stepping aside so a farmer and his donkey could get by. That put her father right next to Caspian—too close. Ebba glared at Plank when he glanced at her. "Give it a rest, little nymph. We decided not to maroon him."

Caspian stopped in his tracks. "What? You were going to maroon me?"

Stubby gripped his shoulder, gray-blue eyes hard as rock. "Plank's just jestin', lad. Juuust jestin'."

By the looks of it, Caspian knew that wasn't the case, but he wisely remained mute.

The pathway grew busier as they worked their way between the thatch houses to the dock, sticking to the shadows in case of navy men. Most navy men liked to frequent the taverns when ashore, though, and it was doubtful they'd be awake so early. If they were, they'd be in no shape to give chase with a head full of pain. Ebba and the others would simply high-tail it back into the bush to lose them.

"Little nymph, is there any point tryin' to convince ye to go with the others to get supplies?" Plank asked.

She shook her head. She was going with Caspian to the dock.

Her three fathers sighed. Ebba and Plank passed over their empty rucksacks and then started down the hill to the docks.

"Thank you for all you've done for me," Caspian said to Plank ahead of her.

Plank dipped his head. "Aye, lad. Ye're welcome, for what it be worth. We're just sorry ye came to harm on Pleo."

"Just a stupid coincidence, wasn't it?" the prince said, bemused. "That the shrapnel hit me. One small movement and it mightn't have hit me at all."

"Aye, lad."

"Though," Caspian added, "I'm not sure if I believe in coincidence after sailing with *Felicity*."

Plank looked across at him. "Why do ye say that?"

The prince shrugged. "You become locked in a war with *Malice* just as magic returns to the world and then happen across two objects of impossible power. I can't believe there's nothing more to it than happenstance."

"I agree," Plank said. "But until the rest o' the crew be comin' around, there won't be any figurin' out."

Caspian smiled, his dimple flashing. "I thought pirates didn't worry about the why of things."

Plank arched a brow. "I preferred ye when ye shook in yer boots at the sight o' us. But between ye and me, I'm thinkin' that ship law be on the way out."

"I still can't believe you knew the entire time," Caspian said, then jolted. "Could you thank Peg-leg for me again? I haven't been as grateful for his help in the last six weeks as I ought to have been."

"Ye don't need to worry yerself, lad. We know what ye went through; there be nothin' ye ought to have done at all. We're grateful for ye bein' there for our Ebba when we couldn't, and when she didn't want us to be."

They fell quiet.

Ebba spent the rest of the journey downhill preparing herself for a goodbye. She hovered near Caspian as Plank headed off to find transportation to Exosia.

"I—" she and Caspian chorused at once.

They chuckled awkwardly, and Caspian gestured for her to continue.

Ebba toed the ground. "When will we see each other again, do ye think?"

"I hope it won't be long," he answered quietly.

His answer told her it *would* be a long time. She'd known it would be, and that was why she'd been so upset to hear the news. Ebba held out her hand and opened her fingers to show the object she'd carried with her from the ship.

In her palm nestled a green-and-orange-striped bead. The one her fathers got for her on Maltu the day she met the prince. "I want ye to have this."

"One of your beads?" His amber eyes flicked up to hers. "Are you certain?"

She took his hand, slapping the bead down on his palm. "Aye, and stop makin' such a big deal o' it."

His fingers closed around the bead. "It's a big deal to me, Mistress Fairisles. I know what the beads mean to you. I must be more important than I'd thought to be gifted one."

"Don't fuss. Ye ain't s'posed to say upsettin' things durin' goodbyes."

Caspian's eyes fixed on her. "How can I not when I don't know when I'll next see you?" He swallowed. "In fact, I . . . I wouldn't forgive myself if I didn't tell you. . . ," he trailed off, biting his lip.

Ebba shifted, watching the color rise up his neck. A burning curiosity to hear exactly what he had to say overtook her. "Tell me what?"

He inhaled sharply. "That I . . . that I think you'll be the greatest pirate to sail the seas one day."

She released her pent-up breath, feeling strangely deflated by his words. What had she expected him to say? Despite the twisting weight in her gut and her current pirate identity crisis, a smile spread across her face. "Ye really think so?" She toyed with one of her dreads.

He stepped closer and took her hand, laying a soft, warm kiss there. "I do. *And the prettiest,*" he blurted.

She stared at him, the weight within her dissipating and spreading as a light sensation through her chest. Caspian thought Ebba was pretty? He'd said something similar about her to Barrels once before. She'd never thought of herself that way. Sure, she enjoyed pretty trinkets, accessories, and doing her hair. Ebba frowned, unsure how to decipher the array of sensations his comment inspired. She'd been so adamant about just being a pirate for so many years. Now Ebba understood that her fathers hadn't left her on Maltu because they viewed being female as a weakness. They'd left her to learn how to best cope with the changes to her body. With all of that added to the whole 'you're a tribe princess' cannon ball, Ebba had no idea how to think of herself. But Caspian's compliment made her happy and . . . uncertain, too, though not in a bad way. More like an exciting way.

Holding all of those mangoes in her basket at once made her head ache more than when Grubby made the grog.

She spotted Plank heading back. "Thank ye kindly," she mumbled to Caspian, drawing her hand away.

"Ye're booked on a vessel leavin' at high tide, lad. Aboard the *Havanna*," he said. "I pointed ye out to the captain, who seems a good man. But ye have the knife I gave ye?"

"Yes," Caspian said, straightening with a glance at Ebba. "I'll stay on deck like Stubby said."

Plank murmured his approval and spat on his hand, stretching it out. "Ye're welcome aboard *Felicity* any time, Caspian." He looked to the sky for a moment. "Unless ye set yer father on us, in which case we'll hunt ye down and slit yer throat."

Caspian spat on his hand and shook her father's in a firm grip. "Fair enough, but you needn't worry. You know I'd never bring harm to Ebba."

Plank assessed him, a curious smile hovering about his lips. "Nay, I don't believe ye would." Plank turned to her. "I'll be startin' up the hill, little nymph. Say yer goodbyes, but don't tally overlong."

"Aye, Plank," she said softly, watching him go.

Ebba turned and jerked, finding Caspian before her. He brought his arm up around her, and she lifted her right arm, hugging him back in their special embrace. A lump rose in her throat. "I'll miss ye," she said hoarsely, feeling tears dripping off her chin. Blasted things. Somehow his compliment had made this parting worse.

"We'll see each other again," he said. "Let's not say goodbye. What we have shared doesn't have a goodbye; it just has a. . . ."

". . . See ye again, matey?" Ebba offered.

He smiled sadly. "Exactly. See you again, matey."

She grimaced at the stilted way he spoke the words. "Still a bit soft."

He grinned, picking up his small bag with a change of

clothes and the knife. "Always a bit soft, Mistress Fairisles. Luckily, you're pirate enough for both of us." He bowed to her, holding her eyes for a long moment before saying, "Please take care of yourself."

"I will," she said, flushing. "Ye too."

Caspian gave her one last dimpled smile and turned for the docks.

Ebba pretended to watch him go, but truthfully, after he'd moved more than twenty feet away, the tears blurring her eyes made seeing him impossible. When she relented and dragged a grubby sleeve over her face, he'd disappeared.

She made for the path after Plank, a little in denial that her friend could really be gone. People gave her a wide berth as she wove through their midst. Ebba wiped at her face again, sniffing hard.

The ship just wouldn't be the same without him.

"Look, lads," a nasal voice called in front of her. "If it ain't fish-lips."

Ebba dashed away her tears again, jumping at the row of black-clad *Malice* pirates before her.

A black bag was pulled over her head from behind, and her legs were kicked out from under her. Ebba didn't waste any time.

"Help!" she screamed. "Hel—"

The butt of a pistol slammed down on her temple with crushing force.

And Ebba knew no more.

SIX

Ebba groaned and rolled to her back, unsticking her tongue from the roof of her mouth. "Missin' teeth o' a gummy shark," she groaned. "Did Grubby make the grog last night?"

"She be wakin', captain."

She didn't recognize the voice. The ground rolled beneath her. Waves slapped against the side of the vessel she was on. A ship, she assumed. It was nighttime, dark . . . but the heat beating down on her body said otherwise.

"Take off the hood," someone ordered.

Ebba froze at the drawling voice. *That* was a voice she'd know in a dark pit. She was wrenched to her feet. The hood was ripped off.

The midday sunlight assaulted her eyes where it filtered between crimson sails and midnight-black booms. Dread settled heavy in her bones. Only one ship was black with crimson sails.

Mercer Pockmark stood before her. "Fish-lips o' *Felicity*," *Malice*'s captain greeted her.

She'd been so upset about Caspian leaving, Ebba hadn't paid proper attention. They'd taken her at the docks. Ebba inhaled sharply. Plank was waiting at the top of the track, and Caspian down by the shore. What if they'd been caught? She had a moment of panic about the *purgium* at her belt before remembering she'd left it on *Felicity* to go into the Kentro village.

Turned out she did care about the magical cylinders ending up in Pockmark's clutches.

Trying to control her flipping stomach, which wanted to remind her how bad this would go for her, Ebba looked into Pockmark's eyes. She gasped at his face. "Blimey, what happened to ye?" The tiny circular scars that had given him the name Pockmark were now ulcerous, as though someone had been digging into his skin and the wounds became infected. His black tunic and slops hung off his frame, a far cry from the lean strength he'd portrayed in Maltu just three months earlier. The feathers of his black tricorn hat were bent and missing half their barbs. His eyes had always been cruel, but now the same eyes were empty, devoid, dull; yellowed and bloodshot.

He leaned in, his breath rank with stale grog and rot. "Power happened to me."

Ebba waved a hand in front of her face. "Have ye considered it wasn't power but a whole heap o' ugly?"

Mercer nodded to his left, and Ebba followed the jerk of his head to Swindles. Swindles grinned and stepped up, socking her in the gut without preamble.

"Shite," Ebba gritted out, doubling over as much as the two pirates holding her arms would let her. That hurt. The pain reminded her about the notion of thinking before talking.

"Where are yer fathers?" Pockmark said in a bored voice.

Why did people always do that? Whenever they wanted something, they acted the opposite. Hope filled her at his words, however. "All six o' them?" she ventured.

47

He gave her a blank look.

Ebba danced inside. Plank was okay. "They be far away from here by now."

Pockmark regarded her, then nodded to Swindles again. Ebba braced her stomach this time, but he punched her in the jaw. Gasping, she blinked back stars, sagging in her captors' arms before locking her wobbling knees.

That one would hurt later.

"Ye always did hit like a landlubber, Swindles," she said, spitting out blood. The thinking first gig was a lot harder than it seemed, but since Ebba also didn't want to be dead, she gritted her teeth against the urge to hurl more insults at the *Malice* pirates' heads.

Swindles' face twisted, and he rushed her, but Mercer stopped him with a lifted finger. The captain sauntered closer until he was directly in front of her. He gripped her chin, thumb digging into the injury Swindles had inflicted. Tears sprang to her eyes.

"Ye'll tell me where yer fathers be," Pockmark said in a low voice. "Or ye'll die."

The answer to that was easy. "There ain't no way I'm tellin' ye where they are."

His eyes widened, then he regained his composure. "Everyone talks." He smiled. "Whether they're wishin' to or not. Time below deck may be convincin' ye otherwise."

There was a snicker from her left, and she turned to see Riot there, Swindles' buddy. Not that they'd seemed all that close when Ebba last saw them on Febribus. At a sharp intake of air from her right, she turned to look the opposite way.

Ebba blinked at Jagger, who had a hold of her right arm. *He was alive.* And he looked terrible. Not as bad as the others, but where he'd always been strong, his uniform hung off him. Usually proudly upright, his shoulders were slouched. His silver eyes had regained their hard edge. He avoided her eyes, watching Pockmark.

"Take her below, boys," Pockmark said with a wave. Glancing back at her, one of the wounds on his face weeping, his lips twisted into a smile. "I will have the *dynami* and the *purgium*. One way or another, I'll be havin' them."

Over her dead body. They could do whatever they wanted. To give up the *dynami* and the *purgium*, she'd have to give up her fathers, and that would never happen.

Riot jerked savagely on her arm, nearly ripping her shoulder out of its socket. Jagger clasped her upper arm on the other side in a grip that was light and tight in turns as though he couldn't decide if he wanted to hurt or help her. Ebba scanned the massive ship as she was marched to the bilge door. *Malice* was a schooner and had a crew of one hundred. The decks were crammed with pirates going about their duties. More swung from the riggings and were dotted up the mast.

How would she ever get away from all this? How would her fathers ever get her back?

They couldn't. Not against so many.

The rags of the crew's tunics hung off their emaciated frames. Sweat poured over their waxy skin as they worked. Yet where they got the energy to work when they looked so weak, Ebba couldn't tell. They were solely focused on their tasks, dark eyes fixed on their hands.

There was no laughter, no whistling or singing.

It was just as Locks had described *Eternal* back in his time under Mutinous Cannon. Something was wrong with this ship.

A tendril of fear slithered up her spine. Jagger shot her a veiled look.

"Ye're alive?" Ebba hissed at him as Riot swung open the bilge door.

Jagger's silver eyes tightened, his gaunt cheeks hollowing

further as he pressed his dry, cracked lips together, but he made no answer, just ushered her down the ladder to the quarters below.

The crew didn't glance at her as Ebba was shoved through the passages, down three more ladders. This ship was huge. There had to be at least four or five decks compared to *Felicity's* two.

"Where are ye takin' me?" she blurted as the passage they were leading her down became darker, and the walls seemed to shrink the farther they walked.

Riot smirked, glancing back. "Ye be goin' into the place no one in their right mind wishes to be. Ain't that right, Jagger?"

Jagger's hand tightened on her arm.

"Ye were in there, too?" Ebba asked him over her shoulder, hearing her beads rattle. The sound did little to alleviate her fears. "What is it? A cell?"

Riot just laughed.

The ship groaned as they neared the end of the passage. The groan was less like the sound of a full stomach and much more like the high-pitched complaint a bone might emit just before it snapped. The echoing noise raised the hairs on the back of Ebba's neck. The soothsayer's groaning house on Febribus was the closest she'd ever heard to such a sound, and that hadn't been anything like this. "Was that people groanin'?" she asked.

Riot unlocked a heavy door and swung it open. A putrid, overwhelming smell hit her, and she dry-retched.

"How long do ye think she'll last, Jagger?" Riot gripped her arm and hauled her into the pitch-black room. "Some only last a single day." He breathed on her, and she gagged again. His breath was nearly worse than the smell of waste in the room.

"Some last a week," he continued, eyes gleaming. "Our

precious Jagger here lasted a whole month afore Pockmark let him out. Should've left him here to rot like the others, if ye ask me."

"Shut yer gob, Riot, and chain her up." Jagger spoke for the first time.

Ebba swallowed. "Chains?"

"Nay," Riot scoffed. "A four-poster bed fit for a king." They guided her over to a wall and placed a manacle around her left ankle.

A quick pull told her it only gave her seven or eight feet of freedom. Could be worse.

A hand found hers in the dark and squeezed. Ebba squinted for a peek at Jagger's face, but there was no light. Worse was the heart-thudding feeling that something else was down here. As though a six-headed monster waited in the depths to devour her.

"Is the other one alive?" Riot asked.

Jagger let go of her hand. "Doesn't sound like it."

Riot shuffled back to the door. "Guess she's dead. Have fun with the smell, fish-lips. It'll be the least o' yer worries when the rats get to ye."

"Can ye at least bring a lantern down?" Ebba croaked.

Another laugh was her reply. "Afraid o' the dark, are ye? Ye should count yerself lucky there's a chamber pot down here."

That explained the smell. A loud boom sounded as the door shut, and the dank, inky room became darker still.

"Shite, I've landed in a good one this time." She released a shaky breath, and felt the area behind her, grimacing as her fingers encountered slime all over the walls of the hull and the wooden floor. Never happier to be wearing boots, Ebba used the heel to scrape at the slime until a mostly slime-free patch was clear to sit on.

Ebba hugged her knees to her chest, shivering as the

ominous pressing feeling grew and her chest tightened. "Ahoy?" she whispered.

The sound hit the opposite side of the hull; it had to be at least twenty feet across. They'd led her four flights down, into the guts of the ship. Was this where they took all their living captives? The room stank and was dark, but Riot was too gleeful about leaving her here. Was it the rats? Or was there something in the slime coating the walls that would make her sick? Something wasn't right about the room.

Her gut was telling her to get out of there fast, like a monster stood right behind her, breathing down her neck.

"Ebba-Viva Fairisles." A frail voice spoke.

Ebba shrieked and leaped to her feet. "Who's there?" The sound had come from diagonally to her left, in the far corner. "How do ye know my name?"

There was a rattle of chains as the person shifted. "Verity."

Verity. "Ye mean Verity the soothsayer?"

"Yes."

"Verity, who gets black eyes when she's mad?"

"Yes."

"Verity, who is in love with Locks, but both o' ye are too stubborn to admit it?"

Irritation crept into the woman's voice. ". . . Yes."

Ebba sat back down. "Well, why didn't ye say earlier? I thought there be a beast in here that would eat me, but it was just ye."

"You have the manners of someone raised by six male pirates."

Pulling her chain from underneath her butt, she replied, "Aye, so I've heard. I'm just glad none o' them got caught."

The soothsayer hissed. "Be careful what you say down here, Ebba-Viva Fairisles. The walls have ears and will tell Mercer Pockmark anything you confess while inside them."

Ebba shifted farther from the wall. "Ye're serious? How can they hear us? There be people listenin'?"

"A darkness rules this ship and those on it. The dark power seeks to uncover what you know. If you didn't have information it wanted to possess, you would already be dead."

"Shiver m'timbers, Verity. Yer sayin' there be dark magic in the bloody *walls*?" That was nearly as scary as a monster. Ebba shifted farther away from the hull.

Verity shuffled again in the dark, sighing heavily.

Ebba frowned at the sound. "Oi, Verity. How long have ye been down here? Are ye hurt?" The woman didn't sound very good. Nothing like the powerful soothsayer they'd met on Febribus. "How did ye get caught by *Malice*?"

It took a long while for the woman to answer. "This is the path I chose."

"Were ye drunk when ye decided?" Ebba asked after a beat.

Verity hummed in amusement, her voice fading. "It was the only pathway to success."

Ebba craned her head to glance around the darkness, wrinkling her nose. She had a different idea of what success looked like. Her version involved a head full of beads and free rein of all the seas with her fathers by her side. At least, it had.

"Can't ye use yer powers to wish us out o' here?" she asked.

"My powers are nearly gone," Verity said calmly. "Most of them. Since I've been here, I've poured all of my power into shielding my heart for as long as possible."

"What do ye mean, 'as long as possible?'" Ebba said, aghast.

"Trapped like this, I cannot withstand the power these walls hold. I won't be able to keep myself from succumbing for much longer. Once they have the heart, the soul is theirs."

Verity seemed half-delirious, and Ebba was struggling to put together what she meant, but if a soothsayer was afraid of whatever was in these walls, Ebba knew *she* should be terrified.

"We'll get out," she said to Verity, biting her lip when she recalled the walls could hear.

Verity's voice was a mere feather on a breeze when she answered. "Our fate is no longer in our hands, Ebba-Viva Fairisles."

SEVEN

Ebba woke, disoriented and surprised she'd managed to fall asleep at all. Nightmares of a six-headed beast had her jerking back to consciousness.

Her cheek was stuck to the slimy deck. "Yuck." Ebba peeled herself off and sat up, rubbing at the area with her sleeve.

She felt unaccountably weary. The events of the last day were catching up with her. Ebba wavered on the spot, frowning. She could go back to sleep right now, actually.

But first. . . .

Ebba got to her knees and then her feet, and set to work scraping back the slime with her boots to make a larger space. Feeling to make sure it was large enough, Ebba nodded and sat back down, arranging her chain beside her. "Verity, ye there?"

No answer came.

How would she ever face Locks if Verity died? Of course, facing Locks depended on her fathers saving her, and that seemed highly unlikely, given the size of *Malice*'s crew. Her fathers had surprised her more than once, however, and she knew by now they had a fair number of tricks up their sleeves. But even with the *dynami*, and Grubby's selkie skills, she couldn't see a way for them to save her. Ebba sincerely hoped she was wrong.

Escaping by herself didn't seem possible either. *Im*possible, according to the slumbering soothsayer. Ebba's heart sank as she thought of the enemy crew between their position and the main deck. And where were they in the Free Seas? She could stay afloat for a day, but anything more than that was questionable unless she managed to steal something to help her drift. And keeping herself and *Verity* afloat wasn't viable.

All of that depended on getting out of the manacle around her ankle, and opening the locked door.

Ebba cursed and abandoned that line of thought, drawing one of her dreads around to play with the beads. She began at the top. It was a turquoise bead with a wavy carved line through the middle. Her first bead. Her fathers purchased it for her when she was twelve and had just started growing her dreads after they shaved her hair because of lice. They got the bead from Neos, and gifted it to her that night. First, she'd thought about making a bracelet, or a bangle, but the wooden bead was so beautiful she hadn't wanted to risk losing it. So, she'd put it in her hair.

Ebba ran her hands over the others, calling forth the memory of how she came to have each bead. She'd given one to Caspian, but the others were all still accounted for. As she ran through her memories, Ebba felt energy returning to her.

Only a day or so must've passed. She had to stay strong. Whatever problems sat between her and her fathers, Ebba knew with certainty they wouldn't rest until she was free. She also knew by now that when the situation demanded courage, she was capable of standing on her own two feet. Somehow, she'd get herself and Verity out of here. Ebba couldn't rely on her fathers for everything, and she couldn't just see herself as part of a crew anymore. Knowing who she was apart from her fathers was important too. That was why, since Pleo, it had felt like she was afloat. Because Ebba had no clue who she was without them. At some point, and in some situations, she had to be capable of surviving on her own.

This was such a time, just like Syraness.

"Ebba-Viva?" Verity croaked.

Ebba jerked, and clutched her chest. "Verity. Sink me. I thought ye might've carked it."

"Still here," the soothsayer replied drily.

"Good, ye need to keep doin' what yer doin'. Locks'll get us out, ye'll see." Ebba paused as something occurred to her. "Hey Verity, why are ye down here then? What does Pockmark want from ye? He want ye to work yer hocus-pocus on sumpin'?"

"No, Ebba. He is feeding the ship."

Feeding the ship. That . . . what?

The door swung open, and Ebba jumped for the second time. Verity made no sound in the far corner.

"Fish-lips? Ye still here? Ye better be; Pockmark don't want the taint to take ye afore he gets his answer."

She recognized Swindles' voice, but frowned at his words. *The taint.* The taint that was in Caspian's shoulder?

Two sets of feet shuffled through the room toward her, and Ebba remained silent.

"Ye get the manacle, Riot," Swindles said.

"Why do I always have to do the manacle?" Riot argued.

"Because I'm first mate now, and I said so!"

Riot muttered, "Ye won't be for long. Pockmark let Jagger out o' here. He's never let anyone out. Jagger'll be first mate again afore ye know it. Mark my words."

Swindles took hold of Ebba's arm and dragged her up as Riot set to work on the manacle around her left ankle.

"Not after what Jagger did, he won't," Swindles said darkly.

"He ain't in charge though, is he?" Riot muttered.

Swindles hissed at him to shut up and shook Ebba roughly. "Bet yer fathers and ye were laughin' fierce-like after dupin' us with that wooden carvin'."

Ebba cracked a smile in the dark, remaining mute by the skin of her teeth.

"Pockmark nearly put us in here, too, when ye tricked us on Pleo," Swindles snarled.

He slapped her. Without light, his arm went astray. Ebba's head rocked to the side as the heel of his palm caught her cheek bone.

Ebba blinked slowly, straightening. She hadn't said anything, sod it! The sting in her cheek was only slightly more painful than the rest of her body, which felt like she'd run all day yesterday. Her muscles ached, her movement slow and restricted, and her stomach rumbled. That must be it; she hadn't eaten since . . . well, the morning of her capture. Time was hard to track down here.

But fear snaked up her spine as she recalled Swindles comment about the taint.

Ebba stumbled after them as they led her to the door. They were taking her out? Even fifteen minutes outside would be a welcome relief, though she felt bad for Verity not getting a break. What had the soothsayer meant with her 'feeding the ship' comment? Verity made it sound like the ship was draining her soothsayer magic away and that Pockmark had caught her for that purpose. That phrase —*feeding the ship*—struck at a memory from not so long ago. The Earth Mother had said the evil power that was locked away 768 years ago had returned to this realm weak and nearly catatonic. That it would gain strength by feeding on mortals, but that it preferred a mix of mortal and magic. Verity was such a mix. Soothsayers were given some magic by the great powers of the realm.

And if Pockmark's cronies were to be believed, the taint was in that place too. She'd seen exactly what the taint could do to a person. The uneasiness under her ribs swelled.

The passages lightened as Riot and Swindles marched her back up the four levels to the main deck. Ebba could feel some of her determination returning, as though she was throwing off the heavy dregs of sleep. The pressing feeling on her chest dissipated as Swindles pushed open the bilge door and Riot shoved her up the last ladder.

Ebba closed her eyes and inhaled the sea air.

The sun was high in the sky. She'd been down there for a whole day. If they let her out each day, it might not be so bad. She'd have a chance to shake off the crushing sensation of the dark room and reset.

The pirates shoved her to the helm where Mercer waited, Jagger at his right side. Swindles glared at Jagger as they approached.

Mercer ignored her, continuing his talk with Jagger before eventually turning to her. "Still alive?"

Ebba arched her brows. "I think yer room be broken."

The captain's face tightened, causing a wound to weep, and Ebba couldn't help screwing her face up in revulsion.

"My face bothers ye?" he asked, sauntering closer. He was without his tricorn hat right now, and Ebba's eyes rounded at the clumps of pale skin where his black hair was missing. The whites of his eyes were a mess of blood streaks and discolored yellow. It could be the light, but his very pupils appeared darker.

She gritted her teeth and contented herself with a shrug.

The blow to her gut didn't take her by surprise, but it still hurt like anything. Thinking before speaking was bloody overrated. Seemed like she should at least get an insult in if they hit her either way.

"I know ye're scared, fish-lips." Mercer sidled up next to her, mouth by her ear. "They tell me what ye say down there."

He dragged a pale finger over her collarbone, and seizing the offered opportunity, Ebba kneed the *Malice* captain in the balls.

Pockmark doubled over, hands between his legs.

Foreboding swept through her, making her regret the rash move, but Ebba forced a laugh. "Can't believe ye got close enough for that."

Riot and Swindles were frozen, their eyes on their captain. Ebba shifted her eyes to Jagger. He watched the *Malice* captain, too, his eyes unblinking.

With fear.

Jagger was afraid.

Mercer recovered his voice, and the sound when he spoke sent chills of terror down her spine. "That was a bad choice. A very bad choice."

EIGHT

"They beat you badly," Verity said dispassionately.

Ebba winced, cradling her side as she sat. Her eyes wouldn't completely open. She licked her lips, tasting blood. "Aye, Riot and Swindles. I might've pissed off Mercer some."

"A foolish thing to do," the soothsayer replied. "You've been unconscious since they brought you back yesterday."

She'd been out that long? A shame the *purgium* was on *Felicity*. It would've been nice to have the healing tube right about now. "Aye, I kneed Mercer in the balls."

Verity snorted. "Was it worth it?"

Ebba thought about it. *Nay*. "Maybe once the pain be gone." She didn't bother trying to sit. The pain to get there didn't seem worth it. "Do ye feel that pressure on your chest, Verity?"

"I do."

"It's worse than when I was last here. Do ye think it's because I'm hurt?" Ebba couldn't get the feeding comment out of her head.

The woman paused. "... Perhaps."

"Ye're lyin' to spare my feelings," Ebba said with a sigh. She hoped she was positioned in the slime-free path she'd cleared, but summoning the energy to check seemed an insurmountable task. "Verity, I ain't never been hurt like that afore. Why did they do that?" Ebba was tired and scared and hurting. A tear leaked from the corner of her eye to the slimy floor. She wanted her fathers.

"Because they are nearly lost to the taint, Ebba-Viva. Their souls are nearly gone to the dark power that lingers within this ship."

The taint—there it was again. "Ye mean the taint that was in Cosmo's shoulder."

"I do."

"Is the thing feedin' on yer powers also feedin' on the crew?" Ebba asked. Was that why Pockmark and the others looked terrible and why Jagger had lost so much weight?

"Yes, the taint is how they feed," the soothsayer whispered. "As the taint spreads, they grow more powerful."

Ebba sucked in a breath as she processed that.

"Are they feedin' on me? Am I tainted?" she forced herself to ask.

"They feed on everything in their path. They will never stop. They cannot; their power is limitless." Verity's chains rattled, and the woman took a labored breath.

Ebba's chest tightened. There were too many coincidences. The power on the ship and the evilness the Earth Mother described were the same thing. "The six pillars."

The ship groaned, and Ebba held her breath as the darkness in the room grew to suffocating levels.

The soothsayer's voice was thin. *"Do not utter their name again."*

"I be gatherin' that," she choked her reply. "How are they on this ship?" The Earth Mother hadn't known where the pillars were located—she'd said that their powers weren't yet strong enough to detect. How long had the evil been on *Malice*? And if

Pockmark was controlled by the pillars, was that why he was hell-bent on finding the *dynami* and the *purgium*? The pillars wanted the magic objects for themselves. The Earth Mother said the cylinders weren't the root of magic, but the tubes had to have something to do with attaining the root or the pillars wouldn't want them.

"The pillars are here because of the dark ambition of one man fifty years ago."

Ebba squeezed her eyes shut as a wave of dizziness assaulted her. "What does this mean for my crew?" If the evil was after the *dynami* and the *purgium*, the pillars themselves, not just Pockmark, would be hunting her fathers down.

"Worry yourself with guarding your heart from evil, not with things out of your control."

"Ye can't talk o' the end o' the realm and then go quiet."

Verity didn't answer.

Ebba huffed. "Real mature. I can hear ye breathin'." The soothsayer didn't speak. Ebba shifted with a groan. "Locks wouldn't appreciate yer attitude, I can tell ye that."

"I couldn't care less," Verity snapped.

"Ha! Got ye." Ebba smirked. "And ye don't fool anyone, by the way. Neither does Locks. He was tellin' me the other day ye be the only woman he could've ever settled down with. Said ye were beautiful and fierce. About turned my stomach with all the gooey."

". . . He said that?"

"I don't know, Verity. Do ye care to explain what ye meant afore?"

Her chains rattled. "I am wary of sayin' too much. But . . . I will tell you what I can."

"Aye, but don't say their name. Say mangoes, instead. The ship groanin' made my chest all tight, and I didn't like it."

"Why mangoes?"

63

Ebba frowned, stomach rumbling. "Because it be the first word that came to mind, why else?"

Verity sighed. "Over five thousand years ago, the world was ruled by the mangoes. . . ."

They both paused, but the ship didn't groan again.

". . . Each mango, powerful in their own right, yearned for unspeakable power. Though retaining their individual bodies, they merged themselves into one entity, one hive mind."

Ebba had heard the same words from the Earth Mother's lips.

"When they joined together, their power was unmatched, as was their depravity. They pitched the realm and all the creatures within into endless night and pain for four and a half thousand years."

She knew the rest, and recited aloud, "They were locked away behind a wall, but now they be back. They slipped through the wall because weak magic came back through first, and they were in a sorry state after bein' ripped from the realm by the root o' magic and the three watchers."

Verity hummed. "I don't know anything about the three watchers, but when the mangoes came back through the wall, the six of them were confined to a single mortal for many years, so weak were they. Then they grew powerful enough to leave that person to occupy this ship. The ship has infected the crew for years; slow at first and then faster and faster as the mangoes power grew. Soon, the crew's hearts will succumb, and the mangoes will regain their shadow forms. Once that happens, they'll become corporeal in mere weeks. Once corporeal, their power will be near unmatched. They will become the most powerful immortal entity in the realm."

There were a lot of big words in that speech. "How long will it take for them to be shadows again?"

Verity fell quiet.

Ebba's eyes searched the dark without success. What did her silence mean? She didn't know, or did her silence mean the pillars would manifest soon? The ship was feeding on the soothsayer. . . . How much power did Verity possess? Enough to grant the pillars their shadow form?

Ebba tried a different tactic. "Until they be shadows, can they only affect the pirates on this ship?"

"Once their taint reaches the hearts of the crew, the pirates will become contagious and will help to spread the taint to any living material they come into contact with—other people, animals, food, trees that aren't on the ship. Though a person can also be infected through injury from tainted material, as with your friend."

She'd been touching the ship which meant she was probably tainted now—or would be soon. Ebba had to hold fast to the knowledge that Caspian had gotten better. "Cosmo healed, did ye know? He lost his arm, but he got better."

"I'm glad. A tainted wound claims a soul faster, but demands less of a sacrifice to be healed. The tainted crew aboard this ship would die if the *purgium* was touched to their skin now."

A shame Ebba didn't have the *purgium* then.

"How do I know if the crew be cont'gious?" The ship was already tainting her; she didn't want to hurry the process along by touching someone whose heart was taken over.

"The eyes are windows to the soul."

. . . Right.

"I am weary, Ebba. And you need your rest," Verity said, her voice increasingly weak.

Ebba needed more than rest, starting with escaping a ship that would take over her will, and then grog, a soft hammock, and Zol.

She recalled their deal. "Locks said that he never knew what love was until he met ye."

The sound of Verity softly crying reached her, and Ebba stayed mute, sure the woman would hate her acknowledging it.

"Thank you," the soothsayer finally whispered.

NINE

"Hold her up," Mercer commanded.

How long had it been? Hours? Days? Ebba supposed it didn't matter. Time didn't change how she felt right now.

She wavered on her feet, held up between Riot and Swindles. Her head lolled, and she vaguely registered that her arms were coated in a black-green mess—the slime from the room.

They hadn't fed her.

They'd given her water, stale and slightly bitter that she'd just managed to keep down. At least that meant she hadn't had to use the chamber pot much—the one it took her ten minutes to find in the dark.

Ebba summoned her strength and lifted her head, squinting at Pockmark. Her left eye opened more than her right. Her bruises were still healing. Maybe that meant less than a week had passed. The thought was flittering and vague.

"Four days down there, and ye're still holdin' up," the captain said. "Not for much longer." He spoke to Riot and Swindles, and she looked past him to where Jagger stood staring at her.

He'd always played both sides. Spineless cur. Darkness

edged her thoughts. He was a traitor. He knew what was right, and he never chose it.

"Her eyes be goin', her skin be losin' its shine." Mercer smirked down at her. "Ye can feel it, can't ye? They all do at the start—afore they don't anymore. My masters be takin' ye." He stared at the ship. "Ye're taintin' her."

Malice groaned, and Ebba swallowed back a jolt of fear as the pressure on her chest squeezed. When she'd last been above deck, the pressure had disappeared entirely. Now it never left. She didn't have the energy to contemplate what that meant.

A weary retort halted on the tip of her tongue. Ebba was yet to recover from the last beating, and it took all her determination just to stand. Her knees shook from the effort. She would've thought she could go a week without food, but the taint down there was doing something, making her weaker and somehow getting inside her head.

Mercer was right. Ebba could feel herself becoming *less*, like the ship was sucking away at her being.

Nightmares assaulted her waking and sleeping. She hadn't spoken to Verity since waking from unconsciousness, but that fact was only occurring to her now. How was that possible? How had she forgotten about the soothsayer, a prisoner in the very same room?

Ebba shook harder. The pillars were feeding on her. The ship's taint was spreading into her. She had no way to resist it. Ebba was losing herself. The pillars were taking her away, piece by piece, and soon they'd reach her heart and seize her soul.

Mercer gestured to the pirate swine holding her, and they stepped back, letting her go. Ebba tried to remain upright, managing only a few seconds until one of her legs gave out. The three pirates laughed, and she gritted her teeth, staring at the deck as Mercer began to circle her.

"Just tell me where to find yer fathers," he said with a smirk. "We won't hurt them, ye know. We can be figurin' sumpin' out."

Ebba squeezed her eyes shut.

"This can all stop if ye just tell me—"

"Nay, ye flamin' sod!" she shouted. "I won't be tellin' ye. Ever."

His footsteps came to a stop behind her, and Ebba tensed, knowing she only had energy to dodge out of the way once, maybe twice. The singing of a cutlass being drawn from its sheath made the breath stutter in her throat.

She lifted her eyes to look at Jagger as the cutlass was pressed against her throat. His silver eyes regarded her without a flicker of emotion, dark smudges of exhaustion underneath.

"I guess ye've outlived yer useful'ness then," Mercer whispered in her ear.

"Are ye sure that be wise, Captain?" Jagger asked. "We haven't found her ship the last month or more. If they be in hidin', it doesn't seem likely we'll catch them."

As she swallowed, her throat pushed out against the blade. The knife dug in, and her eyes widened. Was this it? She'd assumed she'd have so much longer.

Ebba waited for Mercer to draw the cutlass against her throat and end it all.

"Ye know once the taint takes her, ye'll have all the inform'- tion ye want." Jagger spoke again.

Pockmark adjusted his grip. "There ain't no time. My masters want it now. They're close, so very close to regainin' their strength. If I fail, they'll cast me to Davy Jones'."

"If ye don't want to fail, ye need to think longer on this, Captain." Jagger took a step toward her. "What will take longer? Waitin' her out another two or three days, or tryin' to find *Felicity* for another few months? Ye know her fathers be wilier than they let on."

"My masters will drain the soothsayer afore three days be out," Pockmark snapped. "Then they'll be able to get the truth from her themselves. *I* need to deliver the truth to them."

Verity only had three days? She couldn't tell how much Jagger knew about the evil within the ship. His silver eyes darted between the captain and the deck. If Ebba had to guess, she'd say he had little notion of what was happening.

She latched on to Pockmark's last comment. "Ye'll never find my fathers. Yer pillars o' six will never come back."

Pockmark reeled back from where he still held the cutlass to her throat. The blade fell to the deck with a clatter, and he stared at her with wide eyes. Ebba sucked in a breath at the darkness of his irises. She glanced at Riot and Swindles and found their eyes in the same condition. There was something about the sight that shouted a warning at her, but the answer eluded her exhausted mind.

"What did ye just say?" he hissed.

Coughing, Ebba fell to all fours, lifting a hand to the small cut on her throat. It came away bloodied. "Bringin' yer evil friends back won't work," she gasped. If she died here, nothing would stop her fathers from finding the root of magic and taking the pillars out. And if she got free, nothing would stop *her* from doing the same.

Mercer kicked out, his boot catching her beneath the ribs. She wheezed and rolled to her back. He drew his pistol, and his hand shook.

"Ye're wrong," he said to her. "I'll be the one to succeed. They picked me because my father was too weak to hold them. *I* did that until they were ready." He cocked the hammer and shoved the barrel under her chin.

Ebba gasped, squeezing her eyes shut. What was he saying? That his father had been the pillars' puppet before him? Was he the one to hold the pillars and their taint inside until they were strong enough to reside within the ship?

"It's just a matter o' breakin' her quick-like, so the taint has no res'stance," Jagger said, still in the same spot, his silver eyes shifting like quicksand.

The ship groaned, and Pockmark jolted, staring down through the deck. The ship groaned again, and Pockmark dragged his eyes to look at Jagger. "Breakin'. Aye, they like that. How are ye be supposin' we do that?"

"She knows the woman in the room. The soothsayer. Kill her."

Mercer snapped, "I ain't allowed to touch her. They want to drain her powers."

"O' course. I forgot that."

Ebba highly doubted that. Was he trying to kill Verity so the pillars didn't come back? *In three days.*

"We ain't fed her, like ye ordered," Swindles piped up.

"No light, no comforts," Riot added.

Jagger pressed his cracked lips together. His eyes moved to her, and as Ebba surveyed his angular features, dread swept through her as she came to realize he was about to do something horrible.

"Her beads," he said quietly.

The three other pirates stared at him as Ebba forgot how to breathe.

Jagger cleared his throat, glancing away from her. "Take her beads. Her fathers gave them to her. That be the way to break her."

A wide smile spread on Mercer's face. His bottom lip cracked, and a drop of blood beaded there.

He peered down at her, and she rushed to smooth her features. "Is that so?"

Ebba shrugged. "Do yer worst. I can always be replacin' them." Her heart took up a wild staccato.

The ship groaned again, and Mercer's smile grew. He leaned over and picked up one of her beaded dreads, rolling it between his grease-covered fingers. "Is that so?" he repeated, whispering, "My masters don't believe you." He tapped his temple. "They think ye're bluffin'. Get her on her knees!"

No.

Ebba struggled, kicking out at Riot and Swindles, but her attempts were feeble after the beating and lack of food. They batted her fists and legs aside as though they were mosquitos.

Mercer laughed and stepped beside Jagger, slapping him on the back. "Good work, matey."

Jagger laughed with him, and fury filled her as she was slammed onto her knees.

"Curse ye, Jagger. Curse the day ye ever stepped foot on my ship, and curse the hole ye crawled out o'," she shouted at him as Riot drew his cutlass and picked up one of her dreads.

Ebba held the pirate's pistol-gray gaze as Riot drew the cutlass through the base of the dread. He held the severed dreadlock in his hand and then turned it upside-down. Her beads clattered on the deck, bouncing in all directions. Riot slid his cutlass down the chunk of her hair, dislodging the rest of the beads. Each clatter was a bullet in her heart.

She forced the lump in her throat back, not moving her stare from the pirate who'd given them the idea.

Swindles picked up the other dread, and Ebba's eyes blurred as he did the same, emptying another strand of beads onto the deck of *Malice*, never to be seen again.

"Licks, it were yer idea," Swindles sneered. "How about ye do the last one?"

Jagger's jaw tightened, but he drew his own cutlass and approached her. *Licks.* She'd felt so sorry for him when she'd learned what the name meant. Now, if someone had placed a whip in her hand, she would have gladly delivered the lashes herself.

Tears poured freely down both of her cheeks as he made quick work of the last dread. She listened as the beads followed the rest, bidding farewell to the memories they'd kept safe for her, to the years she'd collected them, and to the possessions she valued most in the world.

A sob broke from her lips, and Ebba bowed her head, shoulders shaking violently.

"It could've all been avoided if ye'd just told me what I wanted to know," the captain snarled in her face. He waved at the others. "Take her away."

TEN

Ebba hadn't answered Verity's questions when the pirates brought her back down to the dark chamber yesterday. Or was that two or three days ago now? Uncaring of the filth any longer, Ebba had lain sobbing, feeling the bristly stubs where her three beaded dreads used to be.

Verity deserved to be alone, anyway. Why should Ebba talk to her? Locks had left the soothsayer for good reason. She'd used him, played with his feelings. Verity was probably the one who'd told *Malice* where they'd be in Kentro. The woman could see the future. If she'd chosen her path, then she must've known this would happen. Maybe everything. The more Ebba thought about this, the more certain she became that Verity had betrayed them.

She wasn't the only traitor either.

Jagger. The black-hearted swine. Ebba would kill him one day. She'd fill him full of holes and latch cannonballs to his legs, and then watch from the deck as he sank into oblivion. He'd taken her beads. She didn't blame Swindles and Riot for hating him. Finally, she could see why they loathed him.

Ebba stroked the bristles again, her face twisting. What did it matter that the beads were gone? Her fathers didn't love her. They'd lied to her, again and again, her entire life. They'd hurt her, kept secrets from her. They probably laughed behind her back about it. Hadn't they done just that with Cosmo the other day? They'd known who he was and kept it from her.

They kept everything from you.

They'd kept everything from her.

Her fists curled until her nails dug into her palms. She was all alone in this world. Ebba could only be happy that Caspian got away.

He was there that day. He could have saved you.

Ebba scowled. The prince had been at the dock that day. Surely he'd seen her capture. He probably witnessed the *Malice* pirates marching her onto their ship. He'd been right there. He let them take her. She clenched her teeth. For all his manners and education, for all his words about how she was pretty, and for all she'd done for him, he'd abandoned her. She should've known he was truly leaving her when he asked to return to Exosia.

He deserved to lose his arm.

You are alone.

"I'm alone," Ebba whimpered.

Everyone leaves you.

"They all leave me," she choked.

"Fight back," a voice called to her from across the dark room. "You mustn't let them win."

Ebba screamed, "They all leave!"

Digging her nails into her scalp, she rocked on the spot as darkness crushed down on her from all sides.

THE DOOR SWUNG OPEN.

Ebba didn't care anymore. Sometimes the door opened, and her fathers stood there, smiling, before laughing and shutting the door again. She hated them. She hated the door.

Hands went to the manacle around her foot.

She hissed and drew her leg in. The person yanked it back and freed her ankle despite her attempt to kick them off. Probably because her attempts were mere twitches.

"Leave me alone," she snarled.

The person shuffled across the room, and Ebba lay immobile, listening as they unlocked the bitch, Verity.

The person came back to Ebba. "Ye need to walk. The soothsayer is barely alive."

To walk? A faraway part of herself called through the black fog, telling her to go up to the main deck. "Leave her then," Ebba said, smirking in the dark. "Carry me instead."

The man reached down, grunted, and heaved her up against his side, wrapping an arm around her waist. Grunting again as he shifted Verity's position over his shoulder, the pirate guided her in the direction of the door.

The ship groaned.

"Hurry," the person urged. "Their eyes are turnin' solid black, one by one. Sumpin' be happenin'. Ye've got to get off the ship now."

Ebba couldn't remember why she should want to be outside, but feet faltering, she obeyed the call of the man. Wavering, held up mostly by the man's grip on her arm, Ebba forced her feet one in front of the other.

The man cursed. "This be yer chance. Push harder."

She did. Though Ebba couldn't fathom why.

They made it out of the room and started down the passage. Ebba wanted to get to the deck. Why was that? The urge to be in the fresh air surged within her. "I ain't goin' to make it."

Jagger's face swam before her, searching her eyes intently.

He sagged afterward for a brief moment. "Aye, ye are. They ain't taken ye yet. But I ain't sure how long ye have."

"Ye gutless swine!" She choked on her rage, recalling her beads.

His black-rimmed silver eyes flickered, but he continued heaving her down the hall as the ship groaned again. "Ye can hate me later. Just get off the ship first."

She was going to kill him before she left. But Ebba needed to rely on his strength to reach the top. She'd kill him once she was there.

They made it to the first ladder, and Jagger disappeared up with Verity, sweat beading his brow. He came back and slung Ebba over his shoulder, pushing up the ladder again. "Come on, we need to make it to the main deck," he panted. Raising his voice, he called loudly, "We'll get the rowboat and escape."

The ship groaned loudly, and footsteps sounded far above.

Beside her, Jagger smiled grimly. He set Ebba back on her feet at the top and picked up Verity once more.

Lanterns were strung down the narrow passage of this deck, illuminating the closed doors which probably led to smaller quarters. She had absolutely no desire to see inside any of the rooms.

Her eyes watered from the brightness of the lanterns after so long in the dark, but after a minute, the light helped her place each weary footstep as Jagger continued hauling her to the next ladder.

He shoved her away from him without warning and drew his cutlass. Ebba hit the wooden floor, bouncing painfully. Verity toppled from his shoulder, hitting the deck hard as Jagger rushed a pirate coming down the next ladder. He rammed the cutlass through his opponent's stomach. The pirate didn't respond. He didn't even blink as Jagger withdrew the cutlass and pushed him to the ground, dead.

Jagger hauled Ebba up and carried her up the ladder first this time.

"Just leave Verity," she hissed in his ears.

"That ain't ye talkin'," he grunted, putting her down when they reached the top.

Ebba licked her lips as he descended for Verity. If she could get ahold of one of his pistols, she could make short work of killing him.

He reappeared with the soothsayer, tunic soaked with sweat, and she used the wall to help as Jagger hauled her upright. Two more decks. She was halfway.

Footsteps pounded above, and feet appeared down the ladder ahead.

Jagger drew in a breath. "Hide."

He ducked behind a beam, lowering Verity behind a barrel. He jerked Ebba, and she sprawled over him, breathing hard.

The footsteps swept past them, and Ebba closed her eyes. She didn't want to be caught. She wanted to be in the fresh air.

"They'll be back. Smart-like now."

Ebba used the barrel to stand, her arms shaking with the effort. Verity hadn't made a sound the entire trip, and Ebba wondered how close to death the woman was. Hopefully close.

Jagger heaved them both up the third ladder, one after the other, but instead of heading up to the main deck, he turned left.

"Where are ye goin'?" Ebba demanded.

He held a finger to his lips, pointing at the walls. His usually golden skin was pale and waxy. The pirate was clearly reaching the end of his own endurance, emaciated as he was. It would make it easier to choke the life from him. He'd put her down in that dark room; he'd taken her beads. He'd started the whole war with *Malice*. He might be taking her where she wanted to go right now, but that wouldn't last. The world would be a better place without him. She'd be the one to do it. She'd shoot him with his own pistol or strangle him. Maybe she'd pull him under the water and hold him there. She'd enjoy every second of it.

Groaning, Jagger lowered Verity to the ground. They were on the cannon deck of the ship, an open deck dotted with posts and lanterns, instead of a passage and rooms like the lower decks. Small trap doors that Ebba knew to be gun ports lined the walls of the hull either side, a cannon set up in front of each one. There had to be at least fifteen cannons down here. The presence of the trap doors told her they were now above water level.

Jagger turned his attention to a cannon. He lifted the back end of the heavy weapon and removed the large wedge behind the wheels. He then hacked at the ropes holding the cannon to the wall of the ship. Wasted muscles straining, the pirate wheeled the cannon back from the wall, clearing the trap door of the gun port.

Ebba watched as he staggered to the nearest post and grabbed a rope coiled there. Weaving back to where she waited, he looped the rope around Verity's waist.

Shouts reached them from farther down the passage.

Jagger carried the soothsayer to the gun port, wrenched up the trap door, and shoved her out without ceremony. A distant splash sounded below. He turned to Ebba, his back to the hole. "I'll keep ahold o' the rope up here until ye find Verity in the water. Put her on her back and float on yers. The tide be goin' in, and we ain't far from Maltu. It'll carry ye. Ye just need to make it three hundred feet, Viva. Do ye hear me?"

Ebba glanced up from his pistol to his face, hearing footsteps pounding behind them. Jagger planned to stay behind? Unfortunate, then, that she had other plans. He'd be dead in a few minutes, gone to Davy Jones' locker where he belonged.

Dropping her shoulder, Ebba used her remaining strength

to ram into the pirate's stomach, sending them toppling through the square hole and into thin air.

He twisted as they fell, but Ebba clutched at him with one hand, reaching for his belt with the other. Where was his pistol?

They hit the water, and Ebba was ripped away.

The cold shocked her, breaking through a haziness she hadn't realized was there. The shock shattered through the black fog around her mind, and Ebba's face slackened under the water as her last moments came flooding back to her. She'd been about to kill someone. Not just anyone—*Jagger*. She'd been ready to shoot Jagger. Failing that, to strangle or drown him. Ebba choked on water and kicked upward as her breathers tightened in warning.

As she burst through the water and sucked in huge gulps of fresh air, Ebba felt the cloudiness over her thoughts receding. The pressure on her chest didn't ease in the slightest, but it was as if she could see the world again. Ebba gasped for more clean, wholesome air, driven by some primal urge to regain her senses. What had happened to her? It was as though she'd woken from a nightmare, or from another lifetime.

Horror flooded her as she circled her legs under the surface to stay afloat, struggling to collect herself. The things she'd thought only moments before . . . it was as though she'd been Swindles or Riot. How hadn't she recognized the taint was at play, making her say and do those awful things? It was like at some point her reason, her very awareness, had switched off.

"Jagger?" she spluttered, suddenly terrified she might have been successful in killing him.

He swam up beside her. "Why did ye push me out?" he said angrily. "I've got to stay on the ship." He began drawing in the rope, and Ebba remembered Verity. She'd told Jagger to leave the soothsayer behind. Ebba swallowed, battling against tears.

"Jagger, what happened?" she whispered.

Verity rose to the surface, and Ebba took hold of the sooth-sayer, who'd been face-down in the water. She thumped her back until the woman coughed up the water. Her eyes popped open for a scant second, showing periwinkle blue, before the soothsayer settled back into unconsciousness. They had to get her help. Who knew how long she'd been unconscious? Ebba didn't.

She'd completely forgotten the soothsayer was on the opposite side of the room, dying.

Jagger handed her the rope. "The taint didn't get ye. That's what. And ye need to make sure it don't. Three hundred feet, Viva. Ye need to make to shore." He pointed directly over her shoulder.

Ebba clamped a hand on his arm and stared at him. "Jagger, ye can't go back."

"I have to." His voice was pained. "My family."

"They be gone, Jagger. Ye know that," Ebba said, eyes searching the deck above. They were already floating away from the anchored ship, but well within pistol and cannon distance.

Jagger shook his head. "Mercer said they be alive."

"And ye believe him?" Ebba said. "If they be alive, why sacrifice yerself? He'll kill them anytime he wants; ye know he will. Ain't nothin' so special about ye that'll stop the darkness on that ship from doin' what it pleases."

The pirate was silent.

Guilt tore through her as she remembered her murderous vows from just moments before. Ebba had to stop him going back to that ship. If she didn't, he'd be taken by the pillars. "If ye go back, ye'll be locked in that room for good. Or just killed. I won't let ye take that on for savin' me and Verity. The crew's eyes were goin' black, ye said so. That means the crew be cont'-gious now. The pillars will take your soul, too, Jagger. Then ye won't ever care about yer family, let alone want to save them."

Ebba assumed black irises were what Verity had meant with her 'eyes are the windows to the soul' nonsense. If the crew's eyes were black, the pillars had taken their souls, and the crew could now spread the taint to any living thing by touch. Jagger's eyes were already black-rimmed. He couldn't last against a tainted ship *and* a tainted crew. Ebba wasn't even sure how he'd held up when the rest of the crew succumbed.

She said, "Come with me, and my crew can take ye to Neos for Ladon to do the job, if ye're still suicidal then. Ye ain't thinkin' straight, Jagger. The taint be usin' yer mouth and mind, not ye."

Jagger looked at her, blinking hard. His eyes seemed to lose some of the black rim, his flaxen hair taking on a new shine in the moonlight. "Aye," he said softly, blinking again. "Aye, ye're right."

He took hold of the neck of Verity's shredded dress and floated on his back, kicking below the surface. Ebba left him to carry Verity, sensing it would be a near thing for her to reach Maltu at all, with how weak she was.

Shouts came from the deck.

"Shite," Jagger cursed. "They've noticed. They'll send a boat out. We have to beat them into Maltu and hide."

A muted pop sounded to Ebba's right. She renewed her efforts, paddling her arms beneath the surface beside Jagger, groaning as her muscles burned. "How far?"

Something touched her leg, and Ebba erupted into a flurry of punching and kicking. "Sumpin' just touched me."

Jagger scoffed. "Ye grew up in the water, and yer afraid o' things in the sea?"

She'd just escaped from the worst experience of her life. She was terrified of everything right now.

"Ebba?" someone said behind her.

Ebba whirled in the water, not believing her ears. "Grubs?"

He looked as shocked as she felt. "Ebba, what're ye doin' here in the water? I thought ye were on the evil ship? I couldn't get in to ye. The water just around it was black and didn't feel right to swim in. I've been hangin' back here for a few hours."

"We escaped, Grubs." Her voice cracked, and she burst into tears, hugging him and treading water at the same time. "I'm so glad ye're here."

"How *are* ye here?" blurted Jagger.

"He be part selkie," Ebba explained. The pirate wouldn't know. "Where's *Felicity*, Grubs?"

"She be at the western point. Close-like. We've been followin' ye since ye were taken."

Sailing on the navy side of Kentro to follow *Malice*? Her fathers had put themselves at too much risk to get her back.

"What's a selkie?" Jagger muttered.

"They're shootin' at us," Ebba reminded everyone, darting a look behind her.

Grubby looked perplexed. "Is that what that poppin' be? It sounds right strange underwater."

Ebba gripped his arm. "Can ye get us out o' here, Grubs? There be three o' us."

"Sure." He gave her a toothy grin. "Just hold on to my belt. Oops, wait a second, better tighten it first."

Jagger jerked in the water. "Sink me, hurry it along, will ye? They're loadin' the cannons."

"That be a mite tighter," Grubby announced. "Hold on now. I'll try to be rememberin' not to go underwater overlong. Just pinch me if I'm forgettin'."

Jagger's mouth was slightly ajar. He shook himself, blinking several times before saying, "Ye'll need to hold her in yer arms." He thrust Verity at Grubby.

Grubby cradled the soothsayer, and Ebba and Jagger quickly took hold of either side of his belt.

"Hold yer breath," her father said cheerfully.

She glanced back at *Malice*, obeying some morbid, fearful curiosity. Her eyes ran along the black ship with the crimson sails, following the lanterns strung up along the bulwark. Her breath caught at the sight of Pockmark standing near the bow, facing them. As she watched, a darkness rose behind him, enveloping him.

Her stomach dropped, horror holding her tight as the darkness coalesced, pulsating, shrinking, and reforming. . . .

. . . Into six looming shadows. The shadows were in the form of a man and twice the size of Pockmark. Each of the shadows rested a hand on the ship's bulwark as they stood either side of *Malice's* captain.

Putting two and two together wasn't hard. Verity had said the evil would regain its shadow form. The six pillars were here. They'd become strong enough to transition.

A scream worked its way up her throat, and she froze in the water, waiting for the moment when the dark shadows would fly at their small group and drag them back to *Malice*. But the shadows didn't budge. The largest of them stretched a hand out toward her, but wrenched back the limb as though stung.

Could they not leave the ship?

None of the other pillars had relinquished their hold on the bulwark. The shadows either couldn't move off *Malice* or were content to let the crew do the work of retrieving Ebba and the others. She wasn't sticking around to figure out which it was.

She unfroze enough to form a mostly coherent word. "Go!"

Ebba just managed to take a breath as Grubby took off under the water's surface. Ebba closed her eyes as he pushed through the sea as easily as she usually ran on deck. It wasn't fast enough. They had to get away. Fear surged within her, and though the six shadows hadn't pursued their group so far, she couldn't help the terrified thought that this was a cruel joke and she'd be dragged back to *Malice* any second.

Grubby took them to the surface again and swam on top as they gulped in air. Ebba wiped the salty water from her eyes and then thumped on Verity's back until she coughed up water again. Drowning was something they could deal with, but Ebba's instincts were screaming that if the six shadows back on *Malice* got hold of them again, they were really goners.

Only once Verity was breathing did Ebba glance back. *Malice* was a good thousand feet behind them. "We have to keep goin'. Fast," she urged. "They're back. I saw them back there."

Grubby doubled his efforts, pushing them through the dark waters.

"Who?" Jagger called over the splashing and slapping they were causing with their bouncing movement.

Ebba tried to slow her breathing. "There were six shadows around Pockmark. They rose up and took shadow form as I watched. They didn't move after us, but that ain't to say they can't. I—"

"The taint is still in ye," Jagger said. "Are ye sure o' that? Six shadows?"

Ebba nodded. "I know what I saw. We have to get away." She couldn't go back there. Ever again. Who knew the monster she'd become.

"Goin' under," Grubby announced.

Conversation seized as they turned their focus toward holding their breath. The next time they came up, Ebba's arms were trembling from holding on against the drag of the water. Jagger was the one to thump Verity on the back this time.

"How much longer?" she asked, blinking slowly. They'd have to tie her to Grubby if it was too much farther.

"Nearly there, Ebba. I'll stay atop the water now we be away. The others'll be so happy to see ye."

Tears mingled with the salty drops of seawater on her face. The things she'd thought about her fathers while on *Malice*. They'd been following her the whole time—of *course* they'd been following. Trying to find a way to save her. How could she have doubted them?

"How long was I on *Malice*?" she asked hoarsely.

Jagger answered, "Ten days."

In ten days, the six pillars had taken over her will. Or very nearly. In ten days, she'd turned her back on her fathers, and Caspian, Verity, and Jagger. She'd tried to kill him! A person who'd saved her life in the past. If not for the water knocking her back to her senses, she would've done her best to finish the job.

What kind of person did that make her? Ten days, and she'd forgotten who she was. There was something ugly in her, something evil the six pillars had latched on to and wedged a splinter inside of to make the ugliness larger. She'd lost herself. *In ten days.*

Ebba wasn't who she thought she was. She inhaled sharply. She'd already been a monster, and the ship had just seized on her weaknesses.

She choked and ignored a look from Jagger. Pressing her lips together, she forced her sobs to stay inside as Grubby tore through the ocean.

Soon, a familiar sight bobbed in the water ahead.

It was the last straw.

Ebba choked on her tears, sobbing and shaking uncontrollably in the water as Grubby took them closer.

"Don't cry, Ebba," Grubby begged, moving faster.

The breath caught in her throat, and her chest seized as the last ten days came crashing down on her. She couldn't stop. The stuttering, high-pitched sobs just continued as she was pulled up on deck by her fathers above, and they continued as her fathers took turns hugging her, every one of them crying too.

"What did they do to ye?" Stubby said hoarsely, gray-blue eyes wide as he searched her for injury. His face slackened as he took in her appearance. Were the bruises still showing? Or was it just her general thinness and grubbiness?

Ebba's teeth chattered, and she couldn't answer. Sally flew over and hugged her face before perching on her shoulder. Her fathers glared at the wind sprite before turning back to her, a question in their eyes.

Ebba shook her head, pressing her lips together. Her fathers hadn't wanted to drag up their horrors, and Ebba now had some of her own. She couldn't tell them. It was too vivid. Too real. Shame and confusion rendered her mute.

Jagger spoke from the bulwark. "I'll tell ye when we're on the way."

Locks' eyes fell on the unmoving form at his feet. "Verity? Verity!" He fell to his knees beside her, gathering her in his arms. "What happened to her?"

"S-she was in there, too," Ebba shivered, the memory of the darkness so real she could touch it. "In the room. They were drainin' her power to feed the ship. The pillars be back. The ones the Earth Mother told us of. I saw them." Her shivers grew until she was shaking like a lax sail.

"What?" Peg-leg asked, horror and confusion etched in the deep lines on his face.

Jagger tried to stand and fell back to sitting. "We need to go. This can wait until later. Where are we headed?"

"He's right," Barrels said. "West or east?"

"West—it's farther from the navy's preferred route. We'll have to sail the southern coast of Kentro in navy seas, or risk *Malice* cuttin' us off at the north end," Plank answered.

"Raise anchor, lads," Stubby ordered.

Locks stayed with the three of them as the rest of her fathers scattered to get *Felicity* moving. He stared at each in turn, Verity still cradled in his arms. "Ebba," he whispered. "Lass, we were so afraid for ye. How did ye escape?"

Ebba still shook uncontrollably, but she tilted her head at Jagger.

Her father turned back to Jagger, who looked about to lose consciousness himself. How long had he been holding on by a thread for? He'd lasted an entire month down in that room and had still been so . . . normal. She'd become a cutthroat in ten days. How had Jagger stayed so together?

There really was something wrong with her.

"Let's get ye all below deck. Ye need food and rest." He stood with Verity and turned to Jagger. "Can ye walk, lad?"

Jagger nodded and gritted his teeth to stand. He nearly made it, but fell back into his crouch. Ebba crossed to him on wobbly legs. His eyes were only black-rimmed. Ebba assumed that meant he was okay to touch. She took hold of his arm, avoiding his gaze. "I'll help ye, like ye helped me."

Maybe if she did the right thing for the rest of her life, she'd atone for what happened. Ebba heaved with all her might.

He didn't budge. In fact, nothing happened. Other than her falling on top of Jagger.

"Right, well, I'll be back for the pair o' ye," Locks said, heading to the bilge.

She lay sprawled on top of Jagger, too weak to move.

"Thanks for nothin'," he wheezed underneath her.

But black closed in on her, and Ebba couldn't be sure if she actually said the words, 'Ye better not be cont'gious,' or not.

ELEVEN

Ebba sighed and snuggled into the blanket. This hammock was perfect, and she never wanted to leave it.

There was a muted thud as someone hit someone else, followed by a hissed, "*Shh*."

Already mourning the loss of her oblivious comfort, Ebba cracked open an eye. Her other eye opened, too, at the sight of four of her fathers a few feet away. All of them staring at her.

"What happened?" She groaned and shifted onto her back in the hammock.

"Ye've been asleep for two days, little nymph," Plank said. "Ye all have."

She glanced left and saw Jagger slumbering there in a hammock, Verity in another hammock on his other side. They were in *Felicity's* hold. The familiar sight of her beloved ship brought the recent events rushing back. Cold and lingering horror planted deep in her veins at the thought of the dark room on *Malice*.

She never thought she'd see her fathers again. Or these sleeping quarters. Ebba hadn't dared to dream of ever swinging in her own hammock once more, or of hearing the welcoming creak and groan of *Felicity* as she sailed.

"Ye've been dead to the world," Plank said.

Ebba shivered, but curled as her stomach cramped. "When did I last eat?"

"Afore ye slept, but by the look o' ye, not much afore that. We were goin' to wake ye to eat," Peg-leg sniffed, his eyes glistening. "I'll go rustle sumpin' up."

"Peg-leg?" she said. He stopped, but didn't turn, shoulders held stiffly. "Just not mangoes, please."

Four sets of eyes landed on her, but she didn't explain further.

"Aye," Peg-leg sniffed again. His voice hardened. "No mangoes. I'll throw the whole lot o' them overboard first chance I get." He disappeared down into the hold.

Grubby took her hand. She attempted to smile at him.

"Thank ye, Grubs. We wouldn't have made it back here without ye."

He wiped his eyes on his stained sleeve and planted a wet kiss on her forehead. "Ye can do anythin' ye set your mind to, Ebba."

Ebba closed her eyes, swallowing hard against threatening tears.

"If ye feel up to it," Locks said, "ye'll feel much better after a wash."

"Aye, I'll do that." Ebba didn't have the heart to tell them that feeling better wasn't going to be so easy. Navigating Syraness had haunted her. The fear of not being able to save her fathers, to be without them and the reason they died had plagued her in the weeks after. But that room . . . it had torn into who she was, dug at her insecurities and left them as gaping wounds. She'd been about to kill someone and leave a friend behind. Ebba wanted to tell her fathers about the taint. About what she'd done.

. . . Except she couldn't.

Her shame over the ugliness within her was too thick to navigate. If she was stronger, or truly good, the dark power couldn't have made her act that way. She should've been able to keep the pillars' taint at bay as Jagger had—to fight back in some way. But she hadn't. It had preyed on her weaknesses, her own wickedness. The feeling was similar to how Locks had described his time on *Eternal*.

If being tainted was akin to what he'd felt while sailing under Mutinous, Locks had been right: Ebba *hadn't* understood what her fathers had gone through. About how they'd lost themselves and begun to like doing bad things without understanding why. His words struck a chord within her now. And she desperately wished that they didn't.

Peg-leg returned with food, gaze flicking between her and Plank. The plate held fresh bread and cheese. "Just a bit, mind ye. How long ago did they feed ye?"

"They gave me water. I can't remember eatin'," Ebba said, swinging her feet down. Plank steadied her from behind. Had Pockmark fed her? So much of her stay was a dark blur of malicious thoughts.

"The whole time? Ten days?" Grubby asked, eyes wide.

Only ten days. "Grog," Ebba said.

Peg-leg held out a goblet. "It's just water. Only a few sips, mind. Then some bread."

She did as he bade, eating a few mouthfuls of the cheese and bread before handing the plate back.

"I'm right sorry for bein' so unpleasant to ye after Pleo," she said, the words bursting from her cracked lips. "I couldn't understand why ye'd lie and why ye'd conceal so much from me.

But I do now. I understand that ye *couldn't* speak o' it, not that ye didn't wish to."

All of her fathers froze, their expressions wide eyed and fixed, unmoving, on her face.

"Ye do?" Plank asked, his voice trembling.

Ebba nodded and blinked, dislodging two fat tears that trickled over the cuts and bruises on her face. "Aye, I do. Really. And I be forgivin' ye for everythin'."

Plank turned away, his frame shaking as he covered his mouth.

"What happened?" Barrels asked softly. "You know you can tell us."

Ebba shook her head. "Nay, Barrels. I can't. And I shouldn't have made any o' ye speak o' it either. I'm sorry for forcin' Locks. I won't be doin' so with the rest o' ye."

Barrels exchanged a long look with Peg-leg, and with Plank when he turned back. "Well," Barrels said, "we mean to tell you everything anyway, if you'd do us the favor of listening. And if, by the end, you feel up to sharing, you can be assured we will listen to you too. Without judgment."

She didn't answer. She knew their change of heart only came from their desire to show her she could speak of the horror.

Was this crushing heartsickness what Caspian had felt when he sank into his nightmares? He hadn't spoken of them either, just like her. By going back to Exosia, had he been trying to absolve his shame? Just like she'd have to find some way of doing?

"Yer beads be gone," Plank said as Barrels went to check on Verity.

Ebba stared at the ceiling. "Aye," she whispered. "They cut them off." She didn't tell her fathers who had given Pockmark the idea and cut out the third strand of beads. But only because

Jagger had gotten her away from that soulless place. He'd probably saved her life when he told Pockmark, anyway. Him doing so saved her from death. And maybe by not mentioning Jagger's actions to her fathers, Ebba was atoning, in part, for the ugliness within her. Though . . . she just felt more shame and darkness at the thought. She should have to feel shame to the fullest degree.

"We'll get ye more beads," Grubby said after a full minute.

Ebba turned away from him, facing Jagger. "Nay, I don't want any more," she said. At their doubtful silence, she added, "I'd like to wash." Maybe if she scrubbed hard enough, Ebba would feel better.

Plank helped her down the passage. "Away with ye, Pillage!" He scolded the cat, who was up to his usual tripping antics. "She be injured, ye furry heathen. Not the time."

Her father led her to where Peg-leg was heating water over the fire pit. They left her with a drying cloth and scrubbing brush. What she really wanted was to immerse herself in water and be fully clean, but she was so weak, she'd likely drown.

Sally flew in as Ebba shucked the last of her clothes. The wind sprite picked up the scrubbing brush, dipping it in the water, and began rubbing Ebba's arms free of the stinking and matted slime covering them. The wind sprite continued moving to and from the cauldron to Ebba, washing her.

"Sal?" Ebba whispered after several minutes of these ministrations. "Why didn't ye come for me?"

Sally mewled and came to float in front of her, shoulders slumping. The wind sprite pointed at herself, and then down the hall. Ebba stepped forward to see where she was pointing.

"Verity?" she asked.

The sprite pointed at herself and then flexed her arm muscles before pointing at the deck and making a scary face.

"*Malice* might've fed off ye if they'd caught ye? Is that what ye're sayin'?"

Sally nodded, and Ebba's heart lightened by the tiniest fraction. Sally hadn't left her there without reason. "I'm understandin'. But I'm afraid the pillars be back anyhow. I saw six shadows form out o' thin air. What happens now they've returned, Sal?"

The wind sprite returned her question with a serious expression, which Ebba took to mean 'nothing good.'

"Verity said they'll grow more powerful now. We gotta do sumpin' to help. If my fathers ain't goin' to, I'll need to find the answers myself."

Sally jerked a thumb at her chest.

"Thanks, Sal." Ebba wouldn't be alone.

The sprite hugged Ebba's face again and went back to her work, washing Ebba from head to toe. The heat of the water was soothing on some primal level, and by the end, she was clean and dressed in fresh clothing.

"Thank ye." Ebba sighed. Plank was right; she did feel less like a rotten cutthroat now.

There was just one thing she had to do before she went back to her hammock. If the *purgium* had been on her when *Malice* took her hostage, it would've been a terrible thing, but that aside, Ebba would never let the *purgium* or the *dynami* out of her sight again. She'd never really cared enough to know why *Malice* wanted these objects so badly. And that was her error. She hadn't taken the threat of Pockmark seriously. Maybe if she or her fathers had, Ebba would have connected the parallels between the pillars and *Malice* sooner. But after what she'd experienced on that ship, Ebba couldn't allow the magic tubes to fall into the pillars' hands. They were too powerful already. *Already* unstoppable in her mind. However the two cylinders fit into finding the root of magic, Ebba could feel that the two objects were vital to bringing down the pillars of six or, at least, preventing the shadows from becoming invincible. If the pillars once had possession of the root of magic and were thwarted by the three mortal watchers, then Ebba highly doubted the evil immortals would allow a repeat of history.

The pillars couldn't get their hands on the *purgium* or the *dynami*. Ever. The healing cylinder was staying in Ebba's belt for safekeeping.

Ebba wrenched open the kitchen drawer she'd hidden the *purgium* in, digging into the back by the spoons. Barrels had purchased the spoons way back when, but even he used his fingers and daggers to eat nowadays, so no one ever ventured here for fancy cutlery. She was the only one onboard who could hold the healing tube. The Earth Mother had warned her that her fathers could never touch it.

Smiling grimly, Ebba's fingers brushed the *purgium*. Her smile was struck from her face as a stabbing pain pierced through her chest.

She screamed as the *purgium* melded to her palm, forcing her fingers closed around it. White pain seared through her body. Agony encompassed her very soul.

And everything went black.

"EBBA!" Someone shook her. "*Ebba.*"

She groaned and lifted both hands to her throbbing head. "Who let Grubby make the grog?"

Sally and Barrels loomed over her. Her father's salt-and-pepper hair had escaped its tie. "You touched the *purgium*. It did something to you, my dear." He shouted down the passage for her other fathers.

Ebba frowned as he crouched by her side again. "It healed me?" Her eyes rounded, and she gasped. "Shite! Do I still have my limbs?" What if the *purgium* had taken her arm, like it took Caspian's?

"Yes. . . ." He wrapped an arm about her shoulders to help her sit.

Ebba listened to her fathers' pounding footsteps down the hall. Despite Barrels' reassurance, she searched herself for missing body parts, sagging when everything seemed the same. Too much *the same*. "I still have my scratches and bruises," she mused as her fathers gathered around her.

The healing cylinder hadn't fixed those when it knocked her out.

The strange expressions on her fathers' faces pulled her up short.

"What?" Ebba demanded, heart thundering. "What is it?"

Sally bobbed behind them, her mouth hanging open.

Stubby rubbed the back of his head. "Ye have some white hair now, lass."

"Really? Where? Let me see."

Barrels hurried back to his office and brought back the small mirror her fathers used to shave on the rare occasion.

Holding the mirror up, Ebba peered at her reflection. "Tired jokes o' a down-trodden clownfish," she breathed.

Six of her dreads, three on either side of her middle parting, had been leached of their ebony black color and were now stark white. The blanched dreads stood out like a star on an inky-black night.

"Did it heal the taint in ye, little nymph?" Plank asked. Did she detect hope in his voice?

The taint. She lowered the mirror to look at him. That possibility hadn't even crossed her mind. Ebba closed her eyes. The crushing shame she'd felt, the haunting darkness, the self-doubt, the drive to do endless right to make herself feel better. . . . "It be gone," she whispered, opening her eyes. She took a breath, and it filled her completely. "I'm feelin' much better. Nearly like afore it happened. The *purgium* got rid o' the taint in me," she said in amazement, utterly certain of it.

She felt as light as a feather in comparison to five minutes prior.

"Thank the oblivion for that," Stubby choked out.

Peg-leg paced. "Ye shouldn't have touched the tube at all after being tainted, Ebba-Viva! Ye're right lucky the *purgium* only took the color from some o' yer hair."

"Aye, I know," she replied, chastened. "I didn't think about that. I've always been able to touch it afore." If she *had* thought about the difference, she'd never have touched the healing cylinder.

"But why didn't it heal her cuts and bruises?" Stubby asked, a furrow between his brows. "Aside from the one on yer neck. That one be gone."

Ebba dropped her gaze to her hands and legs. The conversation she'd had with the prince after Pleo came back to her. After finding out the truth of how she'd come to be with her fathers, Ebba had wondered why the *purgium* wouldn't heal her of sadness. Caspian had supposed it was because the magical object knew she'd get better by herself. "The *purgium* only heals things ye can't be healin' yerself," she said slowly, adding, "And Pockmark nicked my neck with a blade that must've been tainted."

Barrels' brows rose. "That would fit. That's . . . very clever of you, my dear."

"Caspian had the thought afore me," she admitted.

The slight confusion disappeared from her father's face.

Ebba mentally studied the lightness in her chest. She felt *grateful*. Impossibly grateful, as though she'd dodged one thousand bullets and was somehow standing, lucky to be alive. She'd lost the color in some of her dreads after being tainted on *Malice* over ten days. Caspian had survived, minus an arm, after the quick-spreading tainted infection of his wound. She knew that tainted wounds claimed a soul much faster than the 'normal' way of being slowly infected by the ship. Though Verity had said tainted wounds demanded a smaller sacrifice. Ebba only lost the color from six dreadlocks, not an arm, which seemed like impossible luck. Then again, Caspian was pretty near the end when they healed him.

Now, Ebba wanted everyone else onboard to feel as she did. Free of oppressive shame experienced by her fathers when they'd sailed under Pockmarks' grandfather.

. . . His grandfather.

The pillars had returned to the realm *fifty* years ago. Pockmark was in his twenties, and he'd killed his father in his teens. "His father can't've been fifty yet, surely."

"What's that, lass?" Locks asked.

She did the numbers again and came up with the same result. "The pillars weren't with Pockmark's father. They were with his grandfather," Ebba whispered, eyes wide on her hands. "That be a parallel too." Just like the parallels she'd missed between *Malice* and the pillars.

Barrels cleared his throat.

"The pillars returned fifty years ago," Ebba said urgently. "Pockmark said the pillars were in his father, but what if they were in Mutinous Cannon, too? What if all the shame ye've carried with ye since desertin' Cannon be the *taint*?" Conviction swelled within her, even in the face of her fathers' baffled faces. "The feelin' ye describe be the exact same. And Verity said the pillars have been able to feed faster in recent years as they grew stronger, so the pillars' taint was weaker back then, but there all the same. Some o' ye sailed with Cannon for near-on twenty years. And nothin' can heal the taint but the *purgium*. That's why ye never got better!"

No one uttered a sound.

Ebba didn't need their agreement. She knew in her very bones that her guess was right. Except something occurred to her. "Were Cannon's eyes flooded with black?"

She was grateful when Plank didn't query the oddness of her question. "Uh, nay, little nymph. Not when we knew him."

"Which meant he can't've been con'tagious with the taint," she said, frowning. "So how'd ye get tainted?"

Stubby opened his mouth, and closed it again. He glanced at Locks and then said, "Ye're sayin' the taint can only be spread when the person's eyes be black, lass?"

"Aye. Verity said that means the heart has been taken and the soul belongs to the pillars. Jagger said the *Malice* crew's eyes had just turned black when we left the ship."

Locks forehead was creased. "And if ye're tainted, it doesn't go away?"

"We already know the answer to that," Barrels answered before she could. "Our own dark thoughts have never lessened. Though, from Caspian's experience, I'd say tainted wounds behave differently." He glanced at Ebba and she nodded.

"They go faster," she clarified.

"Ye'd think the pillars would just wound everyone on the ship then and take them over quick-like," Plank mused.

Peg-leg grimaced. "Six minds in one. I'd say if they didn't, there be nasty-like reason for it."

Apparently, her ramblings had them believing too.

"Do ye think she could be right?" Plank said quietly. "We ain't been on *Malice*, but we all saw what happened to Caspian. And Ebba, even Jagger."

Stubby shared another look with Locks. "And I'm thinkin' that me and Locks have an inkling o' how Cannon might've managed to taint the crew."

They all turned to the pair.

"He used to give us a thimble o' blood to spread between the grog barrels," Stubby admitted.

Ebba's eyes widened. "Why'd he give it to ye?"

Stubby's lips mashed together before he forced out, "I was his first mate."

"And I hated blood. No doubt assignin' me the task amused him." Locks reminded her. "We'd put a drop in each barrel. Each time we filled the hold, it were the same."

Barrels' face was ashen. "I drank his blood?"

"Aye, matey. All o' the crew did," Stubby admitted in a low voice.

Peg-leg grunted. "That makes me feel right ill. But there be the answer. Cannon knew exactly what he was doin'. We're all tainted and have been all these years." He grunted again. "Taint be a good word for what I feel."

"Logic checks out to me, if the grog were tampered with his blood," Plank said, shaking his head. "The theory be worth considerin' at least."

Barrels was staring at her. Then he shifted his gaze to the *purgium*. All six of her fathers did.

She could tell by the envious way they looked at the healing cylinder that they wanted the same relief from their heartsickness. But Jagger had been on the ship for years, Verity for weeks, and her fathers? Who knew how long the taint had managed to work on them. That was why the Earth Mother had warned her about them touching the tube. The sodding Earth Mother must've known her fathers were tainted. She'd mentioned that their souls were crying for absolution, but she could've spoke plain and saved them some bloody trouble. Cryptic wench. For her fathers, the sacrifice to heal would be bigger than what she'd paid—maybe bigger than what Caspian had paid. Possibly the ultimate price. As much as Ebba wanted them to feel as she did, none of the crew could touch the *purgium*.

"What if ye'd lost yer arm or leg?" Peg-leg exploded, making her jump. He left the hold in a flurry of temper, his wooden stump tapping down the passage as he went.

Grubby squeezed her hand. "I think yer hair be lookin' right nice."

She smiled at him. "I like it, too. I ain't never seen a pirate with white dreadlocks afore. Though I feel right lucky it weren't more, and I'm just glad that we finally know why none o' ye ever got better," Ebba told them.

"Aye, me too," Locks whispered, rubbing his chest. "I've never understood why I felt the way I did. Even if we can't touch the *purgium*, just knowin' there be a reason for the dark in me feels. . . ."

"Validating," Barrels offered.

Her fathers chorused, "Aye."

"Validatin'," Stubby repeated.

Ebba sighed, closing her eyes briefly. "I could never connect any o' ye to the cutthroats my blood mother described. I feel like everythin' is back where it ought to be."

Plank gripped her shoulder. "We be right glad for that, little nymph."

Her fathers dispersed back to their posts, and Locks helped her back to bed. The *purgium* certainly hadn't healed her aches and physical pains. Stupid thing. She'd forgive it, seeing as the magic object healed her soul, though.

For the rest of the day, Ebba slept and ate, watching as Locks and Grubby woke Verity and Jagger every couple of hours to feed them. The emaciated pair drank and ate in a half-stupor and were asleep again before their heads hit the hammock. It amazed her that they could even be alive after their ordeal. Verity had lasted a month before nearing death. Jagger had lasted a month and was somehow still standing. And he'd been willing to return to *Malice* after saving her and Verity.

Even healed, Ebba was disturbed by how quickly she'd succumbed in comparison to the others.

"Barrels," she bellowed later that night. A day in bed was enough. As weary as her body was, Ebba was bored.

Jagger rolled in his hammock, dislodging Pillage, who leaped off with a backward glare at her.

"That's for tryin' to trip me this mornin', ye fish-faced weasel. Ye ain't got the *dynami* anymore," she hissed after him. He was a traitor for choosing to sleep on Jagger over her, anyway —though Jagger's chest was larger than hers, she supposed.

A light wrinkle appeared between Jagger's flaxen brows. When he didn't look like he was waking, she bellowed for Barrels again. Her father was in his office, but tended not to hear a thing when adding numbers and whatnot.

Jagger cracked his eyes open. She watched as he transitioned from disoriented to alert in seconds and sat bolt upright.

He groaned and clutched his head, sinking back into the hammock. "What happened?" he croaked.

"Oh, are ye awake then?" she said brightly. "We got away from *Malice*. We be back on *Felicity*."

Jagger smiled, appearing younger than she'd ever seen him. "Good," he mumbled.

He was going to fall asleep again. "Thank ye for savin' me," she said loudly.

A silver eye slid toward her, the barest trace of black around the edges. "Ye tried to kill me."

Her cheeks heated. The air between them tightened. "I know. . . . I'm fierce sorry, Jagger. The taint took me in its hold, and I got some wicked ideas in my head, I'll admit. Happened easier than I'd like. Probably because ye told them to cut the beads out o' my hair?"

He blinked.

"What?" she asked.

His mouth bobbed before he said, "I've never heard anyone speak o' the taint so open-like."

It looked like he wasn't going to own up to the bead thing. "Aye, I a'cidentally touched the *purgium*." She gestured up to her hair, and Jagger's eyes lifted and widened.

His face dropped into a scowl. "Ye could've died, ye eejit."

"Aye." She held back from telling him how much better she felt now. He'd spent two years on *Malice*. Didn't seem fair to rub that in his face.

He looked at the ceiling and muttered, "I'm sorry about yer beads, Viva."

Why did he just call her Viva? She wasn't sure what to make of it. Wouldn't put it past the pirate to be saying it just to mess with her head. Ebba stared at the post by her feet. "Maybe the beads were a scant bit foolish for someone my age."

"Nay, not foolish," he said softly. "But they weren't worth yer life."

That wasn't how it felt to her, but he was right. Though Ebba was fairly certain he'd said her beads were stupid in the past. She swallowed the retort, considering she'd recently been ready to pull him under the water and drown him. "I really am sorry for tryin' to kill ye."

Jagger closed his eyes, and the crackling air between them returned to normal. "Yer attempt was feeble at best. Hardly an attempt at all. Ye ain't strong enough to kill me, only about the size o' a child as ye are."

"I could kill ye if I really tried," she countered. "And I ain't child-sized. I'm just right."

He hummed, glancing down her body. "Not all o' ye, I agree. And weren't ye apologizin'?"

Heat rose in her cheeks. "Aye, I was. But not anymore, ye dolt. Bloody would've deserved bein' dead."

He grinned at the ceiling, and she eyed him askance. Was he riling her on purpose? He was!

"Ye went a whole month down there and still seemed so. . . ." Ebba cleared her throat. "How did ye go that long, Jagger?"

He gritted his teeth and didn't answer for so long she nearly gave up on a reply.

"I ain't sure," he said. "Some things helped. Sleepin' up on deck or in the riggin', not gettin' cuts and scratches, seein' the sun, feelin' the spray o' the water. Gave me more clarity or sumpin'. Down where ye were, it be a lot harder to recall the way things are." He accompanied the words with an uneasy glance about the sleeping quarters.

"If ye got injured, wouldn't ye have been taken by the taint though?" she asked.

"I never was, nay. Mine always healed up. Others weren't so lucky, and they were killed when they stopped screamin' so the rest o' the crew weren't infected faster."

Ebba shuddered, recalling when Caspian had stopped screaming on Pleo not so long ago. "Why kill them then? Wasn't the whole point of the pillars bein' in the ship to feed on the crew and grow stronger?"

"I can't speak for any o' that," Jagger said with a sigh. "Pockmark started talkin' to the ship more and more in recent times. I figured there was sumpin' dark he answered to, but I didn't have a name for them. I always got the sense the ship was waitin' for sumpin'—just from the odd thing Pockmark would mutter about."

She remembered the Earth Mother saying that the pillars' power was untraceable. Had they remained weaker on purpose to escape her notice? "I s'pose when Verity came along with all her power, they didn't have to hide anymore."

"Mayhaps, Viva. Mayhaps."

"I couldn't have gone a month." Ebba spoke her fear aloud.

He'd lasted a month; Verity had lasted a month. If Ebba's theory was correct, her fathers had lasted years in the presence of a much weaker taint. She was susceptible to the pillars' darkness. If she was captured again, she'd succumb once more, just as easily.

He opened his eyes with what appeared like colossal effort. "Some people don't last a single day. Hardly anyone more than a week. Depends what memories ye've got to help ye and how healthy ye be, I guess. People without sumpin' special helpin' out don't stand a chance," he said.

Ebba's eyes flicked past him to Verity and what she'd said about putting all of her power into protecting her heart.

"I've seen men three times yer size chucked in there and pulled out hours later, mind and soul gone to the taint," Jagger added. "Ye ain't weak. Ye're about the smallest pirate I ever saw, but ye ain't weak."

She blinked back the burning in her eyes. His words were more a statement than a compliment, but even healed of the taint, the horror of the pillars was still tangible. His words were the words she needed to hear. Ebba shifted to look at him. "Jagger, ye didn't answer my question. How did ye go so long without becomin' like everyone else?"

He turned his head to her and then rolled away. "I don't know. But it don't matter from what I can tell."

"Why?" she pressed.

His reply was low. "The taint be inside o' me, Viva. I won't ever be free o' the dark."

TWELVE

Ebba stumbled out onto the deck sometime in the middle of the night. Most of her fathers were asleep, but one of them would be on deck, keeping an eye on *Felicity*. Probably Locks; he was captain of the month.

"Ahoy," Locks called softly.

"Ahoy," she replied, padding over to him, wrapped in Stubby's holey woolen jersey.

She perched on a barrel behind him. "Where are we?"

"Tomorrow evenin', we'll reach the west point o' Kentro. We'll head back to our bay there for a bit in case *Malice* attempts to cut us off around the south side o' the island. We'll head back to Zol after a couple o' weeks. Grubs said the selkies will escort us."

"We'll take Jagger back to Zol?" Ebba asked in surprise.

Locks swung the wheel left. "I don't rightly know. What d'ye think on the matter?"

That she was being invited to discuss it took a moment to process. She'd always just gone along with the will of the crew, voting where she had to, and voicing her occasional dissent. But in the room, Ebba recalled thinking that she needed to start asserting herself more. She chose her words with care, eventually saying, "He saved my life, but I'm never sure what his game be. He only acted the way he has to protect his family, but he was on that ship for a long time. Part o' me be wary o' what that could've done to him. We should get the measure o' him while we be docked in our Kentro bay."

A glimmer of approval crossed Locks' face. "A good notion, lass. We'll do just that." He paused. "What do ye know o' how Verity came to be captured by *Malice*?"

"I ain't sure, matey. All she said was that she chose her path, and it was the only way to win." Ebba frowned. "When we were at her place on Febribus, Verity said sumpin' strange, though. I asked her if she had a message for ye, and she said there wasn't no point now. . . . Do ye think she knew what would happen even back then?"

Locks growled under his breath. "I'll be findin' out."

"Just . . . be careful with her, Locks," Ebba said. "I wouldn't have made it if not for her. She was the only other person down with me in the dark. She told me the pillars was takin' her powers. Her eyes ain't black, so they didn't get all o' her, but I think drainin' her powers be how they became shadows again."

Locks sighed. "Guess we better get to work then, lass, so we can kill those pillar buggers."

She glanced up. "Ye want to fight them now?"

"Aye. We'll talk more when we arrive at Kentro safe and sound, but I doubt any o' yer fathers will be against figurin' this mess out." His face twisted into savage lines. "No one, and I be repeatin', *no one* hurts our daughter and gets away with it. We'll make the pillars wish they never got out o' that magic wall. And I'll kill the lot o' Pockmark's crew with my bare hands afterward."

"The pillars were so strong, Locks. I didn't even know they

were takin' over me. They just crept in and covered my thoughts."

His emerald eye blazed. "I'll drag them to Davy Jones, if that's what it takes. Ye have six fathers; we'll each be draggin' one down each."

Ebba smiled, grimacing at the pull on her dry lips.

"Make no mistake," Locks said in a hollow voice. "They'll pay for what they did to ye."

Despite her decision to fight back, Ebba wrung her hands in her lap. She didn't want any of her fathers near that ship. They were all battling their pasts already, and already carried the taint within them. What would the ship turn them into? And how fast? Simultaneously, part of her had to wonder if they always would have arrived here. The Earth Mother had spoken of their murky path like the crew's destiny was set. What if the crew of *Felicity* had accepted their responsibilities after Pleo? Would Ebba have been caught on Kentro? Would any of that have happened?

Ebba supposed knowing the answer to those questions didn't really make a difference.

Locks made a noise. "Do ye see that?"

He squinted at the water ahead of the ship. Ebba leaped off the barrel and joined him at the wheel, peering into the night.

". . . Nay," she replied. A tiny speck flickered. "Wait. Aye, I saw a light."

"Up the shrouds with ye," Locks said urgently.

Tying a knot in the bottom of Stubby's jersey so the garment didn't flap about, Ebba crossed to the nearest rigging and swung up onto the ship's side. She climbed the lattice of rope squares to the crow's nest only a tad slower than usual.

Ebba swung into the nest. Her eyes took a moment to adjust after focusing on the rigging on the way up. She looked far into the distance to help the adjustment before scanning the ocean closer to their ship.

A light flashed once, twice, three times. She waited, squinting as the light appeared again and repeated the three flashes.

The intermittent sparks were almost like a. . . .

Ebba whirled to look behind her and gasped at the lights back there flashing in the same odd sequence. The lights were a signal!

Leaning over the side of the crow's nest, she hollered, "Locks, we got company."

Her father wasted no time. Racing to the bilge door, he bellowed down for her fathers to wake.

There was at least one ship in front of *Felicity* and maybe two ships behind. Judging from the lights flickering to life across the ships' lengths, they were huge. Only one *pirate* ship that large existed, and they'd left *Malice* behind two days ago.

If these ships weren't *Malice*, then they belonged to the navy.

Plank was the first to appear out the bilge door, then Grubby, and the others. Jagger stumbled out last, pale-faced and looking still mostly asleep.

Ebba shouted down, "I think it be the navy, lads. There be two behind and one in front."

"How far?" Stubby shouted.

It was hard to tell distance at sea at the best of times, but even harder at night. "We'll easily outrun the two behind," she called. "But we'll have to get past the one in front for that." Another light caught her eye from ahead. "Uh-oh, make that *two* in front."

Her fathers' cursing floated up to her. She leaned over the edge of the crow's nest to listen.

"We need to turn inland and skim the shallows by the shore

to get around the front ships," Peg-leg said. "*Felicity* can sail far closer to the coast than the big navy ships. It be the only way past without gainin' a hull full o' cannon holes."

"They're not far away. I'm not sure that we have time to get to the shallows," Barrels said.

Stubby spoke. "We've got to try. Or else Plank be right. We'll be facing their cannons. Smart-like now, raise the topsail and the foresail!"

That was her cue. Ebba clambered up to release the reef knots holding the furled topsail neatly against the boom. That done, she leaped back down into the crow's nest and reached for the topsail sheet. She unwound the sheet from the belaying pin, dealing the rope out slowly until the topsail filled—not to bursting point, though. She looped the end around the belaying pin again.

"Stay up there, little nymph," Plank hollered. "We'll be needin' yer eyes."

She returned her vigil to the surrounding seas. Sally joined her in short measure, cobalt-blue eyes huge on her tiny face. The wind sprite disappeared beneath Ebba's hair, clutching the sides of her neck.

Ebba gripped the side of the crow's nest, listening to the thuds and shouts of her fathers below as they raised the foresail and directed *Felicity* into Kentro's shoreline. Barrels was right, they mightn't have enough time to reach the shallows to evade the heavier navy ships. But her fathers had gotten them out of impossible situations before.

And everyone knew what the alternative was. King Montcroix made no secret of it.

Ebba kept an eye on the topsail though it didn't really require attention. She was coiled for action. Her muscles were tensed, but there was no outlet as she was carried by *Felicity* closer to the shore. The ships ahead had altered in response to

Felicity's new trajectory. The two ships were angling closer to the shore, too, to cut them off. Unfortunately, the navy only had to get within cannon distance to force *Felicity's* surrender.

"We need another half an hour to reach waters shallow enough that they can't follow," Locks shouted, his frustration evident.

Plank shook his head. "We don't have that long. This wind ain't doin' us any favors."

Ebba's heart thudded. She searched behind. The ships there had fallen back, though they never would've caught up. That wasn't their purpose. Their purpose was to box *Felicity* in.

She leaned over the side to watch as her fathers gathered in a huddle. Jagger lurked by the bilge door, head cocked to their group, clearly eavesdropping. After some minutes of terse nods and whispered words, they separated, faces grim.

"Let's get her ready then," Stubby announced. "Barrels, make sure Pillage stays down in the hold."

Their group dispersed across the deck.

Plank called up to her. "Take down the topsail, little nymph."

"Take it down? Why?" she demanded.

"Aye, we ain't outrunnin' them today. We need to surrender, or we'll be shark fodder in less than an hour."

Ebba met his eyes. "Surrender *Felicity*?" That was the clear alternative to not reaching shallow waters and losing the navy vessels by sailing the Kentro coastline, but giving up their ship seemed implausible. *Felicity* wasn't just a ship. She was their home.

"Aye, little nymph," he said hoarsely. "But better that than have her sink to the bottom o' the seas."

Even he seemed unsure that was true.

Stubby worked the sheets of the mainsail. "We need ye to

stay up in the crow's nest during whatever happens next, Ebba-Viva. Do ye understand?"

No, she didn't understand. "I ain't leavin' ye to be caught by the king's men."

"We need ye safe," Stubby called up. "Please promise us ye'll stay up there? We can't bear anythin' more to happen to ye. We'll handle this."

Ebba couldn't bear if anything happened to them either. She'd known it from the first time they'd left her on Maltu, and again when they were locked in the gaol while she was taken to the governor's mansion. Even after Ebba found they'd lied to her for seventeen years, she wasn't able to tear herself away. On Maltu, before the war with *Malice* began, she'd made a mistake that pitched them into a danger that didn't seem to have an end. One single slip, whether they were destined to be on this path or not, and she'd set her fathers on this course. If they'd failed Ladon's riddles, they'd surely be dead and devoured by now. If Grubby wasn't a selkie, they might all be colder than a mother-in-law's kiss. If not for sheer luck and surviving by the skin of their teeth, everything could be over. Because of her. Ebba wouldn't fail them again. Her fathers expected her to stay out of the fight, to leave them to their fate. They should know better by now. They had to stay together. Bad things happened when they didn't. Ebba would hide here. For now. And then trail after the navy men. She'd save her fathers when the chance arose.

Both sails were lowered, and Jagger heaved up the rigging toward her, dark smudges beneath his eyes. He passed her the white flag that the crew of *Felicity* had never had cause to use. Ebba took it and attached the flat to the mast, hoisting it halfway up.

"Lad," Peg-leg called to Jagger. "Ye need to get in there with Ebba, too."

Jagger glanced at her, then to the crow's nest. Shaking his head, he began climbing back down to the deck. "Nay."

Her fathers frowned at him.

She leaned over to watch as he landed at the bottom. He shrugged in response to her fathers' scrutiny.

"Nay," he repeated.

What was he planning? It didn't seem within his character to make a stand; he was too much a pirate. He switched sides as easy as a cannonball on a pitching ship.

Her fathers' gazes trailed after the pirate before they too shrugged and went about setting their array of weaponry on the ground.

"Drop anchor," Locks called.

Soon, *Felicity* bobbed in the light swell, a sitting duck. What happened next was inevitable. The navy drew alongside them a short while later. Ebba crouched in the crow's nest, heart thudding and ears strained for any sound. Below, her fathers didn't stir from their passive position near the mast.

Ebba could hear the foreign snap of sails on either side of *Felicity*. They were sandwiched between two ships now. She could all but feel the navy men's hands closing around her arms and shoving her into a cage.

Her hand tightened in the space where her pistol usually sat —the pistol tucked away in her trunk in the hold with her cutlass and daggers. Perhaps it was a good thing she hadn't thought to grab her weapons. Taking action right now was more likely to get her fathers killed than anything else.

A booming call crossed the small gap between the starboard ship and *Felicity*. "Hear ye, corrupted men and half-beings—"

Ebba rose her brows at Sally, who appeared amused by the greeting.

"—The royal navy hereby accepts your surrender on behalf of the esteemed King Montcroix. Lay down your arms and accept your impeding trial with whatever dignity, if any at all, still resides in your blackened hearts and rotten souls."

They weren't trying to make friends; that was for sure.

Holding her breath, she attempted to keep as motionless as possible, listening to the bustle of the navy men boarding their ship. They did so with much yelling and stamping—unnecessarily, in her opinion; must've been part of their training. She winced at her fathers' grunts and yells, listening to the clang of the chains no doubt being fastened around their ankles.

"Commodore Tinkleman," one called out. "Look what I found hidden on this misbegotten creature. It appears to be a tube of some fashion, but see the pearly movement beneath the surface. Have you ever encountered such a thing?"

The *dynami*. Ebba's eyes widened. They'd taken the *dynami* from Grubby!

There was a pause, and the man Ebba assumed was the unfortunate possessor of the name Tinkleman replied, "We will seize this for King Montcroix's perusal, Weatherby. Smashing job."

Frantically, Ebba felt along her belt and found the *purgium* still in place.

Now she had to free her fathers *and* get the *dynami* back. Ebba swallowed. Preferably all that would be possible before her fathers reached the king, who hated piratekind.

"Clear the crow's nest," the captain boomed. "Search the hold."

Ebba tensed and felt Sal retreat once more to burrow into her dreads.

A lazy voice called out, "Pointless to; I just came down from hoistin' the sur'ender flag."

Jagger. She placed a hand against the inside of the crow's nest, listening hard for the captain's answer.

"I did see him coming down from the shrouds through the scope, captain," a navy man called.

Tinkleman sniffed after a moment. "Nevertheless, a navy man always dots his i's and crosses his t's. Search everything."

"Sal," Ebba whispered. "Don't come out from my hair for nothin'. Ye understand?"

Sally patted her neck as the creaking rigging announced more than one sailor ascending. Being caught like a cowering rat didn't appeal. Ebba extracted the *purgium* from her belt and after a quick debate, shoved the cylinder down the middle of her chest, into the valley there caused by her skin-tight jerkin. Who knew breasts could be useful?

As the sailors neared, Ebba slowly stood with her arms raised. "No need for a fuss now, lads."

One of the sailors screamed, and just caught hold of the rigging in the nick of time. The other fumbled for his pistol, and by the time he'd retrieved the weapon, Ebba had swung over the side and was making her way down.

She landed on light feet and straightened. *Shite*. The navy ships either side were huge. The port side vessel around three times the size of their ship. The starboard vessel, larger still.

"Oh!" Barrels said in a strangled voice. "You have found our prisoner, Lady Maybell's companion."

Lady Maybell's what now? Ebba wrinkled her brow. Lady Maybell was the Maltu governor's wife. Ebba wasn't her companion.

Stubby stared at Barrels for a long moment before his brow cleared. "Aye, ye scallywags have found the wench we were set to ransom. Curse ye all."

Ebba shifted her eyes to the captain. He was older than his high-pitched voice suggested, and appeared to have a rod located somewhere uncomfortable.

He surveyed her in doubt. "You . . . are Lady Maybell's companion."

Locks trod on her foot, and Ebba cleared her throat. "Aye, I be Lady Maybell's esteemed-like matey."

A low groan came from Peg-leg's direction.

The captain held a hand to his chest. "I rather do doubt that considering the lowliness of your speech."

Ebba narrowed her eyes. "I be crossin' my i's and dotting my t's just like ye."

"We took her from the tribes on Pleo," Jagger said. "Made her our servin' wench." He smirked at her as he said *wench*.

Flaming sod would've enjoyed that. She scowled darkly at him.

The captain arched an eyebrow at Jagger. "A rather long time ago, judging by her be-pirated appearance. Search her."

A pimply-faced sailor neared and patted her down as she bore holes into his face with her eyes. Inwardly, Ebba was focused on where Sally hung in the middle of her dreads, and where the *purgium* was lodged under her jerkin. The sailor's face burned bright red as he felt up her torso, arriving at her chest.

Ebba breathed again when he abandoned the search and stood back. Interesting. . . it was as if he'd been mortified by the idea of feeling her chest. Good to know.

"Sir! We found a real lady in the sleeping quarters. Unconscious."

A large sailor exited the bilge door with Verity over his shoulder. He placed her on the ground near the captain. Plank shot Locks a warning look, extending a hand out to hold her father back. Ebba didn't blame him; Locks looked murderous.

"I do say," the captain said. "This is most assuredly a real lady."

The sailor sucked his finger, wincing. "There's a demon cat down there, too, Captain. Couldn't get hold of him."

"A cat doesn't concern me," the captain sniffed.

A wise choice. Woe to any man who chose to remove Pillage from his ship. He wouldn't even leave to follow Barrels. She'd certainly learned her lesson not to attempt it at a young age.

"I've thwarted your attempt to catch me in your web of half-truths, scallywags." The captain adjusted his ridiculous feathered hat. "*This* is Lady Maybell's companion, I am certain. Let it not be said that Captain Tinkleman is a fool. I would know a real lady anywhere." He glanced at Ebba and sniffed in disdain.

What did they mean *real* lady? Not that Ebba was a female, but if she wanted to be, she'd damn well be a real one. She may not have luscious blonde hair to her waist, but she was woman enough to make a sailor red-faced as he searched her. And that was without trying. Jagger was smirking her way again, and she shoved down her rising temper, seeing that Tinkleman's assumption might save Verity's life.

Ebba followed her fathers' attempts to appear cowed, slumping her shoulders and widening her eyes fearfully. Grubby was the only one who managed to pull the look off. The rest of her fathers appeared crazed, and Barrels looked like he'd been reading all night.

"Weatherby, take the lady to our guest quarters and fetch her some smelling salts. Place the rest in the holds—behind bars, of course." The captain smiled at them, covering the curve of his lips with his hand again as though smiling was against the law. "You will face trial at noon tomorrow, miscreants."

"I s'pose the trial will be fair-like?" Stubby asked drily.

"As fair as you deserve," the captain answered, mounting the plank extended between the navy ship and *Felicity*. "Do not expect to see out the week."

THIRTEEN

"This be a right pickle," Peg-leg observed aloud, his face resting between two bars of their prison.

One sailor stood guard in the area they were locked—a square space with vertical bars for walls that extended from floor to ceiling. The space was just large enough to fit the eight of them shoulder-to-shoulder. Which was the only thing holding Jagger up. He'd promptly fallen asleep, or lost consciousness again judging by the lolling of his head.

The navy sailor glanced over at Peg-leg's comment, but quickly found something else interesting as Peg-leg glanced right back.

Plank lowered his voice. "We've gotten out o' worse scrapes than this. And remember our royal friend."

Ebba straightened. She'd forgotten about Caspian. He could get them out of this. He was a royal-lubber.

"I'm not sure what good that will do us," Barrels said, pale-faced. "On Exosia, people of importance do not attend trials. We won't see the king, or go anywhere near the castle, before our sentence is carried out. But the common folk and middle class will see us. They *all* come to watch." He swallowed.

"Wind sprite," she reminded them.

Her fathers stared at her. Ebba jerked a finger to her hair, where she could feel Sally slumbering. Six grins flashed her way.

"Handy-like for carryin' words once we know where we'll be caulkin', am I right, lads?" Locks said.

Aye, they'd send Sally to the prince with a message and location when they reached the land prison.

The sailor approached. "Enough talk."

Grubby gave him a toothy smile, and the man blinked and stepped back from their cage.

Taking her father's hand, Ebba said in an undertone, "They took yer *dynami*, Grubs."

Grubby nodded sadly and slumped where he sat, hands twisting. It'd be tearing him up inside that he'd lost the cylinder after promising his selkie kin so faithfully to keep the thing safe.

"We'll get it back, Grubs," she said quietly in his ear. Not just for Grubby, but to protect the realm as she knew it. "Don't ye worry." None of them would be worrying much over anything unless they found some way to get away from Exosia and the pirate-hater, King Montcroix.

Conversation was spotty after that. Most of her fathers fell asleep. Barrels was the only other person awake before long. Even the sailor was slumbering, snoring in the far corner of the room.

The journey to the mainland should only take half a day at the most. The strip of sea between Kentro and Exosia wasn't large. She jerked as Jagger stirred, uttering a string of crazed, nonsensical mutterings. She could only make out 'deck' and 'rigging.' She felt sorry for what he'd been through. Part of her even felt sorry for Swindles and Riot, but her words to Locks were true: Ebba would keep an eye on Jagger and decide if he was too tainted to be safe.

"I always wanted to see Exosia," she muttered to Barrels. Despite what might be their imminent death, Ebba was intrigued to see the king's lands, a place she'd never expected to visit. She wondered if the navy men would march them past the castle. She wouldn't mind a wee tour.

Barrels didn't answer, and she turned to him. His eyes were fixed on his clasped hands. He was barely blinking.

"What are ye thinkin' about, Barrels?" she asked. His peppered hair had fallen down about his face, and his cravat was crumpled, yet he hadn't moved to fix either. Something was wrong.

He lifted his head and watched her, eyes distant. "I am from Exosia. *Was*," he corrected himself, "long, long ago."

Ebba knew that. There was no way to miss it with the way he spoke and dressed. And read. "How long?"

"Nearly forty years have passed since I last set foot there. I can scarcely believe it."

Barrels was the oldest of her fathers at fifty-eight. "Ye've been off longer than ye've been on."

He crooked a humorless smile. "Yes, I suppose that's true. Yet, I can still see how it all was in my mind. I still recall the smells and the feel, the music and the etiquette. Or just that there was etiquette."

Ebba wasn't sure she liked the wistful undercurrent of his tone.

He smiled. "I was son to a baron, did you know? A lesser noble in the king's court."

"Ye knew King Montcroix?"

"His father, yes."

"I forget how ancient ye be at times," Ebba remarked with an impish grin.

Her cheekiness didn't make him smile as she'd intended. "His father was a beloved and just king," Barrels said. "Nothing like Montcroix. I was a second son and had no aspirations to become an officer in his navy. So, I apprenticed to his quarter-master, to the shock of the court, being rather learned and inter-ested in numbers. It was *quite* the scandal," he chuckled briefly, trailing off when he caught sight of her baffled expression.

The only scandalous thing about his interest in numbers was that he was interested in numbers.

"Anyway," he continued, "a year into my apprenticeship, my master commissioned me to travel to Maltu in the king's name and audit the governor's reports, many of whom he suspected of dodging their duty to the king. Maltu was the only governed island at the time."

Ebba leaned forward, belatedly realizing Barrels was telling her his story. She'd said she wouldn't ask them to speak of their pasts, and though she was now healed, Ebba still meant it. But if her father wanted to talk, Ebba wouldn't stop him. She wanted her fathers to heal as she had. If they couldn't touch the *purgium*, talking seemed the next best thing. "Then what?"

"I noticed a discrepancy in the ledgers. I queried the governor of the island at the time about the discrepancy to allow a full report to my superiors, but I'm afraid mentioning my find-ings was a grievous error. The navy ship I traveled on had not sailed one hour before we were boarded by pirates."

"Mutinous Cannon?" she guessed.

Barrels flinched. "Yes, Ebba. It was he. I later learned he was paid by the Maltu governor to get rid of me. The governor was skimming money for his own coffers."

She gasped. "So the Maltu governor set Mutinous on ye?"

Her father grimaced. "Mutinous wouldn't have lowered himself to paid work of that kind without reason of his own. I expect he knew from the governor I was an apprentice quarter-master. As you know, we are highly valued by pirates. He merely took advantage of the situation to secure me as a bonus.

He killed the crew and kept me alive, and so I became enslaved on his ship for twenty-two years."

Twenty-two years. Ebba couldn't fathom such a number. That was longer than she'd been alive. She'd been a prisoner for ten days, a mere blip on Barrels' experience. "Ye must be fierce-strong to have lasted that long."

Barrels glanced up, brow raised. "Strong?"

"Aye, strong," she said with a firm nod. Ebba hesitated before asking, "Locks said ye tricked him onto the ship, but he didn't blame ye." That there might be a festering grudge between two of her parents didn't sit right with her. Stubby and Peg-leg had a mostly competitive-sometimes angry relationship, but nothing spiteful.

"I did many things I'm not proud of, my dear. Through me, Mutinous grew rich, and his power grew with it. He used my unthreatening person and youth to con many young men onto the ship. If I had but hidden some opportunities from his notice, or worked the numbers to ruin him, he might not have been allowed to do what he did. But the figures before me became an obsession until I would have done anything for one more dollar. And I did do many terrible things. I don't know how the numbers came to be so important to me, more important than my morals. Only that they did." A ripple of shame ran through his face.

"Whatever ye did wasn't yer fault," Ebba said, gritting her teeth. "The ugliness makin' ye do that didn't come from within ye, and it wasn't there afore. The taint entered ye until it took yer mind and told ye what to do. I understand, Barrels, I really do, and ye need to know none o' that time was yer doin'. Ye're kind-hearted and a smart thinker, and I love ye."

He surveyed her. "You do understand, don't you? I'm sorrier about that fact than I am for every misdeed or harm I've ever caused. I wish you could've been spared from the horrors you underwent."

As the memory of black slime coating her arms flashed across her mind, a lump rose in her throat, and she forced it down with considerable effort. "Aye, but if there be anythin' good that's come o' it, it's that I know why ye did the things ye did back then." Ebba cleared her throat and plowed on. "So, then ye stole me and raised me. . . ."

"We did." Barrels quirked a brow. "Have you really forgiven us, just like that?"

She shrugged. "The lyin' is what bothered me most-like about the whole s'tuation. I didn't believe there could be a good enough reason for ye to conceal such things, but there was in the end—the taint. Part o' me be glad for that. Though—" She paused, and decided to let Barrels in further than she'd let in any of her fathers since Pleo. "I'm still stuck about who I am after findin' out where I came from. It kind o' . . . opened my eyes, and I can't seem to close them again."

Barrels smiled. "Maybe opening your eyes isn't a bad thing?"

"Caspian says I learned to pretend from the six o' ye."

His eyes narrowed. "Did he now?" Then he tipped his head back to look at the ceiling. "Probably right. He's rather discerning about other people."

Other people, but not himself? "He be a book person, just like ye. But what did ye do after stealin' me?"

He glanced at her. "My heart yearned to see Exosia again, but I could not bear to leave you, and . . . I was not sure of my reception in Exosia after traveling at Cannon's side for so long. I was more refined than any of my fellow crewmen, a fact that set me apart all those years on *Eternal*. However, I was not as I once had been. My appearance, for starters: tanned, weathered skin and the rough hands of a sailor. My own family would not know me, and if they did, they could only be deeply ashamed of such a relation."

Ebba studied the deep creases on his face. "Is that what yer worried about now?"

"It is, my dear. Though most of my family will be dead and gone by now. Call me a silly old man, but after all this time, that is what I fear."

"Ye're the smartest person I know, Barrels," she said with a reassuring smile. "Ye survived the most fearsome pirate to ever sail the Caspian Sea. Plus, ye still wear cravats and buckles on yer shoes," she added. "If yer family can't see past yer old skin and slightly rough-like ways, they ain't deservin' ye."

Barrels reached back and gathered his salt-and-pepper hair, confining it with his tie. Then he set his attention to his cravat. "You're right, my dear. Quite right. Besides, it is uncertain that we'll happen upon them—if any still live. And unlikelier still that they should recognize me."

"That's the spirit, m'hearty."

He dropped the ends of his cravat and sent her a thoughtful expression. "Thank you, Ebba-Viva. You've made me feel much better about returning to Exosia."

Ebba cocked one ear as the trill of a seagull sounded from outside.

She hoped Barrels really did feel better. Because by the sound of it, they'd reached the mainland.

FOURTEEN

There was no sign of Verity as the crew of *Felicity*—and the watchful Jagger—were shuffled off the navy ship with their wrists bound in front of them, a manacle around their left ankles.

The sun was bright after the dimness of the lower deck, and Ebba was forced to squint through watering eyes around the goliath wharf. They'd seen many a navy ship at Maltu over the years of steal-trading, but she'd never seen so many of the navy's man-o-wars in one place. The section of the wharf they were shuffling through seemed dedicated to the navy, stretching as far as she could see down the coastline.

Ebba tilted her chin up, and felt her jaw slacken.

A hulking stone structure loomed far above, erected on the highest point of the only cliff. The king's castle, where it lurched high above the village and wharf, had an ominous presence that Ebba assumed was purposeful—the place gave her the shivers anyhow. She'd never seen such a huge building in her life. How many people lived in there?

"Impressed?" Jagger sneered.

She watched the way his eyes followed the sailors at the

front and the way his jaw tightened upon glancing up at the castle. "Ye talk while sleepin', did ye know?"

He swung to look at her, and Ebba sniggered before shuffling off ahead.

The navy men directed them up the wharf, and they were shoved through the bustling fish market at the port. Exosians turned to look at them, and Ebba stared back at the strangely clad people. The women, even being peasants, or so she assumed, wore layers and layers of clothing. Weird open-rimmed hats sat upon their heads, framing their faces amidst tightly sprung curls that reminded her of piglet tails. The men appeared rather like Barrels, though they all wore hats too: caps, top hats, and a few wore Monmouth caps like Grubby.

"After you, Lady Bethany," a woman said demurely. She stood aside from a doorway of a fancy-looking shop for a woman with a larger dress hoop.

"No, Lady Gertrude," the second woman said, opening her fan with a *snap*. "After you."

Was everyone a lady here?

The first woman curtsied low and simpered, "But I insist. Please do oblige."

"What's wrong with them, Stubby?" she whispered. Why didn't one of them just walk through the bloody door?

Stubby sniffed in disgust. "They be over-polite, lass. There be pleasant manners, and then there be politeness like theirs. For folk like these, it's all about face; what ye earn, how ye dress, and who yer friends be. Sometimes, rich landlubbers be so desperate-like to appear a certain way they're forgettin' who they really are."

"And what's that?" she asked.

"Human, lass. They need to eat, drink, breathe, and shite just like the rest o' us. When it comes to survival, we're all the same. People go too long without strugglin', and they're forgettin' that. Then their minds move to useless things like ye just saw."

That made sense to her, but also didn't. She had liked the thought of a fierce pirate reputation, but had only ever contemplated that it could be gained through dangerous quests, witty escapes, a sleek ship, and glorious deeds. Maybe the important things for a landlubber were dress hoops and connections with other fancy people. Except Ebba couldn't imagine forgetting who she was in pursuit of her dreams. Then again, she didn't *have* a fierce reputation, so maybe if she became a swashbuckling pirate, she'd turn into a sod.

Ebba wrinkled her nose, scanning the oddly dressed Exosians again.

"No talking, miscreant," a sailor snarled.

These navy men sure had a lot of words for lowlifes.

They exited the fish market and were led through double-story *stone* buildings. She'd never seen so many tall buildings not made of wood. Only the governor's mansion, really. Tilting her head back, she stared beyond the high buildings again to the castle up on the cliff. Caspian was all the way up there, and they were all the way down here. How would they ever get up there so he could free them?

She had an idea.

Ebba cleared her throat. "I would like to talk to Prince Caspian."

Jagger groaned, and Barrels threw her a warning look. She ignored it. How else were they meant to see him? "I be wantin' to talk with your leader's son, miscreants!"

One of the sailors rounded on her, and Barrels edged between them.

"What my crewmate is unsuccessfully trying to enquire is whether you would allow us to seek an audience with the esteemed King Montcroix and Prince Caspian," Barrels said, executing a bow.

The captain had turned to see what the ruckus was about. "You don't speak like a pirate. You speak like an Exosian." His features settled into disdain. "I suppose *anyone* can be lured into a life of debauchery."

Another sailor stepped forward. "Not this one, Captain. Not lured. I heard him talking in the lockup. He was the royal quartermaster's apprentice and got caught by pirates and forced into servitude."

Ebba took a closer look at the man and saw it was the sailor who'd guarded them—not as asleep as he'd seemed, apparently. "Ye'd make a decent pirate," she told him.

His face flushed pink. He appeared chuffed at the thought.

The captain circled Barrels, eyes narrowed. "Forced to serve, you say? A noble-born Exosian. This is . . . unprecedented."

Plank slid nearer, dropping his voice to the ominous one he used for storytelling. "If I may? We were droppin' Barrels here at Kentro when ye came across us. He'd met the Prince Caspian in Maltu recent-like, and the prince had assured him o' a pardon after hearin' o' his trials and sufferin'.'"

Ebba cut in. "That's why we need to see Caspian." If that didn't work, they still had Sally as a backup.

The captain whirled on her. "*Prince* Caspian to you, scoundrel." His face trembled with rage. He broke away and resumed his place at the front of the procession, muttering, "Wrongdoers, reprrrobates, *malefactors*."

"Where to, Captain?" their guard called after him.

"To the castle," Tinkleman snapped.

They resumed their march through the high buildings.

"I don't think he likes us," she remarked to Barrels, who shuffled in front of her.

"No, I rather think not, my dear." He reached up his bound hands to pat his hair.

Ebba ran her eyes over his elderly yet straight frame. "Yer hair is all back in the coil, and yer cravat be straight."

Barrels' shoulders relaxed. "Thank you, Ebba-Viva."

Soon, a burning in her calves told her the ground sloped upward. She lifted her chin and leaned to peer down the side of their single-file procession. They were scaling the hill to the castle.

"Easy now," Plank warned her from behind. "Let's not celebrate just yet. Caspian may not be able to do anythin'. Don't be gettin' yer hopes up."

The well-worn path turned to light gray cobblestones. Sturdy shoulder-high stone walls appeared either side, which served to shelter them somewhat from the rising wind at the increasing height. The wind not held back lifted her dreadlocks, and Sally squeaked in complaint, leaving her place at Ebba's neck to crawl under the hem of her tunic. She curled into a ball over Ebba's heart.

Ebba peered down to the village and saw the fish market they'd passed through was just a distant blur from here. She stumbled slightly and faced forward, focusing on the path.

The castle loomed larger and larger, casting their procession into shadow. If she'd wondered how they made a double-story house of stone before, Ebba had no idea how they made this gigantic thing. The castle was as tall as fifty pirates stacked on top of each other. From her position at the bottom, she couldn't even see the top.

She stopped, and Jagger called from behind Plank, "Are ye seriously stoppin' to look at the castle o' a man who's about to sentence us to death?" he muttered.

"Aye, never seen a castle afore," she replied. Pausing a few beats more to annoy him, she continued forward.

There was a parapet ahead. An armored row of the king's soldiers lined the gangway above.

Ebba quietened as they marched beneath the opened portcullis, a dozen soldiers scowling at them from overhead. Two dozen more gathered to flank their crew and Jagger the instant they passed underneath. They were now outnumbered by navy men and guards four to one.

Locks whistled low from ahead as he exited the other side. Her lips formed an O as she followed in his wake, the same amazement echoing in her mind. They stood in a cobbled, rectangular courtyard longer than two frigates set end to end. Grains of sand scattered over the cobblestone, but piles hadn't been allowed to accumulate despite the castle's proximity to the sea. Ebba spotted a woman sweeping in the far corner. Poor slave. At the far end sat two heavy wooden doors that appeared as though they'd need a whole crew to get them open. Everything was so oversized.

"On your knees, ruffians!" Captain Tinkleman shouted once they were halfway down the stone courtyard. The captain whispered furiously at another sailor. The sailor ran off in the direction of the heavy doors.

Peg-leg sighed. "My only knee be bung, do we have to kneel?" He jerked his head at his right limb, which Ebba knew hurt him something fierce in the cold, or when the rain was coming in.

The captain drew himself tall, puffing his chest out.

"Do ye think that be an aye?" Stubby whispered to Barrels.

Barrels cleared his throat. "Yes, I believe so."

The captain shot him a look and deflated slightly, just enough that his chest didn't jut out farther than the rest of his body.

Ebba sat down cross-legged on the ground, the chains clanking. The sooner Caspian got here, the better. She listened to the moans and grumbles as her fathers lowered themselves to their knees. They were putting on a bit of a show, really, considering not a day went by when they didn't have to get on their hands and knees to work on the ship.

Her fathers had just finished grumbling when the heavy doors were drawn inward with a booming crack, and a small party of men ambled out.

"Montcroix," Jagger hissed on the other side of Plank.

Ebba squinted at the man in the middle of the party of men. She assumed that was the king. His purple cape looked heavy and fur-lined. About his head was a light crown that glinted in the sun. He was bald, possessing a stark-white beard and a set of rusty eyes that gave Ebba the sense they'd snap into serrated pieces and cut her if she made the error of trusting them.

Unfortunately, the eyes, though hard, were an all-too-familiar color.

Shifting her focus to the young man on the king's right, Ebba whispered, "Caspian."

"Easy now, Ebba. We can't drop him in it," Locks said from her left.

Aye. If she acted too familiar, the king would grow suspicious. From his hawked appearance, suspicious seemed to be his middle name. Ebba bit her lip. The king had power to spare, and they were in his clutches. He was known for his hatred of pirates. There weren't many people who gave her the willies, but the way the king surveyed each of them as he approached sent a cold shiver up her spine.

But they weren't just any pirates, she reminded herself. Maybe he'd see that, like his son.

Sally shifted beneath her tunic. "Keep still, Sal," Ebba muttered. "We may still be needin' ye to free us later."

The king and his men stopped ten feet from where she sat. The rest of the men with the king seemed like elevated slaves.

Their clothing was better than that of the woman sweeping, but they possessed the same subservient look about them.

Ebba stole a peek at the prince, but didn't know what to make of the rapid darting of his eyes.

"Scum," the king greeted them.

Sally squeaked indignantly. The king's eyes shot to Ebba, who quickly cleared her throat. Her cheeks warmed under the utter loathing she detected in his rusty glare.

Mostly, when Ebba was hurt, her grudge toward whomever had caused the hurt lessened over time until one day it was gone. Other grudges, like the one she held against Pockmark and *Malice*, she'd harbor until the day she died. Ebba suspected that the king's grudge against pirates for killing his father fell into the latter pile.

King Montcroix shifted his attention to the navy captain, and Ebba sagged, catching a sympathetic glance from Caspian. He could save them anytime now. She shot him a scowl.

"Why are you wasting my time, Captain?" the king asked coolly. Not a fleck of emotion softened his face. Ebba cast a worried look at Barrels, whose tight smile did nothing to reassure her.

The navy captain appeared to need more reassurance than Ebba. He wilted under King Montcroix's attention and stuttered as he scrambled for an answer. "One of the men is from Exosia, Your Majesty. The pirates say the man recently met Prince Caspian and that t-the prince g-granted...."

The king's voice could've frozen the whole mainland. "Granted what?"

Ebba caught Caspian's wide-eyed glance and mouthed 'pardon.'

"You," the king said sharply, making her jump. "You just moved."

"I did never," she blurted.

His face didn't change color. He didn't make any angry gestures or shout, but the entire courtyard vibrated with unreleased tension in such a way that left Ebba in no doubt that the monarch was coiled to strike. Jagger fidgeted, and the king diverted his focus to the flaxen-haired pirate.

The king's eyes flickered, widening slightly.

"The captain is correct, Father," Caspian said, stepping forward. "I met this man in Maltu while staying with the governor."

The tension didn't dissipate. Ebba didn't dare look at any of her fathers, or Jagger, who was breathing as though he'd run a race.

"You met a pirate. In Maltu," the king said, voice leaden. He shifted his gaze from Jagger to Caspian.

The prince did not wilt visibly as the captain had, but Ebba knew him well enough to catch the flicker in his amber eyes. "Yes, I did. The soldiers there apprehended this man, Barrels, and I caught sight of them dragging him to the gallows. I recognized his accent."

For the umpteenth time in their friendship, Ebba was glad the prince was so smart.

"Which of you is the pirate Barrels?" the king said. His bored tone belied the flash of contempt in his eyes.

Barrels answered, "I am, Your Majesty. I was apprentice to the royal quartermaster under your father's rule many years ago. A pirate took me hostage while I was traveling around the Caspian Sea, auditing the governor's records."

The ruler paused at what Ebba assumed was Barrels' accent. Plank had told her once that was what know-it-alls sounded like.

"My name was Jonathan Schnikelwood."

Sally choked under her jerkin. Ebba froze, but the king didn't look her way again.

"Schnikelwood," another of the king's comrades mused.

"Jonathan Schnikelwood," Barrels replied. "Second son of Baron Schnikelwood."

Sally snorted a laugh, and Ebba jerked up a hand over her mouth to cover the sprite's none-too-quiet amusement over her father's name. Sink her, Barrels had definitely traded up when he became a pirate. *Schnikelwood*. If they didn't die, Ebba would never let him hear the end of it.

"The baron and his eldest son helped me a great deal in the Battle for the Seas," the king said, eyes fixed on her oldest father.

Barrels slumped. "They are dead then, Your Majesty?"

The king waved a hand, turning to his son. "You would vouch for this pirate?"

Caspian looked like he didn't dare believe his ears. "Yes, Father. I spoke to the man at length."

"How came you to be with these pirates, Barrels?" The king didn't remove his eyes from Caspian's face as he spoke.

Barrels replied smoothly, "They saved me from the governor's soldiers and agreed to bring me to Kentro so I could buy passage to Exosia."

"Out of the goodness of their hearts, I suppose," the king said, tilting his head.

Ebba stiffened, sensing a trap. Stubby also tensed on her right.

"Father, this man has spent many years as a prisoner to pirates. He is one of our people," Caspian said softly.

The way this was going, Ebba didn't expect the rest of them would get off the hook, but if one of her fathers could be spared from whatever fate lay before them, she'd never stop thanking the prince.

"The baron and his eldest son died during the war," the king said, ignoring his son to address Barrels. "You did not know, which means you were captured a *long* time ago. Tell me—" The king's face hardened. "What ship did you sail upon?"

The courtyard hushed.

"*Eternal*," Barrels admitted. "I was taken hostage by Mutinou—"

"Do not utter that name here!" the king roared.

Sally squeaked again. Captain Tinkleman cut Ebba a look, frowning as Sally shifted position under Ebba's jerkin.

"What are you hiding?" the captain asked, striding forward. His eyes were bright, and his steps eager.

Sharks' teeth, he was looking for a way to save face. "Nothin'," Ebba blurted, high-pitched. Sally stilled.

The lie hung thick in the air.

"Search her," the king ordered.

Ebba surged to her feet, hissing, "Fly for it, Sal."

Her fathers erupted into shouts to the ringing and rattling of chains as soldiers surrounded Ebba. Sally didn't budge from underneath her tunic. Flaming disobedient pet!

"Get yer hands off me, ye Exosian pigs," she snarled at them.

"Wait," Caspian said loudly. "Really, there is no need to treat a lady in this manner."

"Caspian," the king called.

The prince ignored his father, and the soldiers holding Ebba stepped aside for him, though they did not relinquish their grip on her arms.

Caspian stood before her, and Ebba stared up at him for a long moment. They exchanged wordless horror over their current predicament.

"Mistress," he said. "If you are hiding something, now is the time to hand it over."

Ebba was aware of Montcroix watching them intently. She just couldn't decide if Caspian meant what he said or not. He didn't know she had the *purgium* stuffed down her top, surely. Did he just think Sally was there? Did he think it best to admit to Sally's presence? Well, he should know better than that; Ebba would never drop her winged friend into danger.

"What did I tell you? There is no reasoning with a pirate," the king said. "They understand only violence."

Caspian's amber eyes bore into hers, and Ebba swallowed. What did he want her to do? "I'll need my hand back."

"Release her." The prince jerked his head at the soldiers.

"Just one arm," the king called.

The soldier on her right released her, and Ebba reached for the *purgium*. No way was she handing over the wind sprite. The navy men already had the *dynami*. As frustrating as losing the tubes was, Ebba could find them again.

Sally batted her away from the *purgium* and clung to her finger. Ebba tried to shake her off to no avail. Noticing that Sally's white glow was pouring out of her jerkin, Ebba sighed and drew the sprite out.

Gasps sounded from the soldiers, and those by the king craned to catch a glimpse as Sally's brilliant light burst out around them.

Ebba scowled at the sprite, who'd just condemned herself for the *purgium*. "Fly," she hissed again.

But the wind sprite merely floated over into Caspian's upturned hand, ignoring Ebba and her kneeling fathers.

"What is it?" the king said, something other than stone-cold anger entering his voice for the first time.

Caspian turned but the soldier still gripping Ebba's left hand spoke. "She's still hiding something, sir."

"Nay, I ain't!"

"I can see the top of it," the soldier pressed, squinting down the front of her tunic.

Ebba wound up her arm to sock him for staring where he shouldn't. Clearly the hiding place wasn't infallible.

"Search her," the king boomed.

No one was searching her tunic. Ebba quickly reached inside and drew out the *purgium*. The loudmouth soldier snatched it from her grip. His eyes rolled back in his head, and he fell to the stones unconscious, the *purgium* rolling from his grip.

Ebba stared at him in shock.

"Is he dead?" Caspian asked.

Captain Tinkleman crouched at the man's side and shook his head. "Still breathing, Your Highness."

He'd clearly had some permanent illness inside of him.

The prince was white-faced as he stared at the *purgium*, and Ebba recollected that the last time he'd touched the magic cylinder, he lost an arm. Sally disappeared up Caspian's ruffled sleeve as he bent down to pick up the *purgium*.

"Son—" The king strode forward.

Caspian took a deep breath and gripped the *purgium*.

Everyone held their breath, the captain surging to his feet, arms outstretched to catch the prince.

But Caspian wasn't affected. Not physically, anyway. As the king came to stand beside his son, Sally reappeared at the open V of the prince's tunic, yet the monarch did not spare the sprite a glance. His attention appeared fixed on the *purgium*.

No one uttered a word as Montcroix stared at the object. To Ebba, the king looked as though he'd witnessed something unbelievable. What she couldn't understand was that he seemed *more* interested by the sight of the *purgium* than the sight of a glowing sprite exploding out of her top. Had he seen magic before, or did he know what the *purgium* could do?

"Where did you find this?" the king said quietly.

Ebba shrugged. "On the ground." She winced. Not her best pirate truth.

The captain spoke. "They had another one just like it, Your Majesty." He nodded to two of his men, who stood over a large chest dragged in from *Felicity*. The sailors opened it and rifled through, one of them taking the plunge to pick up the *dynami*.

She heard Stubby's muffled curse.

The king reached into his pocket and drew out a heavily embroidered handkerchief before taking the *dynami* from the sailor.

"You are guilty by association," the king said slowly, taking several seconds to break his unblinking stare to look at Barrels. "You will suffer the same fate as the others." The ruler shifted to look at Jagger. "And you, boy? What is your name?"

Missing teeth of a gummy shark, Jagger was breathing heavy. Was the climb up here too much for him? Ebba darted a look at him and found the flaxen-haired pirate's attention was on the king. And not in a good way. If Ebba was the object of that seething attention, she'd be running as fast as possible in the other direction.

"Jagger," he answered tightly.

Ebba couldn't glean anything from the king's expression. Did he recognize Jagger? If so, why ask his name? Did this have something to do with why Jagger hated Caspian?

Caspian was looking between them. He glanced at her, and she read the same questions in his eyes.

"Where are you from, boy?" The king asked the question wearily, as if angry at himself for giving way to curiosity.

Jagger smiled a wide smile that Davy Jones himself probably gave to new guests in hell. "I was raised on Neos, *Your Majesty*."

Only because she was watching so carefully did Ebba see the king's tiny jolt.

"I see," he breathed.

Caspian stepped forward. "Father. . . ."

Montcroix turned back to the castle. He was silent for a space where Ebba could only listen to the thudding of her heart.

Icicles dripped from every word when he did speak.

"Take them to the cages, Captain. Caspian, come with me," he said.

"That's stupid," Ebba said angrily. "If Barrels be guilty for a'sociation, so is yer son. He spoke to Barrels, after all."

Stubby didn't quite manage to bite back his groan.

The king turned back. Briefly. "Pour boiling oil on them at dawn."

"Yes, Your Majesty." The captain bowed. "It will be done."

FIFTEEN

Ebba pressed her face between two of the bars of her cage and blew a white dread off of her cheek. "These things don't have much space."

They'd been escorted back down to the town and shoved into human-sized birdcages. Now, Ebba was suspended above a sludgy brown canal filled with writhing crocodiles. The canal looked man-made, lined with stone walls, and about two hundred feet wide—probably purpose-built for the cages and to add more of a fear factor for those contained within. Why anyone would want a stinking pit of water in the middle of their town was a mystery to her, though the jeering Exosians below didn't seem to mind.

"Ye be the smallest and the youngest. Ye don't get to complain," Peg-leg grumbled in the cage next to her. They were strung out in a line and hanging from the stone parapet above, Ebba in the middle. Most of her fathers were watching the leering and booing crowd on the far side of the murky water, but Barrels had his back turned to them, lost in his own thoughts. The throng of Exosian towns-people had dwindled in the last hour as the sun set, and hopefully once they were all gone, Barrels would come out of his funk.

Honestly, after hearing the terrors of how pirates were tortured on Exosia, she didn't find the cages so bad. Ebba supposed after a week of no water, she'd change her tune, but they might not even make it that long, with the boiling oil tomorrow. That seemed kind of . . . final.

Her plan to free everyone had failed well and truly. Now they didn't even have Sally. She should have sent the sprite to Caspian straightaway, instead of waiting to arrive at the prison. Sod it, hindsight was a fat load of use.

She swallowed, suddenly realizing her life expectancy might have been greatly reduced by recent events. "Do ye think Sally will be okay?" she asked.

"Aye, Ebba-Viva," Grubby said, smiling at her. He seemed the least worried of her fathers, and Ebba wondered if he fully grasped the situation.

"Cosmo will take right good care o' her," he added, leaning back against the rusted bars of his cage.

"I be more concerned about the look in Montcroix's eye when he saw the *purgium* and the *dynami*," Stubby said.

"Ye think he knew what they were?" Locks asked.

"He knew enough to rush forward to try to intervene when Caspian gripped the *purgium*," Plank replied. "I guess that could be coinc'dence; the healing tube had just dropped that navy man." He pushed at his raven black curls.

"Ye don't sound convinced o' that," Ebba noted. "How would Montcroix be knowin' what they are?"

"I don't rightly know," Stubby said. "But I didn't like the gleam in his eye one bit."

"Aye, he was a mean one, all right," she agreed. "How is Caspian so nice-like with that for a father?"

Peg-leg stretched his peg out of the cage with a loud groan.

"Not everyone be as lucky as ye. From the look o' it, Montcroix has been caught up in revenge for a long time. That changes a person. But Caspian turned out just fine on his own, and when Montcroix passes, this world will be a better place for not havin' a Montcroix junior in charge."

Ebba pursed her lips. "I be forgettin' Caspian will be king."

Stubby threw her a glance. "That's what princes become when their fathers cark it."

"I know that," she withered. "I just mean, it's hard to tell my skull that he ain't a prince slave."

"Aye," Grubby said with a deep frown. He blinked several times.

"Don't think too hard, Grubs. Ye know it gives ye a noggin' ache," Locks reminded him gently.

Ebba watched the last of the sun's circle disappear below the horizon. "Can't be complainin' about the view, though."

Plank snorted. "Nay, we can't at that."

"Oi, Jagger," she hollered down the row of their swinging cages. "Why'd the king know ye?" No time like the present to ask a few questions. He might even feel amenable to answering because they'd all be dead in a matter of hours.

"He doesn't," Jagger replied after a beat.

Stubby snorted. "Aye, he recognized ye, all right. Thought ye were goin' to run him through and get us all killed."

Jagger muttered darkly. "It weren't me he recognized."

"How about ye just spit out why ye hate the royal-lubbers?" she ventured, holding her breath lest he should reply.

He didn't.

"Well, I for one would like to know how we mean to get out o' this," Locks said, hammering his cage with a fist. A cage was the epitome of Davy Jones' locker for her impatient father. "The sailors took Verity somewhere, and she was still injured. She needs me."

The soothsayer had gotten by pretty well without Locks so far, in Ebba's opinion.

"I gotta get the *dynami* back," Grubby said. "My seal kin'll be angry with me."

"And the *purgium*." Plank sighed, rubbing his temples. "I'm afraid I ain't got any bright ideas."

"Could we swing somehow?" Peg-leg said. "Maybe a chain will break?"

"Sure, let's drown in our cages," Stubby scoffed, rolling his eyes. "Or be eaten by crocs. Have ye ever heard a crocodile's jaws snapping shut? The power will kill ye in a second. And if it doesn't, their death roll will. We ain't got a hope o' outswimmin' them either. Not by a long shot."

Something clinked by Ebba's head, and she rubbed at her ear.

"Peg-leg has his wooden leg," she said.

"Maybe he can be gnawin' at his peg to use it for a key," Locks said drily.

With that attitude, the plan was bound to fail. Ebba scowled at him. "Ye come up with a better idea then." She rubbed at her ear again.

"Have we got anythin' to pick a lock? Ebba could climb up and escape," Plank said.

"I ain't leavin' any o' ye."

What was that sodding plinking sound? Ebba twisted and squinted at her cage in the dying light. Trust her to be put in the broken bloody cage. She— "A key," she said thickly.

"Aye, Ebba-Viva, that's right helpful," Stubby muttered.

"No," she said louder. "A real key."

A key dangled just outside of her cage, knocking against the bars every so often. She stretched her arm through and carefully took the metal key, tugging at the yarn it dangled from. She traced the yarn up, up, and up some more to the stone parapet above. A shadowed figure was leaning over, but without a torchlight present, she couldn't make out the person above.

She grinned. There was only one person on Exosia who'd help them—who didn't glow. Actually, Ebba frowned. Why wasn't Sally here with the key?

"Is that Caspian?" Plank asked.

"Aye," she replied. "I'm thinkin' so."

Jagger snorted derisively, the first noise he'd made since they were shoved into cages and lowered over the side of the castle wall. "Skulkin' about in the dark instead o' standin' up to his father? Sounds about right."

She understood he had something personal against the royals, but Caspian was different. "Didn't seem to me like there was anythin' else he could've done at the time. This be smarter."

"Have ye truly got a key?" Stubby stared at her between the bars.

Ebba held up the key, which gleamed in the dark. "What say ye? Time to get out?"

The others encouraged her in hushed voices.

Ebba winced as she turned the key in the lock, sure the entirety of the king's army would descend upon them at any second, even though the torchlight of the two sentries overhead had moved away several minutes prior.

"Imagine if I dropped the key?" she whispered, chuckling.

Jagger's answer was immediate. "*Don't* drop the key."

Ebba frowned. Did he even have a sense of humor? "What d'ye think I am? An idiot?" She rushed to add, "Don't answer that."

She held the key tight and shoved her door open. The hinges screeched in protest, and her sharp inhale was echoed by those of her fathers.

No one budged an inch for a full minute, all of them

listening for the sentries. Ebba let out a shaky exhale when there were no shouts of discovery. She leaned out of her cage and passed the key to Stubby. After a further seven clicks of locks, they were all free.

Of a sort.

They were still hanging over a canal filled with crocodiles. "Now what?" she asked. "Are we climbin' the chains to the top?"

"How young do ye think I am?" Peg-leg asked.

She thought that they were definitely over thirty. And that people over thirty couldn't do much. "Only me, Grubby, Jagger, and Plank'll be able to climb to the top," she said. "So how will the rest o' ye get up?"

Plank replied, "I don't think they'll be goin' up, little nymph."

Ebba poked her head outside of the cage and glanced down to where the brown, crocodile-infested water shimmered. "Don't much like our chances down there with the snappers, mateys." Not after what Stubby had said.

"I could talk to them," Grubby offered.

"Ye're kiddin' me," Jagger muttered.

The pirate knew by now that Grubby was a selkie, but he was clearly having trouble with the concept of her father talking to water creatures. Ebba guessed he hadn't known that—just that Grubby could hold his breath for far too long, and swim far too well. She wondered what the pirate would say about the conversations Grubby had with the octopi in Zol.

They all ignored Jagger. Locks asked, "Ye sure, Grubs?"

"Aye, crocodiles ain't my favorite. They be a bit mean-hearted for my likin'," Grubby explained. "But they always keep a promise."

The creaking of their cages was the only sound as Ebba assumed the others did their best to absorb that little tidbit.

145

"Right." Stubby drew the word out. "Well, if ye think they'd listen, Grubs."

Ebba shook her head. "Ye can't send Grubby down there with the crocs." She gestured to his cage only to find it empty. She gasped and peered down. "Grubby!"

A huge splash disrupted the still night air.

"Don't worry. He's a good swimmer, remember?" Barrels said.

"Shite," Plank said, scanning the parapet above. "Did he do a bloody belly-flop? He'll draw the guards back."

Stubby shifted in his cage. "Best get ready to move whether it be up or down, crocs or not. We ain't the only ones who would've been hearin' that."

"Ye can jump now." The thin tendrils of Grubby's shout reached them.

Peg-leg blew out a breath. "Ebba, I be thinkin' ye and Jagger should still climb up."

Ebba wasn't going a different direction to her fathers. If they were falling fifty feet through the air into crocodile territory, so was she. "Nay."

"Well I be headin' upward. I'll see ye back at *Felicity*," Jagger said. He pulled himself over the top of the cage and began heaving himself hand over hand up the thick chain.

No surprise there.

"Ready?" Locks asked, though the question seemed more geared toward himself.

Barrels groaned. "I'm too old for this."

"Now!" Ebba jumped out of her cage into the black night, windmilling her arms as she plummeted toward the dark water.

As the air rushed past her ears, she had no idea where her fathers were or if they'd even jumped. She broke the surface of the water, and thick sludge swallowed her whole, invading her ears and clothing. Ebba kicked, chest tightening, and pushed her arms down in frantic strokes.

She resurfaced, sucking in a huge gulp of air. The fetid smell of the water—if it could be called water—overwhelmed all else, and she swiped at her eyes. Ebba shrieked as something huge reared underneath her, pushing her up.

Grubby appeared by her side. "Settle yer seas, Ebba. It be our new friends."

"*A crocodile?*" Ebba glanced down in horror at the thick-scaled creature she now sat astride.

"Aye," Grubby said happily. "They be goin' the extra yard for us in exchange for a favor."

She didn't venture to ask just what that favor was.

Yells erupted across the surface of the sludgy canal.

"If ye could just be droppin' us away from the guards, that'll do nicely," Grubby said to the monster underneath her. The crocodile swung its great head toward her father.

Grubby grimaced, shrugging. "Well, I ain't seen the normal guard, so I can't be commentin' on his thinnin' hair."

Ebba registered the crocodile's sinister smile, but craned to look up as shouts reached her from the gangway above the cages they'd escaped.

"The guards," she called out.

The crocodile began swimming through the sludge with her on its back, tail swishing side to side, its powerful body a constant reminder the creature could probably eat her in one bite.

A subtle splashing to her left alerted her to Peg-leg's presence atop of an even larger creature, looking utterly relaxed.

"How can ye be so calm?" she demanded.

Peg-leg shook his head. "There ain't nothin' about this s'tuation I be okay with, apart from the survivin' o' it."

Aye, she'd forgotten about that. They were surviving. Ebba set her sights farther left and counted two more of her fathers on crocodiles, and to the right where she found two others. That only left Grubby in the water.

"Do ye think Jagger got to the top okay?" she asked Peg-leg.

"Aye, Ebba. That one don't need any help gettin' out o' a tight corner. I'd guess puttin' faith in Grubby speakin' to crocs was a bit much for him."

Couldn't blame a pirate for surviving, and even their crew had hesitated before joining Grubs in the canal.

"Look smart now," Locks called from her right. "We're nearly to the other side."

Her crocodile pulled up next to a stone outcrop, and Ebba hoisted herself up onto the ledge. She backed away a safe distance. "Uh . . . thanks?"

A shiver ran down her spine as the crocodile slid over to Grubby.

Still in a crouch, Ebba glanced up at the parapet across the canal. The gangway was lined with torches. More torches were moving either side around the canal, no doubt carried by sprinting soldiers racing toward her and her fathers. "We gotta go."

"Hold on," Grubby called. He disappeared, and moments later, a series of loud clangs ensued.

Ebba pursed her lips. "Should we be worried about that?"

"Only that Grubby be tellin' the guards exactly where we are," Peg-leg said with a growl.

To her, it sounded like a gate being destroyed. If that was the favor they owed the crocodiles, Ebba had a strong feeling her father had just released the powerful creatures on the towns-people of Exosia.

"To the docks?" Plank asked as Grubby reappeared. "We shouldn't tarry in this spot."

They couldn't go back to *Felicity* yet.

"Nay, we need to get Sal and the two cylinders back," she

said. There was no way she'd leave the *dynami* and the *purgium* behind. Not without a fight. And Ebba certainly wasn't leaving her friend. Who knew what they were doing to her in the castle. Sal had to be locked up, too.

Stubby shook his head. "Aye, that we do. And the navy men will be headin' to the wharf. We'll have no chance to be gettin' to *Felicity* just yet, and I doubt we'd have time to get out o' cannon range if we did. Then there still be the navy-infested waters to navigate between here and Kentro."

"I know of somewhere we might go until we can find a safe way off Exosia," Barrels croaked. "Only to gather ourselves because I'd wager the king will look there soon enough."

Ebba shot a look at him, blinking at his forlorn expression.

He sighed heavily. "Someone I haven't seen in a very long time and who I hope very much is still alive." He sighed again. "My sister."

SIXTEEN

"Ye're sure this be the place?" Ebba tilted her head back, taking in the columned house that extended upward for several stories. "It be awful grand."

Barrels was retying his hair. She wasn't sure why he bothered when brown, stinking mud covered him from head to toe, but she suspected the thought of seeing his sister for the first time in forty years might have him out of sorts.

"It is grand," Locks answered. "Barrels' father was a baron, remember?"

Ebba replied, "I ain't knowin' what a baron is."

"Baron just mean there ain't no grog left," Peg-leg said.

Barrels jiggled his sopping wet cravat. "That's barren," he corrected.

Peg-leg shrugged. "Guess I don't know what a baron is either."

"A person with too much money," Stubby grumbled.

The door swung open. A man stood there gaping before promptly slamming the door.

"Who was that?" Plank asked.

"The butler." Barrels groaned, patting his hair again.

"The governor had some o' those folk," Ebba said. "I don't think he recognized ye, Barrels."

They paused to listen to the screeches inside.

Stubby muttered, "I be more worried they'll tell the soldiers exactly where we are."

"Marigold wouldn't send soldiers after me," Barrels protested, though he glanced back at the solid door with a small wrinkle between his brows.

"Little nymph," Plank said, "shimmy up the column here. Ye're lookin' for Barrels' sister."

"Doe blue eyes, a head shorter than me," Barrels said miserably.

Plank's lips trembled with what looked suspiciously like laughter. "Tell her that Barrels be here."

Stubby grabbed Locks and Grubby. "We'll go round the side and be makin' sure no servants are sent out with an alert."

Ebba eyed the column before walking up and wrapping her arms around it. The first level was ten feet above. She went on tip-toes and held tight, jumping to place her feet either side of the column. "All right," she puffed. "Find Marigold."

She shifted up the column as Plank had instructed, wishing the soldiers hadn't taken her belt—she could've wrapped it around the back of the column to make climbing easier. The stone scraped against the soft part of her forearms in the absence of the strip of leather. Wedging her feet tight into the crevices and hugging the column for dear life, Ebba made it to the top and shuffled along the ledge of the second-story windows.

A servant stood on the other side of the window, and both of them jumped upon sighting the other. They lunged for the bottom edge of the window at the same time, and as Ebba made to wrench the window up, the servant turned the latch.

"Ye bloody bugger," Ebba shouted at the woman.

She edged to the next window, but the woman had pre-empted her move.

"We'll see about that."

Leaving the servant to continue running about locking windows on the second level, Ebba returned to the column and began shimmying to the top level of the house. Her arms and legs burned as she skirted upward as fast as she could without dying.

Ebba made it to the third level and, when she lifted the first window, had the triumph of seeing the same servant racing into the room. Ebba flung the window fully open and vaulted inside.

"Ha! Beat ye," she said smugly.

"Pirates in the house," the woman screamed.

Ebba frowned. "Oi. I just be lookin' for Marigold." She paused. "Can ye really tell I'm a pirate just from one look?"

The woman backed out of the room as Ebba strode toward her. Holding up her hands, the servant stammered, "Y-yes."

Ebba beamed, following the woman's retreat. "Thank ye. But where be Marigold?"

"I am she," an imperious voice boomed.

Ebba turned, glancing down at an elderly woman standing at the base of the stairs. One fine-boned hand rested on the balustrade, her hair was coiffed up in night curlers, and a quilted robe sat over the blooming powder-white lace of a sleeping gown.

"Ye're Marigold?" She couldn't see much of Barrels in her. The woman was much prettier.

"Samson," the woman said, turning her nose up. "Fetch the pistols."

Definitely not related to Barrels. She had a feisty way about her. "Hold on now. I only came in to tell ye that Barrels be outside. Keep yer hair on."

"Barrels?" the woman said shrilly.

Ebba winced. "Aye. Sumpin' an octave lower would do the trick, though."

"Who is Barrels?" Marigold demanded.

"Sideways swimming codfish! Ye don't know his pirate name, o' course." Ebba racked her skull grog for his real name. "He did mention his real name, he did. It were right rid'culous. I'm just on the spot. I can't rightly remember it. His father be a barren."

"A barren?"

"Aye, someone with too much money." Ebba floundered. "Uhhh, he wears cravats. And he's Exosian. Oh!" She slapped her forehead. "He's yer brother."

The woman's face paled. "My brother?"

"Aye." Ebba nodded frantically. "Not yer dead one."

The woman clutched at the stair railing now. She swayed on the spot as she repeated Ebba's words. "Not the dead one." She glanced past Ebba and blanched. "Brigetta, no!"

The initial sharpness of a heavy blow to Ebba's head was accompanied by the shattering of whatever had caused it. Ebba swayed before, blinking slowly in a last attempt to focus her vision, black coated the insides of her eyes, and she crumpled to the polished wood floor.

"YE BE ALL RIGHT, lass. Rest easy now."

Ebba recognized Stubby's murmur through the throbbing pain in the back of her head. "Was it the servant who struck me?"

"Aye, lass."

Had to respect her perseverance. Ebba was sure she would. Later. "Is there blood everywhere?"

"Nay, the vase didn't break the skin."

"What? No blood at all?" The pounding jabs stabbing her skull were worthy of the whole room being sprayed with blood.

"None. Ye'll get a mighty bruise, I'll be expectin'."

Ebba opened her eyes, feeling mildly better at that.

She was still in the same spot, but three of her six fathers loomed over her. "Ye got inside," she said. "Did ye have to kill anyone then?"

Stubby cleared his throat, glancing over his shoulder. "Barrels' sister let us in to help ye."

"His *name* is Baron Jonathan Schnikelwood," a woman answered.

A suspicious wheezing sound began in Peg-leg's chest.

Ebba sat up with Grubby's help. Her crowding fathers parted, and she peered between them to an elegant lounge suite and its occupants. "Repeat that one more time?" she asked Marigold.

"Baron Schnikelwood," Plank called from where he sat on the couch. "It's even better than Jonathan Schnikelwood. Why in Davy Jones' do landlubbers choose such names?"

Barrels' face was bright red, and at Plank's remark, the rest of her fathers fell into fits of laughter. Knowing how important the reunion was, Ebba checked the majority of her laughter, feeling more than a little sorry that one of her fathers had such a horrible name.

She got to her feet, weaving toward where Barrels sat next to Marigold.

"I think ye should stick with Barrels," she confided in him.

He glared at the rest of the crew before his brows lifted. "Strangely, so do I."

"There will be nothing of the sort. You are returned, Jonathan! Exosia shall rejoice. The king—"

"—Put me in the cages, Marigold," Barrels interrupted her gently. "I cannot stay. But I came to seek your help to get off the mainland."

"Forty years, Jonathan," she whispered, bottom lip trembling.

Ebba stepped over to the woman and hugged her. "I'm sorry yer brother was stolen and at sea for so long."

The woman glanced at Ebba in shock.

Barrels tugged her back. "You are covered in filth, my dear. Marigold doesn't want that all over her."

With a snort, Ebba gestured to where her father sat on the couch. "Or on her couch."

"Oh," Barrels said, standing abruptly. "Sister, I do apologize!" He gestured at Plank, who rolled his eyes and stood.

"Jonathan."

"I'm afraid my manners are rather rusty. I—"

"*Jonathan.*"

Barrels slumped and faced his sister. "I'm so sorry, Marigold. So very sorry for everything."

Marigold stepped closer to him and cupped her hands around Barrels' filthy face. "My brother miraculously returns home after I've thought him dead for nearly forty years, and you think I'm worried about a dressing gown and a silly couch?"

He stared back at her for a long moment before his shoulders relaxed, and a small smile graced his face. "I guess not."

Ebba liked Marigold. She glanced around the spacious room, counting her fathers. "Where's Locks?"

"He went with Marigold's footmen to search for Verity," Stubby answered. He cleared his throats. "Apparently the town be in an uproar over some escaped crocs."

Her eyes rounded and shot to Grubby.

Marigold stood, looking exactly the same as when Ebba had first seen her. Completely dignified after rediscovering her brother was alive, *and* in the presence of six fearsome pirates, too. Ebba really liked her. "Is Locks knowin' where they took her?"

"They likely dropped her at one of the sisters' hospitals. Finding her won't be hard," Marigold said. "Now. Each of you must wash and dress in clean clothes. If you plan on escaping, you won't get two steps looking like that."

"We got more than two steps to get here," Ebba pointed out.

"Ebba-Viva. Manners," Plank said.

Barrels gave her a look and then stood beside his sister. "I'm afraid our departure is not so easy as merely leaving, sister. We must retrieve a number of items from the king and prince."

Sal!

"Poor Sally must be right terrified," Ebba said, pacing. "They'll have her locked up and starvin'. She'll be missin' me sumpin' fierce."

Grubby wrapped an arm about her shoulders. "We'll get her back. Ye just wait and see."

"What precious items?" Marigold asked.

Peg-leg ticked off his fingers. "One glowin' wind sprite. One tube that can heal right bad stuff. Another that makes ye strong."

Barrels' sister stared at her fathers and Ebba, face going slack momentarily before she drew herself up. "I see," she said. "Then once you are bathed and dressed, I shall call for tea."

SEVENTEEN

"One does not *saunter* into the castle," Marigold said as Ebba entered the room. The woman gasped upon seeing Ebba still in her pirate clothes. "You are still in those rags."

"Aye, I washed and put my dirty clothes back on," Ebba said. "Ye only sent me a nightgown."

"'Twas not a nightgown," Marigold scolded. "Young ladies wear dresses."

She knew her fathers wouldn't willingly enter a conversation about dresses and what Ebba should do with one. She'd taught them better than that by now. They'd been dressed by Marigold rather like Barrels dressed every day. The bunch of them looked utterly ridiculous, and she gathered from their constant fidgeting they knew it. Barrels was the only one who seemed comfortable.

"I ain't wearin' no dress. Ye wouldn't be the first to attempt gettin' me in one either," Ebba countered. She softened her tone because, truthfully, Ebba did have female parts, and she could understand how landlubbers would get confused on the matter. They seemed stuck in their straight lines—like horses with blinders on who missed most of the world. For all that she'd worried over the subject for weeks, in the end, the answer to who Ebba was slid naturally from her lips. "I mostly be a pirate," she explained. "Though I'm a bit o' a tribe princess, too, did ye know?" The thought struck her with odd strength as she spoke. She'd never particularly thought that a person could be more than one thing. Yet Ebba wasn't just a pirate. She was from the Pleo tribe, too.

"I gathered you were from the tribes. But a princess?" Marigold asked, patting the seat next to her.

"Aye, Miss Marigold," Ebba said. "My fathers stole me from the chief and chieftess when I were naught but a baby."

Marigold threw a look at Barrels, who confirmed Ebba's statement with a small shrug.

"I were steamin' mad at them for a while," Ebba added. "They didn't tell me anythin' about it, ye see."

"Oh, you poor child," Barrels' sister said, taking one of Ebba's hands.

Ebba smiled sadly.

"But you will still wear a dress while you're on Exosia," Marigold added, arching a brow.

Her smile slipped away. This one was wilier than anticipated. "Nay."

"Yes."

"Nay."

"Yes."

Through the open entrance of the lounge, she watched as the front doors burst open. Locks stormed into the circular lobby, Verity clutched in his arms. Ebba and her fathers stood as Locks caught sight of them and altered his course. He was dressed fancy-like, too.

"Found her right across town. Ye were right. She was in one of the hospitals."

Verity's blonde hair fanned out over the couch cushions as

Locks lowered her. Whoever had cared for her in the day's interim had done a good job. The soothsayer was clean and in fresh garments, and her cheeks looked to have more color.

Her eyelashes fluttered open, and Locks dropped to his knees.

"Verity," he whispered.

Her periwinkle blue eyes landed on his face, unfocused, but entirely free of black. "Locks?"

"I'm here, Verity. And I'll not be leavin' ye."

"You saved me," she sighed, melting into him.

"Sink me, I don't want to listen to this shite," Peg-leg grumbled.

Ebba had to agree, though she saw Marigold wiping under her eye as Locks helped a sighing Verity to sit.

"So what be the plan? We can't dally here overlong. The king's guards'll come here once they've searched the wharf and town," Plank said, exchanging a sudden and feral grin with Stubby. Her fathers got excited about danger at the oddest moments.

They all took seats, Ebba plonking herself on the ground, despite Marigold's stern look. Maybe because of it.

A knock sounded at the door, and they all tensed.

"Sister, are you expecting someone?" Barrels asked quietly.

Marigold stood. "No. I'm not. Samson," she called to summon the butler, her face paling, "whoever it is, turn them away. I am indisposed."

The rest of them hushed as the butler they'd terrified last night gave a composed incline of the head and strode forward with a stiff spine to open the door.

Ebba held her breath, watching the butler's profile go from composed, to shocked, to terrified all in the span of five seconds. He appeared almost as scared as he'd been to encounter seven filthy pirates the night before.

Shite.

"Hide," Stubby hissed as the butler stood aside.

Ebba got to her feet, ready to dive behind the nearest couch, but paused when a cloaked man stepped inside. He pushed back his hood as the butler closed the door.

"Caspian," Ebba shouted, darting over to the prince.

She threw herself against his chest, hugging him with her right arm and smiling as she felt him return the one-arm embrace. "How did ye find us?"

"I had assumed you'd go directly to *Felicity*, but when you didn't appear, I looked up Barrels' family tree." He smiled down at Ebba, amber eyes warming before he glanced away. "I'm so sorry I couldn't stop Father from putting you in those horrible cages. He won't listen to reason when there are pirates involved."

Ebba bit her tongue. She hated when people insulted her fathers. It was best not to be telling Caspian his father was a heartless brute.

His eyes flicked up. "I couldn't ask you up at the castle. Why are some of your dreads white? And why are you so thin?"

Oh. She stepped out of his embrace. "So much has happened since I last saw ye, Caspian. I'll tell ye o' it soon, but right now we're in a pickle."

The prince searched her gaze, his smile fading.

"Y-your Highness," Marigold interrupted. Barrels' sister sank into a deep curtsey.

"Chh." Ebba waved her hand. "Ye don't need to do that around Caspian. He ain't a snob."

Marigold's eyes widened. "He is the crown prince of Exosia. I would never dream—"

Caspian cut her off with a smile. "We are in the presence of seven pirates and a soothsayer. I believe we can dispense with formalities."

The woman relaxed after a beat. "Yes, I suppose so."

"And you can be assured that no one will come searching for you here."

"How'd ye do that?" Ebba asked him.

He cast a look at Marigold before carefully saying, "Being a prince has its . . . perks. And the crocodiles from the lake somehow got loose and are currently being rounded up by the army."

The prince arched a brow at her, a knowing gleam in his eyes as he handed his cloak to the butler. Ebba smiled sheepishly and led him into the lounge where her fathers had collapsed again.

"We were just discussin' how to get our stuff back," Peg-leg said, shifting so the prince could sit.

The prince sat next to her father without pause. "Yes, it won't be easy. My father has locked the *purgium* and the *dynami* in his personal treasury. And Sally. . . ."

"Is she okay, Caspian? Please tell me yer father didn't cook her up and eat her," Ebba said, wringing her hands.

"He wouldn't do that," the prince replied with a wry smile. "Sally is comfortable, I assure you."

Though the wrinkle between his brows as he *assured* her didn't assure her at all. What wasn't he telling her?

"I believe it best if one of you come in to search the castle while I distract Father," Caspian said.

"I'm sorry," Marigold said with a regal wave. "How do you all know the prince?" She stared at where he sat wedged between Peg-leg and Stubby as though staring at a puzzle she couldn't solve.

"We thought he were a prince slave for a good long time," Grubby explained. "Took him with us, and then he got black gunk in his shoulder so we healed him with a magic tube which stole his arm and won't give it back."

Ebba pursed her lips, then nodded. That was pretty accurate.

"I see," Marigold said faintly. Her eyes briefly came to rest on Caspian's empty sleeve. "It must have been a life-threatening wound, Your Highness."

The prince nodded. "To fall victim to the wound would have been a fate worse than death. I owe the crew of *Felicity* a great debt. They have saved my life many times."

"You could argue we put you in danger in the first place," Barrels countered.

Blimey, they were going to start one of their smart everything-has-two-meanings discussions. "We didn't put him in danger. We just took some o' the soft out," she said.

She inspected the prince closely for the first time. He wore hugging breeches of a rich forest green; an embroidered tunic with gold buttons rested tight against his skin. Ebba surveyed his knee-high boots, billowing sleeves, and cravat with a critical eye. He looked handsome and as a prince might. Caspian had a regal way of standing that she'd always noticed, but that was more pronounced in his fitted clothing. She tore her gaze from his thighs and continued her perusal.

"Ye've lost some o' yer hard already," Ebba finally noted.

"On my honor, Jonathan. Have you raised her with any manners at all?" Marigold blurted.

Barrels colored, but the slight tilt of his chin told Ebba it wasn't in embarrassment. "We raised her to be honest. That's a quality very few have."

"Yes, but you can be honest and polite."

"Perhaps, sister. But I would thank you to keep your opinions about our daughter to yourself. We are extremely proud of her, and you have no idea what she's been through."

Ebba blinked at Barrels, who was all but frothing at the bit he was so angry.

Marigold's mouth fell slightly ajar as she glanced around the rest of her fathers who had fallen into a heavy silence. "I do apologize for criticizing your parenting."

Ebba replied, "I probably am a wee bit rusty with fancy manners." She was willing to admit her faults. Sometimes.

"I find Ebba-Viva's manners very refreshing," the prince announced. "And she is right. It's easy to fall back into, uh, soft habits. However, Mistress Fairisles, you may need to soften yourself if we are to carry out my plan."

"Never," Ebba scoffed, glancing away. She'd take a bullet in the innards before that happened.

"There is to be a ball for my return tomorrow night," Caspian said. "I would like Ebba to be my guest. She can retrieve Sally, and I shall steal father's treasury key so she can grab the *purgium* and the *dynami*."

"I can't hold them at the same time," Ebba reminded him. When she'd tried, white light exploded, and she was thrown across the room.

That wasn't Stubby's worry. "Ye want to take our daughter to a ball?"

"There'll be dancin', will there?" Plank asked, coming to stand beside him.

Locks had been murmuring in Verity's ear but lifted his head at this. "Why Ebba? Why not one o' us?"

"A man is more suspicious," Caspian said, red creeping up his jaw. "Many of the women at these occasions are. . . ." he glanced at Marigold, who answered for him.

"Occupied with the finer things in life?" she suggested.

The prince smiled at her. "Exactly. If Ebba is caught while searching the castle, she can merely pretend she is lost."

"I ain't no codfish," she said, rounding on him.

"Not a codfish, but the art of distraction. Never underestimate the power of a pretty dress, my dear," Marigold said. "If properly wielded, it can be the equivalent of stabbing a dagger into a man's side."

Stabbing people? That put a different spin on things, to be sure. "I ain't wearin' no dress," Ebba said mulishly.

The woman glanced at her brother. "I'm afraid the larger problem is how we can make her fit in."

"Ah, yes. I did not think of that," Caspian said, turning to look at her. "Your coloring is far more exotic than the other women in the court. Though most will just be jealous, don't you think. . . ." He trailed off, catching the older woman's expression.

Marigold regarded him in disbelief. "She has dreads, a golden hoop earring, and her hair is arranged in clumps. Not to mention the way she speaks."

He studied Ebba again. "You're right. I've only seen Ebba on the sea." The prince shrugged. "She's beautiful, but you're right; she does not look like the other courtesans."

He'd called her pretty on Kentro. She'd even heard him telling Barrels that she was beautiful one time. But Ebba had never been called beautiful directly to her face. Her gut reaction was to lash out as she did when people called her fish-lips, but Caspian wasn't a random stranger or a heckling pirate. He meant the compliment genuinely, and the respect she held for him had her floundering on how to best respond.

Heat rose into her cheeks at the furious whispered conversation several of her fathers were having on the far couch.

"He be takin' her to a ball *and* called her beautiful," Peg-leg hushed in an ominous tone. "I don't like it. Not one bit."

"Aye," Stubby said, glaring over his shoulder at Caspian, who stilled.

Ebba ignored the mounting heat in her face and spoke. "Well, how hard-like can it be? I can be mindin' my manners."

Caspian winced. "We need another plan."

"What? Now ye don't want to take me?" she demanded.

"I'm too weak to go, but I can disguise her," Verity said. The soothsayer rested her head against Locks' shoulder. Dark bags hung under her eyes but did little to hide the fair woman's natural beauty. Ebba wondered how Marigold would react if Verity went soothsayer on them.

"How?" Plank asked, pulling out of the discussion with Stubby and Peg-leg.

"I'll make her a charm. While she's wearing it, anyone who glimpses her will see only a well-bred lady."

Ebba wrinkled her nose. "I ain't no horse."

"What about how she sounds?" Caspian asked the soothsayer.

"She will sound genteel, with an Exosian accent."

"What about her movements," Stubby asked as Ebba plonked down on the floor again.

Barrels added, "And her smell?"

"What about my smell," Ebba exploded.

"All anyone will see, hear, smell, or feel is a lovely young woman with impeccable manners. I can have the charm ready by tomorrow."

Marigold was whispering to Barrels. "What does she mean by charm?"

Locks gripped Verity's hand. "It be too much. Ye shouldn't be exertin' yerself in any way."

"I thought the ship drained most o' yer magic," Ebba said.

"Not all of it," Verity said. "Just most. I can still do small things like this. It won't be taxing." Her face softened as she glanced up at Locks. "I will be able to rest when we are back on *Felicity* and away from here."

Caspian stood. "It's sorted then."

"Hold on just one moment," Peg-leg said to the prince, standing.

165

Marigold surged to her feet, waving at Ebba. "Come with me, my dear. We must start getting you ready."

"But I'll have a charm," Ebba complained as the woman ushered her out of the room. She glanced back to see her fathers surrounding Caspian.

"It never hurts to have a backup plan," Marigold answered.

"Ye just want to dress me up like a doll."

"I've got four sons. Of course I do. Plus, what did I tell you before?"

Ebba shrugged, and the woman gave her a stern look.

"*Never* underestimate the power of a pretty dress."

EIGHTEEN

She sat with her fathers and Marigold outside a room, ignoring the periodic flashes of red emanating from beneath the door, and the occasional wisp of smoke.

Caspian had left yesterday without saying goodbye, leaving only a cream envelope with a gold trim that would gain her access to the castle. If Ebba could walk into it in these ridiculous shoes.

"But honestly, Jonathan. Has she never worn shoes in her life?" Marigold hushed at her brother.

"She doesn't like them. It's easier to climb the shrouds in bare feet," he answered.

"I'm not sure a lady should be climbing ropes and gallivanting around in such a manner!"

"Sister," Barrels said in warning.

Ebba took pity on the woman, not taking her eyes off the flashing light, which had just changed to purples and greens. "Don't be feelin' sorry for me, Miss Marigold. My fathers did drop me off with some females once. It was an awful time bein' in dresses, so I made them promise never to leave me at a brothel again."

Marigold jerked, and her teacup fell to the polished wood floor, smashing. "Jonathan Schnikelwood!"

Ebba smirked evilly.

"It's not what it sounds like," Barrels hurried to say, standing with his hands raised.

"*Schnikelwood*," Stubby wheezed, pounding his chest. "Gets me every time."

The flashes turned brilliant gold, and Verity emerged amidst a plume of silver smoke, a ruby necklace in her hand, one that Marigold had donated to their plan.

"Does it work?" Plank asked, drawing closer.

Verity shot him a look. "What are you saying?" she snarled at him.

Disappointingly, no cracks appeared on her skin.

Locks cleared his throat, and the soothsayer tore her eyes from Plank to walk over to Ebba. "Watch," she muttered.

Ebba lifted her dreads so the woman could clasp the ruby necklace around her neck. Ebba wasn't happy with the shoes or the stupid frilly dress she had on, but *treasure* was something she could get used to.

Her fathers gasped.

"What?" Ebba asked, staring at them. "Ye look as though a fly flew in yer gob."

"*You are shocked. Might I inquire as to why,*" Barrels said, mouth open. "Those exact words just came out of your mouth."

Really? That wasn't what she'd said, but Ebba supposed the meaning was the same.

Barrels turned to the rest of their crew. "The charm works."

"Are ye sayin the charm is changin' my words?" She couldn't hear anything.

Peg-leg gasped. "That be mighty strange, but ye're right. Ebba never spoke so fancy a day in her life."

"Is Ebba still there underneath?" Stubby demanded. "Her hair ain't that long."

"Her hair?" Peg-leg scoffed. "She ain't dark brown, for starters."

"I be white?" Ebba asked. "My skin be fair?" That *was* strange.

Verity leaned into Locks' side. "The prince may think you exotic, Ebba-Viva, but a tribesperson will stick out in the castle as much as a pirate. While I'd usually be all for shocking some ignorance out of the Exosians, now is not the time to be noticed."

Barrels came over and patted her hand. "Rest assured, my dear, you look nothing like your usual self, but this guise will help us get our lost items back."

"Where did Ebba go?" Grubby asked, entering the room.

Plank pointed. "She's right there."

Grubby tilted his head. "I ain't sure I like what ye've done with yer hair this time, Ebba."

Plank took pity. "It ain't really how she looks, Grubs. She's wearin' a magic charm that's changin' her appearance."

His brow cleared. "Oh. Thought ye were awful pale."

Her fathers groaned.

"Get up and move," Marigold said, eyes narrowed. Ebba suspected the woman was awed but didn't wish to show it.

Ebba stood, wincing at the pinch of her shoes, and wobbled across the floor, nearly falling twice.

"As graceful as a butterfly," Locks breathed.

Verity snorted.

"Ye can see the real me?" Ebba asked. At least something about her was the same.

The soothsayer grinned in response, exposing all of her teeth. "No."

"Well," Plank said, blowing out a breath. "Will she pass inspection?" he asked Marigold and Barrels.

The two Exosians surveyed her in silence, glancing at each other before Marigold answered. "Yes, she'll pass inspection. And set the courtesans aflutter."

"There'll be no aflutterin' o' any kind," Stubby glowered. "She goes in, finds our stuff, and comes straight back out afore ten o'clock tonight."

"Aye," Locks joined in. "And no dancin' closer than two feet."

Plank watched her. "If ye drink anythin' stronger than grog, we'll be knowin'."

Ebba scanned them, and looked at the women in the room. But Verity and Marigold seemed to be having trouble keeping a straight face.

Verity gave mercy first and strode forward to unclasp the necklace from Ebba's neck. "This will only last eight hours at the most while on. We must conserve the charm for tonight."

"When will I be leavin'?" Ebba slumped, resigning herself to the ball.

Marigold inspected a grand pendulum clock against the far wall. "The prince's horses will come for you in two hours." Her expression hardened. "Just enough time for me to run you through the layout of the castle."

"BLIMEY, I stick out like a sore thumb," Ebba said, nearly falling out of the carriage in her stupid heeled shoes.

One of Caspian's slaves had jumped off the back and bowed before her. "Someone of your grace and charm could never be anything but welcome."

Ebba thought he might have been having a laugh but then

remembered the ruby necklace about her neck. "Aye, cheers, matey." The slave melted like ice in a hot pot after she spoke. What the heck had the charm translated her 'Aye, cheers, matey' to?

The carriage had stopped within the castle gates in the huge rectangular courtyard where she'd knelt beside her fathers two days prior. Determined to get this over and done with, Ebba stormed up the steps where the king had first appeared, using both hands to hold up the stupid white dress with silver embroidery Marigold had forced her into. At the top, she clunked through the wide castle entrance in the pinching white shoes with the silver buckle. The clothes she wore were of fine quality, definitely not for rags. The women at the Maltu brothel would sell their hair to wear such luxury against their skin, but Ebba just saw the dress as a way to limit her stride. The material would get tangled in her knees if she had to run. And the shoes were just a painful nuisance that would give her blisters and a sprained ankle *if she had to run*. She was about to steal from the king of Exosia. Running seemed likely.

But Marigold's statement about the dress being a weapon had stuck with her. As Ebba pushed past the rows of gaping people in the entranceway, she wondered if Barrels' sister might actually know something about survival. Ebba might not be above using a female thing or two for that purpose—surviving was the pirate thing to do, after all. She just objected to it otherwise. Like right now when Verity's charm was doing the majority of the work and being in a dress was pointless. Ebba wasn't planning to still be in the castle when the ruby necklace ran out of juju.

"Oi, where be Prince Caspian?" she asked a slave decked out in purple and gold livery.

The slave bowed low. "The prince is in the ballroom, madam. Might I escort you there?"

"Yeah, I s'pose." Ebba wiped her nose on her bare forearm and then grimaced, wiping her arm on the hoop skirt that could probably host a circus underneath. The neckline of her dress was wide across her shoulders and didn't possess sleeves. Ebba missed the nose-wiping capabilities of her stained tunics. And slops, she missed her slops.

"Not to worry, madam. You shan't get lost while you're with me," the slave said.

Ebba stared at him. "I be thinkin' yer grog has fallen out o' yer skull."

The man laughed and bowed again before leading her through the thickening throng of fancy people. Ebba trailed behind in silence, taking in her surroundings.

The inside of the castle was much prettier than the outside. The ceilings were high, the walls draped with purple and gold curtains. Torches sat atop ornate stands at intervals, lodged in intricately welded settings. The flooring was the same stone as the outside, but in here, the hard gray was polished to a shine with rugs bearing golden tassels covering the majority of the floor space. Chandeliers with hundreds of white candles hung above their heads, casting a romantic light through the hall. The soft light bounced off the gathered people beneath, showing Ebba just how much Marigold had held back while dressing her.

Grand feathers jutted from headdresses, skirts ballooned, and cravats were tied so flawlessly Ebba knew they had to have taken hours. Even in the governor's house, Ebba had never seen such lavish luxury or flaunted wealth. Caspian's world was utterly foreign to her. How was he so normal when he'd grown up around this? Ebba snorted, recalling him in stained slops washing the deck.

The slave she was following glanced back and smiled at her as they exited the grand hall into something even larger.

Ebba's mouth hung ajar as the ceilings pushed higher, the chandeliers gained a hundred more candles, and the thicket of people crowded more densely. Was this endless? Did each room beat the last?

"The ballroom, ma'am." The slave bowed. "You will find refreshments to the left and the balconies to the right."

He disappeared through the crowd, and Ebba continued to gape. Bay windows covered the wall to her right. The balconies, the slave had said. The large glass doors were flung wide, yet a drip of sweat still trickled down the back of her neck from the cloying throng of landlubbers.

To the left were the 'refreshments'—if you could call a fountain of pink liquid falling into narrow glass chutes refreshments. The crowd was thickest there, and Ebba had no urge to join them. Instead, she ran her eyes along the wall directly in front. Two rows of soldiers with hats so oddly shaped Ebba had to wonder if their heads were that shape, too, stood guard by a roped-off area. Inside the cordoned space were three fancy seats, high-backed, with clawed armrests. In the middle and largest seat sat King Montcroix. *Sour brute*. To his left sat a beautiful young woman who appeared a few years younger than Ebba but who, even in the way she sat, possessed a grace Ebba only felt while swinging on the rigging of a ship. Her resemblance to Caspian couldn't be missed, so she had to assume the young woman was the elder of his two sisters.

Ebba shifted her eyes to the right where Caspian sat, straight backed, his gloved right hand on the armrest of his seat. Outwardly calm, the only sign that he might *not* be was the tapping of his forefinger against the chair, and the trawling of his amber eyes across the crowd.

She navigated the crowd toward him, ignoring the few fancy people who tried to talk to her. Nearing the two rows of guards,

Ebba couldn't help reaching up to ensure the ruby necklace was in place.

"I need to talk to Prince Caspian," she told the nearest guard. "Sooner rather than later."

The soldier bowed. "Evening, ma'am. If you wish to speak to the royal family, you must get in the line." He pointed behind her, and Ebba surveyed the queue with no small measure of disbelief.

People *lined up* to see Caspian. Laughter bubbled up inside her. "Shite, that's right hilarious. No wonder he be soft." She wasn't about to wait in line to see him. "Oi, Caspian!" Ebba lifted a hand high and waved.

The soldier cast her a look that was equal parts amused and admonishing. The onlookers, even those she'd shoved in front of, glanced at her affectionately, as though she was a toddler playing in a field of wildflowers. Flaming eejits.

"Oi!" she called at the royals again.

Caspian's eyes landed on her, and Ebba placed her hands on her hips, giving him an expectant look. The prince frowned, but when she stayed where she was, he hesitantly got to his feet and drew closer. He wore a tight tunic and breeches like he'd worn yesterday, except the brown and green had been replaced with green and gold. His boots had tassels, and a classically tied cravat occupied the open V of his tunic. He looked . . . handsome.

Ebba's stomach flipped.

"How can I help you, Mistress. . . ?" Caspian asked.

"It's Ebba, ye dolt." She rolled her eyes.

His eyes widened infinitesimally as they swept up and down her frame. His face smoothed, and he swept a low bow. "Lady Fairisles. How could I forget such a face? I hope you fare well tonight."

"Yeah, all right. Let's get on with it then." Ebba jerked her head over her shoulder. She wanted to be back in the open air where pirate tribe people were supposed to be.

Whatever Caspian was, he'd never been slow. "One moment," he said. Striding back to his father, the prince whispered in Montcroix's ear. The king's eyes settled heavy on her before he nodded to his son.

Caspian held out his arm as he neared her side once more. Ebba frowned at him. A small smile graced his face before he held out his arm and looked at her expectantly. "Place your arm through mine."

She did as bid, and he led her through the throes.

The staring crowds parted for them, and Ebba was suddenly glad for the ruby necklace around her throat. Hopefully, the charm would conceal her fidgeting as they looked between her and Caspian. Talk about uncomfortable. Like bloody seagulls.

"You look nothing like yourself," he murmured to her.

"Thanks," she said drily.

"I don't like it," Caspian said, scanning her again through the corner of his eye. "I can't tell what you're really saying. I wager that it wasn't 'you flatter me, Prince Caspian.'"

He led her out onto the balcony, and Ebba sighed as the sea air hit her face, even if it was warm sea air and not accompanied by sea spray.

He didn't stop, leading her down wide curved stairs into a garden that overlooked the cobalt ocean.

Ebba stared at the turquoise blue, and her surroundings faded away. If everything went to plan, she'd be back out there, the water rolling underneath her, the waves breaking on *Felicity*'s figurehead.

"That look in your eyes right now is real," Caspian whispered, breaking the ocean's spell.

With a cursory glance around, he tugged her behind a tree. Ebba pulled the ruby necklace off, and he blinked.

Caspian stared at her face, then his gaze dropped to the dress Marigold had forced her into. "Ebba," he breathed.

"What?" she asked, oddly nervous to hear his reaction.

"You look *breathtaking*." His amber eyes raised to hers.

That was the third time he'd complimented her.

. . . Why was she keeping count? And did he mean something by the compliments, or was that just an Exosian thing?

Ebba broke off their stare, pretending to check for company. "Aye, Marigold put it on me in case the charm wore off. Not that it's solvin' anythin' else about me on the list o' issues she mentioned."

"I don't like the charm," he said after a beat.

"Aye, ye should be under here, talkin' like normal but havin' all the fancy people simperin' and smilin'. Right weird, it is."

"Strangely, I can relate to that. But I wish to hear what happened to your dreads. Why have some turned white?" he asked, searching her face.

Ebba sucked in a breath. Right. That. She'd promised to tell him. How would Caspian react? Would it bring up painful memories for him? "Right after I left ye at Kentro, I was captured by *Malice*."

He stumbled back a step, his eyes wide. "*What?*"

"Aye," she said in a low voice. "They wanted to know where the objects were, obvi'usly, and when I wouldn't tell them, they shoved me down in a dark room with Verity. They'd captured her from Febribus after we left her."

"I didn't see them take you," Caspian said frantically. "I purposely didn't look back because I was worried I'd lose the courage to return here. Fool," he said to himself, lifting his chin. "I'm so very sorry, Mistress Fairisles."

She shook her head. "There were too many o' them anyway. They hurt me pretty bad, I'll admit. But worst was the room they put me in. Ye know the six pillars that the Earth Mother spoke of?" The prince knew everything that had transpired in the Pleo cavern. When he nodded, she continued. "The six pillars *are* the taint. It be their evil. The taint is how they feed on us. They were the blackness that was in yer arm. And the pillars were on *Malice* this whole time, inside the ship, feeding on the crew."

Caspian appeared dazed, but he was anything but slow with connecting the dots. "That's where the evil has been hiding and gaining its strength after escaping the wall?"

"When I was shoved in that room, the taint took me," she told him. "And it nearly won. Ye . . . ye don't want to know the things I thought."

The blood drained from his face. "You were tainted?"

"I was there for ten days, and I swear one more day, and I would've been theirs. I was in a sorry, dark state."

Caspian's chest rose and fell in quick succession. He lifted his gloved hand to rub his forehead. "This is a lot to take in." He dropped his hand. "Are you okay?" The prince frowned. "How are you okay?" His confusion cleared. "The *purgium*. It took some of the color from your hair as sacrifice."

He stepped closer and picked up one of her white dreads. "I wish you hadn't gone through that. Ever. You may be healed, but I know how haunting those memories are. You aren't telling me everything."

"I wish ye hadn't gone through what ye went through, too," she said, simply. "But we both have, and now we have to make sure as few people as po'sible go through the same."

His brows arched. "Your other fathers have changed their vote then? You'll find the root of magic that the Earth Mother spoke of?"

"Aye, they weren't impressed with how I was treated on *Malice*, that's for sure. None o' my fathers will stop at just finding the root after what Pockmark did to me. And I surely won't. We'll fight *Malice* and the pillars to the end."

The prince whistled. "When your crew decides to do something, they go the whole way."

His voice had an edge to it, and Ebba shrugged. "I know ye've found it hard to understand why my crew voted against trackin' down the answer afore. But to us, a promise be a promise. I get the sense that people on Exosia might give their word willy-nilly; forgive me if I'm gettin' that wrong. My crew don't make an oath we don't intend to keep. And by votin' to go after answers, we would've been promisin' to see this through to the end. Maybe we didn't see how serious it was for a while, but after a fashion, Plank was ready to vote aye, Grubby second, and me third. The others have joined, too, because now, they've got a reason to be makin' such a vow. This be personal to my fathers and to me after what happened to them on *Eternal,* and me on *Malice.* But more than that. . . ." She shivered, recalling the six shadows touching Pockmark. "The evil I felt and saw on that ship, the taint *ye've* felt and seen, can't be allowed to rule this realm. When Jagger saved me from *Malice,* I looked back an' saw the pillars take up their shadow forms. I felt their emptiness. I felt that the realm would be empty if they were allowed to take over. That evil has no place here, Caspian, and I'll do whatever I can to be rid o' it." The taint had to be extinguished. No matter the cost. Ebba wouldn't wish that fate on anyone. Not even Pockmark himself.

Caspian's face had paled, but his jaw was clenched. "Jagger saved you?"

That was about the least important part of what she'd said. Ebba stared at him. Was he serious?

He sighed. "I just wish I could figure out how the Earth Mother intended your crew to locate this root she spoke of. Success seems centered on that."

"Aye, same here. I'm guessin' I'll have to return to Pleo and ask more questions o' her."

Ebba turned to the prince in the quiet that followed her comment, squeezing his hand. "Caspian, I just wanted to say that I understand why ye returned home to win yer father over to fight *Malice*. I wasn't totally understandin' afore, but I do now."

He sighed heavily and smiled at her. "Thank you, Mistress Fairisles. That means a great deal. You have no idea how I doubt my every move."

"Ye're too smart for yer own good," Ebba said, and grinned. "Can't say I be havin' that problem. But there ain't nothin' wrong with lookin' at sumpin' for holes and whatnot. That's what I have my crew for. Maybe ye just have our entire crew in yer head all the time." She frowned. "No wonder it gets noisy."

Caspian chuckled softly. "I've missed your logic. And I'd hoped to hear more of it before the night is over. However, my father will greet the guests shortly. I suggest you excuse yourself to the ladies' room and promptly get yourself lost. If anyone asks, you couldn't find the right room."

The castle had a poop room just for ladies? "Aye, okay." She frowned at the crown on Caspian's head. "I know ye be a prince and all, but it's odd to see ye being a prince, if ye know what I mean. I'll always see ye as Cosmo."

His amber eyes regarded her, and Ebba blinked into their burning depths.

"And I would have it no other way," he said seriously. "I shall always see you as Ebba the pirate."

"Tribal pirate," she corrected him.

"Tribal pirate," he repeated with an arching smile. "You'll always keep me on the straight and narrow."

"Ye be speakin' soft again already." Ebba glared at the prince. All her hard work, undone.

179

He made a face. "It's easy to fall back into old habits, I fear."

Voices called out, and she and Caspian shared a look as Ebba lowered the ruby necklace back in place. Caspian presented his arm, and Ebba wound her arm through his and strolled by his side. They passed by a gaggle of feathered and tasseled women who erupted into whispers upon sighting them.

"I'm afraid the castle will be talking of you for quite some time," he said.

If that were the case, they didn't have nearly enough to do. "Where be yer father's treasury?" she asked.

"Fourth floor, at the very end of the hall." He slipped his hand into his shining boots in a graceful swoop and straightened, pressing something into her hand. "This is the key. There will be a guard, but I've arranged for him to be taken care of."

That sounded far too ominous for Caspian. "He won't be back while I'm there, will he?" She'd have to stick the guard in the gullet, if so. "And where's Sally? I'll need her help to carry one o' the cylinders."

Caspian hesitated. "Sally has her own chambers on the third floor."

Wait. "Did ye say she has her own chambers? Like a cage?"

Caspian blanched and bowed over her hand as they re-entered the throng of the ballroom. "Mistress Fairisles, should all go well tonight, I do believe it will be some time before we see each other again."

Heart sinking, Ebba took him in.

There had been a gap in her life since Caspian left. He didn't even know the details of what had happened to her on *Malice*. Ebba found herself desperately wanting to tell him everything. He'd understand the horror she'd gone through. The subject seemed more approachable with him as her peer than it did with her fathers. There was no time, however, and Ebba wasn't sure there would ever be time with how different their lives were. Ebba watched him sadly, saying, "I'll miss ye sorely, Caspian. It just doesn't feel right when ye ain't around."

He smiled sadly, peering over to where couples twirled in time to music. "I'll miss you, too, Mistress Fairisles." His face shadowed. "More than you know. And . . . I-I know such thoughts are not in your mind, but I regretted not telling you how I felt at Kentro, and I promised I wouldn't make the same mistake when I saw you again."

Ebba's mouth went bone dry at his serious expression, and her stomach erupted in sudden nerves.

"For a while now, I've wished we could be *more* than friends," he said, darting a look at her lips. "If ye were ever open to such notions, I'd rather hoped to have the honor of courtin' ye."

He was speaking like a pirate, so Ebba knew not to laugh. But court her? She didn't know what that meant. However, she didn't have to know what it meant—the 'more than friends' part was *crystal* clear.

"Ye're attracted to my body?" Ebba croaked, mind awhirl.

His color deepened, and he rushed to say, "Well, yes, but it's more than that. You don't need to say anything. I know that's not how you see other people. I just wanted you to know I feel romantically for you, in case a long time goes by before we're together again. I just . . . wanted you to know."

She should say something, but not a single word rose to her lips. She stared at him.

A few heavy seconds ticked by, and then the prince dropped his gaze and pressed a lingering kiss to her hand, causing an elderly woman who stood close by to nearly expire on the spot.

"Fair well, won't you, Mistress Pirate?" he whispered.

NINETEEN

Marigold had spent two hours going through the layout of the castle with Ebba, regularly lapsing into descriptions of the curtains and chaises. The living quarters of the castle wrapped around three sides of the rectangular courtyard—the last side being the guarded entrance they'd first been marched through. The castle had six levels, each accessible via a grand staircase, which wound all the way to the top.

Ebba needed to get to the third level to save Sally, and to the fourth level to find the *dynami* and the *purgium*.

She puffed up the stone stairs in her cumbersome dress, past the first and second levels, nodding at the few servants and guests she encountered. A guard marched past her, and Ebba held her breath, but no one seemed to think her out of place. She continued climbing and then stood at the top of the stairs on the middle of the third level, looking left and right while catching her breath. Caspian had said Sally had her own chambers. Left or right?

Caspian had also said a whole heap of other things that included the word romantic. But he was right about one thing. They likely wouldn't see each other for a long time, and Ebba would need at least that long to mull over his confession and decide what to do with it. She couldn't deny that his words had excited her on some level. And also couldn't deny that those were the words she'd wanted to hear on Kentro before he left. But *doing* something with that knowledge was where things got tricky. And her identity had just recently been in crisis; Ebba wasn't eager for another one so soon.

Hiking up her skirts, and wincing at the growing pinch of her shoes, Ebba set off to the left, opening chamber doors at random.

"Sorry," she muttered to a man dressing in front of a mirror.

He smiled at her. *At the ruby charm.* Sink her, if Ebba didn't have self-esteem to spare, the ruby charm might dig away at her after too long. Were people seriously so susceptible to the polished look she'd been given by Verity? Landlubber logic just didn't make sense to her.

Ebba slammed the door shut and continued down the left wing of the level without success. "Where are ye, Sal?" Ebba knew that the wind sprite had a few cards up her sleeve. She was strong, and had a glowing white light that kept evil magic away. But Sally was her friend, and Ebba couldn't help worrying about her.

Retracing her steps to the grand stairway, Ebba continued past it down the right wing, flinging open the doors. She muttered a hasty apology to a barely clad couple who were in the act of drinking tea. Thankfully, most of the guests appeared to be below, enjoying the festivities.

Ebba threw open the final door at the end of the wing, and scanned the chamber.

The room was large, and where the other chambers on this level had seemed standard with their canopy beds, trunks, and wardrobes, *this* room belonged to someone special. The canopy of the bed was a sheer white, and the bed itself was filled with gold and silver cushions that Ebba thought she could sink into forever. Stately pedestals sat at intervals with gold cushions atop them, and the same sheer white material from the canopy was strung throughout the rafters of the room, giving it a light, relaxed feel.

Voices sounded from behind her.

Ebba slipped into the room, pressing the door closed. She swept material out of her face as she ventured farther into the chamber, and her eyes fell on a golden platter perched on a large window seat.

As she watched, a tiny hand reached out from behind a propped silver cushion to snag a green grape.

Ebba gasped. "Sal."

The hand froze and slowly retreated.

Ebba frowned. "Sal?" How many tiny hands were there in Exosia? But if the tiny hand belonged to the sprite, why was she hiding?

Ebba took three striding steps to the window seat and plucked the silver cushion away.

Sally fell flat on her back.

"I found ye!" Ebba said, grinning.

The wind sprite sat, rubbing the back of her head, and glared upward.

"Ain't ye happy to see me?" Ebba's grin faded as she ran her eyes over the sprite.

Sally was dressed in a white toga with a golden circlet about her head. Her gut bulged out of the dress. "Wow, Sal. Ye've packed a few on. It's only been two days since I saw ye. Have you been eatin' the whole time?"

Sally rolled onto her front with difficulty, struggling to her hands and knees before standing.

"Wait." Ebba's hands flew to the charm about her neck. "How do ye know it's me?"

The sprite rolled her eyes and pointed at the charm, holding her thumb and forefinger close together. Then she pointed at herself and held her hands far apart.

"Yer magic be stronger than the charm?"

Sally shrugged and casually inspected her nails.

That seemed like an aye. Ebba glanced around. "Have ye just been in this room then? There be windows. Sal . . . ye could've gotten free."

There were many windows to the room. One of them was even propped open. Sally had wings—though whether they worked with the sprite's new weight was anyone's guess.

Ebba fingered the ruby necklace, and Sally's eyes tracked the movement, the perplexed frown she'd worn cleared. Ebba removed the necklace, though certain the sprite could see through the soothsayer's magic regardless. "Sal," she whispered. "Why didn't ye come for us?"

Sally gestured around the room, and at the platter of food. With a self-depreciating shrug, the sprite pointed to the corner, at what appeared to be a pink champagne fountain.

Red crept up Ebba's neck. "Ye left us in the cages because there be a champagne fountain in yer room?"

Sally shook her head, pointing to the floor and then holding her hands up either side of her head, murmuring in a high-pitched voice. She mimicked unlocking a door with a key.

"Ye knew Cosmo would get us a key?"

Sally pursed her lips and then shrugged again.

What did that mean? "And so ye stayed here with yer champagne fountain and yer grapes instead o' liftin' a finger to help?" The king had ordered boiling oil to be poured on the crew of *Felicity*. They'd had to jump into a canal filled with crocodiles. She was wearing a *dress*.

The sprite flew over to the fountain, her wings working double time. Sally waded into the bubbling basin, under the cascade of champagne, and tipped her head back, gulping the bubbling drink back.

The heat in Ebba's cheeks flared as the sprite stood fully under the waterfall of alcohol and began to wash.

"Ye flamin' addict! Ye abandoned the crew for a soddin' drink?" Ebba shouted, lunging for the sprite.

Sally squeaked, and in her bid to escape, she slipped, disappearing under the surface. Tiny arms flailing, she managed to drag herself to the curved lip of the fountain and heaved herself over the side. Ebba's hands clutched at thin air, and she jumped after Sally as the sprite took flight. "Ye shite o' a pet."

The air chilled. Sal turned back, and her eyes narrowed.

"That's right," Ebba said, puffing. "A pet."

Clanging footsteps sounded down the hall, and both Ebba and the wind sprite locked glances. Sally flew at Ebba, hands flung out in a pushing motion. Ebba lurched backward to escape her waving limbs.

Sally stopped and pointed behind the bed. The clanging footsteps grew louder.

"Ye want me to hide?" Ebba asked, already crouching.

She didn't answer, zipping back to her perch by the platter a scant second before the door was opened. Jolting, Ebba remembered the charm and threw the necklace back on.

"Lady Athena," a soldier greeted Sally.

Athena? Terrible name for a pet. Ebba raised her head to peek over the cushions littering the bed.

Sally waved regally at the soldier.

"The king would like to introduce you to his guests, if you are agreeable."

The wind sprite appeared to ponder the request at great length before lurching to her feet. She waited imperiously as the soldier held out a purple cushion with golden tassels. Ebba simmered as the tiny woman stepped onto the cushion, and the soldier returned to the door and disappeared, wind sprite in tow.

They'd been swinging from cages, riding on crocodiles, and been scratching to survive for two days, and Sally had been in the lap of luxury, gorging herself on cheese, grapes, and *pink champagne* while being displayed like a prize animal for the king's guests.

Ebba should have paid more attention to the sprite's drinking problem. Things would be changing when they got back to *Felicity*. If the sprite was willing to mend her ways, Ebba would think about allowing her back on the ship, but not without a damn good apology. That was if Sally could be torn away from her champagne fountain.

When the clanging footsteps disappeared, Ebba stood and dusted her dress off, reaching up to check the necklace was in place before cracking open the chamber door.

The coast was clear.

Ebba returned to the stairwell and climbed to the next level, the fourth floor. Marigold had told her the king slept on this level. She assumed Caspian and his sisters did, too. A quick detour to gawk at Caspian's room was tempting, but Ebba's fathers would be sweating barnacles right now. She had to be as quick as possible.

The prince had said he'd handle the soldier outside the treasury. A wary peek around the corner of the stairwell proved him right. The level was empty.

Sally had been in the chamber on the right, so Ebba set off this way first, obeying her gut. Superstitions were a thing where she came from. Ebba hobbled as quickly as she could and, upon reaching the end, pressed her ear against the heavy wooden entrance.

Nothing.

Ebba tried the handle, but the door didn't budge. Recalling

the key, she dug into the top of her dress and drew out the gold object Caspian had palmed off to her. She inserted the key in the lock, relieved when it opened as easily as Stubby's brandy bottles when the music was playing.

With a quick glance back the way she'd come, Ebba cracked open the treasury door and slipped inside, releasing a slow breath as she closed the door behind her.

She turned to inspect the room, and her jaw dropped open. "Well would ye call me Bonny and whisper sweet nothings in my ear."

Cabinets and shelves occupied every space in the chamber, rows and rows of them. And every cabinet and shelf was filled with a countless, jumbling arrangement of sparkling *treasures*; a pirate's dream.

"This might take a while."

She picked up a mosaic vase and replaced it. Was all this stuff precious? Silver and gold glinted from every corner. Gems sparkled wherever she looked. Crossed weapons covered the walls, one huge sword outdoing them all.

Ebba tore her eyes away from the sword and began working through the room systematically. Gilded frames. Emerald ring. Stuffed monkey. This room was full of heir-looms, ripe for plunder. She eyed a jade snake with diamond eyes at the end of the first wall. That would go for a pretty penny at the Kentro market. Her crew were steal-traders, after all. Fulfilling the stealing half of their occupation was tempting.

But she wasn't here for that. There had to be at least twenty rows in this treasure chest; searching the place would take forever. How long would the guard be away for?

Her eyes shot to the huge sword on the wall again. Why did it twinkle so much? She drifted in that direction for a better look. In a chamber full of gleaming finery, the sword was the shiniest object by far and was displayed as a central piece of the collection. The weapon had to be really important.

Really expensive, too.

Ebba stood beneath the blade and reached up on tip-toes, leaning on a carved box to push herself a little higher.

She only managed to graze the sword with her fingertips, but the flashing edges beckoned to her. Ebba searched and located a box of solid ivory with inlaid sapphires. Grunting, she shifted it beneath the sword, and climbed on top. She reached higher and pushed to extract the blade from the hooks it sat upon. Ebba needed a closer look.

Her fathers wouldn't want her to waste time inspecting the shiny sword while all their lives were on the line, but Ebba gritted her teeth and took hold of the hilt anyway.

"We love you, Ebba-Viva Wobbles Fairisles," said a much *younger Barrels. "Don't you ever forget it. We love you more than life itself."*

Ebba gasped, entirely focused on the vision of Barrels in her head. Utter surety of her fathers' love for her spread unchecked through her chest, to her very toes. A soft smile quirked her lips before she frowned at the mistimed emotion. Ebba stared at her hand on the sword's hilt and jolted as a second vision flashed across her skull.

"I'll kill anyone who harms ye, lass," a brown-haired Locks *said with a snarl. His patch was in place, the thin scars covered his cheeks, and his emerald eye was ablaze, but there were far fewer wrinkles around his eyes.*

With a yell, Ebba jerked her hand away from the sword. "Slithering sirens!"

But the sword didn't land back on its hooks. The weapon came away from the wall with a ringing slide, and she shouted in earnest, throwing her body clear of the sharp weapon. The sword collided with a vase and a gilded frame, and the shatter and ring burst throughout the treasury. Ebba wasn't so worried about that as she frantically windmilled her arms, perched precariously on the very corner of the ivory box. Too precariously.

With a wordless shout, Ebba aborted the box and twisted in the air to land gracefully on her feet.

Or so she planned.

The heel of her buckled shoes slipped. Ebba catapulted back into the cabinet behind, sliding down the heavy furniture to the floor in a heap. She froze as the cabinet that broke her fall creaked. Spinning on her back, Ebba's eyes widened as the cabinet began to tilt. And tilt. Until the cabinet was tipping past the point of no return.

"Nay, don't do that," she whispered.

Ebba leaped to her feet, clutching the sides of her face as the cabinet tumbled into the cabinet behind it. The second cabinet toppled into a third and then a fourth. Glass smashed, gems were scattered, and heavy furniture fell with belly-deep groans and the boom of wood on stone.

She squeezed her eyes shut as the last of the cabinets plummeted to its echoing doom.

"Shite," she mumbled, cracking open a moss-green eye. "Ye bloody eejit, Ebba. All for a shiny sword." Were there guards running her way right now?

Ebba whirled frantically.

Where was the sword? When she'd touched the weapon, she'd seen. . . . What *had* she seen? Either the last few days were catching up with her, or the sword had just shown her two memories with her fathers. They'd been visibly younger, but more than that was what she'd felt—their love. When she'd touched the sword just now, Ebba was completely certain of her parents' devotion. Even now she felt the glow of their adoration in her heart.

Ebba turned away from the devastation she'd caused and scanned the area for the blade, but her eyes fell instead on a shiny cylinder—tarnished silver but for the pearly sheen that swirled under its surface.

"Ebba-Viva Wobbles Fairisles, yer a bloody *genius!*" She cackled gleefully.

A cylinder sat next to the ivory box she'd stood on to reach the sword. After her tumble, the box now sat open and upturned.

Gleaming happily as though uncaring of the trouble it constantly caused was the *dynami*.

TWENTY

She could tell by the rounded end of the cylinder it was the *dynami*. And if one cylinder was here, surely that meant the *purgium* was close by.

Ebba fell to her knees and searched under the cabinets, scanning the ground left and right. She'd just caused a racket to end all rackets. There was no way someone hadn't heard that.

"There ye are," she whispered, spotting the *purgium* twinkling on the stone floor two toppled rows over.

She swiped the *dynami* up, and kicked off the pinching shoes to dash around the row. Reaching the cabinet in the middle of the now not-so-orderly rows, Ebba dropped to the floor and stretched her fingers out. Her hand stilled at the painful memory of when she'd last clutched the two cylinders at once.

She'd been so angry at her traitorous pet, she'd forgotten why she needed Sally to help. Ebba couldn't hold both of the magical tubes at once. Last time she'd unintentionally done so, white light had exploded, and she'd been picked up and thrown by an invisible force.

Shite.

Holding both of them on Pleo hadn't worked. Maybe that was no longer true. Ebba hesitated and then set the *dynami* by her side before reaching to take hold of the *purgium* under the low cabinet. Dust tickled her nose and as she drew out the tube, she sneezed a few times.

Ebba placed the *purgium* next to its tarnished-silver cousin and studied them, cross-legged on the cold stone floor. Maybe she could grab Caspian, or whisk Sally away from wherever the guards had taken the wind sprite.

Maybe. . . .

Ebba scooped up the *dynami* and shoved it down her front, between the silken dress layer and her corset. Maybe if the magic wasn't touching her skin, they wouldn't react to each other. She tried to remember if she'd held both in her hands last time, but couldn't recall.

Worth a shot. She hoped.

Holding her breath, Ebba extended her forefinger toward the *purgium* where it glittered menacingly.

Turning her face slightly away, she touched the *purgium*.

A brilliant white light exploded, and her body was lifted by the invisible force and flung backward so quickly that Ebba only just realized she was *in* the air a scant breath before the back of her body and head smacked into the far stone wall. Ebba cried out, clutching at the base of her skull as pain erupted there.

She toppled forward from the wall to the stone ground, her flailing legs upsetting an open chest of sparkling gems on her descent. Ebba managed to get one arm forward to stop the front of her face from striking the ground but cried out again at the bruising impact on the front of her hip bones and knees.

Ebba rolled onto her back atop a bed of uncomfortable gems, eyes wide as she attempted to suck air into her chest again.

"Ouch," she wheezed.

She lay there until her lungs recovered from the shock and then hoisted her dress to get on her hands and knees. Ebba peered back the way she'd come. The blasted thing had thrown her halfway across the treasury. Suffice to say, her experiment hadn't worked, but she had her answer. Ebba could hardly parade through the castle with a giant sapphire-inlaid box. The charm likely wouldn't make her charming enough to pull that stunt off. Another person would have to help her. And that meant the prince or Sally.

Ebba stood, straightening with the help of her hands on her thighs, and limped back to the *purgium*. She'd take the *dynami* with her for now. Power would be more helpful in this situation than the ability to heal. Unless she could heal Montcroix of being a dolt. Perhaps he'd help them then.

Another boom rocked the castle, and Ebba clutched the back of her head, tensing in preparation of being flung again. The entire castle shook again, and when she wasn't thrown back by the invisible force, her eyes tracked dislodged dust as it floated from the ceiling to the ground.

The castle was shaking from something else. Unless she'd caused some kind of damage just now. But Ebba didn't think so.

The treasury didn't have a window to look out of. Another blow shook the stonework, nearly throwing Ebba to the ground, and her stomach twisted with foreboding. Someone was attacking the castle. Unless King Montcroix had a number of shady dealings going on, Ebba could only think of one other person who had reason to attack the king. A person who'd long been a slave to six masters.

Her mouth dried. As the jolting shocks continued, Ebba skirted back to the door, never happier for her sea legs. She patted her chest to make sure the door key and the *dynami* were in place under the front of her dress before opening the door to peer left down the level.

No one was in sight.

Ebba pulled the door closed quietly behind her and set off to the grand stairway to return to Sal's room on the floor below. There were several windows in there. She just wanted to look at the dock, just to make sure the terrible warning rippling up her spine and raising the hairs at the base of her neck were unwarranted; that the remnants of her time on *Malice* were driving her imagination in the wrong direction. Surely. . . .

Guards appeared at the top of the stairway.

Nearly there herself, Ebba skidded to a halt and lunged for the closest door.

"Halt!"

Ebba froze, letting go of the handle. Armored footsteps clattered toward her. Schooling her features, she turned to the guards, wondering if the charm was working. Verity had said the charm would last eight hours. That meant until somewhere in the early hours of morning. What was the time now?

Twenty armored guards milled up the grand stairway, surrounding her. Those closest to her parted, and Ebba gulped at the sight of King Montcroix in their center. His amber eyes blazed in a way that told her his next words could be, 'off with her head.'

The soldiers stepped aside as someone pushed their way through.

"Mistress Fairisles," Caspian blurted.

Ebba glimpsed his sister behind him, and her eyes dropped to the younger look-alike at the princess' side. His second sister, she assumed. "Prince Caspian," she answered, heart beating fast —not just because she'd been caught, but because of their last conversation.

His eyes were fixed on her. Was he thinking about what he'd said as well? *Ugh*, she'd banked on having a few months until they met again.

"I . . . got lost?" she offered weakly, her cheeks burning.

The soldiers relaxed, though the king's murderous expression didn't ease.

Caspian gripped her arm with his gloved hand, staring at her pointedly. "The castle is being attacked by pirates."

"By *Malice*," his father hissed.

Ebba tensed, and her gaze shifted from the king to Caspian. Her embarrassment disappeared, and she wet her lips. "*Malice*?" But it wasn't *Malice*, not really. Not even Pockmark. Pockmark was cruel in his own right, and he could be depended upon to go after the magical tubes at all costs, but only for the pillars. And attacking the castle certainly wasn't his style. Mercer moved through alleyways, shoving a blade into your back, not into your face in plain view. He cornered. He taunted. He poisoned. He didn't boldly declare war on the king. No, even if Pockmark was the face of this attack, he wasn't behind the move.

The shadows were. The pillars. They clearly felt strong enough in their shadow forms to usurp the king.

While Ebba might scoff at one ship's crew taking down the castle, she'd experienced the creeping, suffocating evil within that ship firsthand, and had no idea what the limits of the six pillars really were. Verity had said they'd regain power fast once in shadow form, and Ebba assumed that was because the crew could now infect others with the taint. She'd said becoming corporeal would take weeks and that's when the pillars would truly be invincible. Yet the king had said *Malice* was attacking, not six shadows. And anyone in their right mind would notice that. Were the pillars still confined to the ship?

The prince shook his head, his grip on her tightening. "One of the guards heard the name 'Pockmark' being shouted on the other side of the portcullis. It's *Malice*."

"My Liege," a soldier addressed Montcroix. "We must get

you and the royal family into the safe room while the threat is dealt with."

The king nodded, jaw ticking. "Caspian, leave her. One of the soldiers will take her to the ballroom to be guarded with the rest of the court." He sure made that sound like she was a pig to be put in a pen.

"Father, I would prefer Mistress Fairisles to come with us." Caspian's eyes were edged and darting. He let go of her and reached out a hand to the wall to steady himself as another blast rocked the castle.

"I cannot allow that. Family only."

Another blow rocked the castle, and his elder sister cried out. The younger one looked like she was enjoying the commotion, if truth were told.

Caspian's gaze firmed. "Father, I intend Mistress Fairisles to *be* family soon." He flashed her an apologetic look and turned to the king. "I asked her earlier if she would consent to wed. And she said yes."

Ebba's brows shot into her hairline. She hoped the charm was working overtime to mask her reaction. Now they were pretending to be betrothed? That veered mortifyingly close to his recent romantic confession and embarrassment flushed through her anew. He was always quick-witted, but she couldn't help observing just how quick he'd been to offer the engagement as a solution. Heat swept up into her cheeks, and she remained mute in the face of the shocked and disbelieving faces of Caspian's family and the royal guard.

Ebba hated to think what their faces would be like if the charm *wasn't* in place.

"Your intended?" the king blurted, stepping forward.

The prince reached back and wrapped his arm around her waist, drawing her forward. Ebba stumbled next to him, her head still throbbing from hitting the treasury wall, but all she could feel was the heat of his arm through her dress.

"As you see," Caspian said, jaw set, "I love her."

He stared down at her, and Ebba glanced between his burning amber eyes, unsure what to say in reply to keep the game going. Mostly because this didn't feel like a game at all.

"With all my heart," he whispered.

Sink her, everyone was waiting for her to say something.

"Me too," she grunted, feeling oddly fluttery inside about uttering such words.

Awkwardness aside, Ebba would rather be with the prince right now, even if that meant being cooped up with the king. If they had to keep up this guise for a few hours, it was no skin off her teeth. And Caspian wouldn't hold her to anything she had to say. Though, she frowned, had Caspian thought about what *he'd* say when she left? If all went to plan, her crew could be out of here at first light.

Ebba latched onto the prince to hold him upright as the castle was struck again. "What are they firin' at us?" she asked underneath the cries of his sisters.

"Cannons," he answered. "What else? They took out the guards on the wall."

She gasped. "They're *inside* the courtyard?"

"Your Majesty, we must get to the safety chamber," a soldier pressed.

Ebba lifted her head and found the king scrutinizing her. Ebba did her best to arrange her face into innocent lines. His amber eyes scoured her from head to toe, and a scowl twisted his mouth. "Very well, bring the woman too."

The woman? *The same woman who broke into your treasure room?*

Maybe she'd keep that tidbit to herself.

"Thank you, Father," Caspian said, bowing slightly.

Taking her hand, he pulled Ebba back in the direction she'd come. The soldiers closed rank around them, and the royal family and Ebba were herded down the right wing of the fourth level. The *dynami* sat heavy beneath the top of her dress, and as the soldiers ushered them down the passage, Ebba winced, wondering if they were going back to the treasury. The treasury which she'd left in an absolute mess.

"You have them?" the prince whispered low in her ear.

His warm breath caused shivers to erupt up the side of her neck. "One," she said.

Ebba waited until the soldier on her right shifted a couple of steps away, and added, "Sally wasn't inclined to be helpin'. I couldn't pick them both up."

Cosmo shifted uneasily. "Yes, about Sally. . . ."

She fixed her moss-green eyes on him. "You knew she'd turned sides?"

He winced. "I don't think she's turned sides as such. More that she's enjoying what luxuries there are on offer. Almost like a vacation. With the consequence that my father has been parading her in front of his court tonight."

A vacation? Yeah, right. "She was here for the booze. Don't be sugar-coatin' it. She has a problem. But Sally be magic. Won't that mean. . . ?"

Caspian's reply was grim. "Yes, it means Exosia is now aware that magic exists. They weren't before, and it was hard to gauge how they took it earlier tonight. From what I can tell, there haven't been any other magical encounters on Exosia." He lowered his voice. "Though my father didn't seem as surprised by her as I'd expected."

She'd seen the king's calm expression when he saw Sally, but had since wondered if his casual acceptance was more due to the *purgium* and *dynami* stealing his attention so completely than lack of wonder over magic's existence.

Ebba eyed the dust and grit floating from the ceilings. "Is it safe to be up here? What if the castle falls down?"

The soldier to her right answered. "Never fear, Lady Fairisles. It is easier to defend ourselves from high ground."

That logic was all well and good until this level *collapsed* to the ground. Then she could see there might be a few holes in his theory.

They were halted, and Ebba raised on tip-toes, sighing in relief when she saw they'd stopped at the chamber just before the treasury. They were ushered inside the chamber. Four soldiers entered the room with the king and searched the large sitting room thoroughly, overturning cushions that they clearly expected to be hiding Pockmark. Another guard rustled the heavy purple and gold curtains. Did they think Swindles and Riot were behind it, ready to jump out?

Landlubbers.

Apparently satisfied that the entire crew of *Malice* wasn't in the room, the soldiers exited with a hushed word to the king.

"Yes, yes." Montcroix waved a hand at the soldier. "I'm aware of the safety word."

"Why is *Malice* attacking?" the prince whispered in her ear, pulling her to a chaise on the opposite side of the room.

The pillars were back, and the pillars wanted power. While the pillars could just be here to take the castle and to attempt to replace the most powerful man in the realm, she couldn't discount that news would have spread of *Felicity's* capture. Pockmark and his masters could be here for the *purgium* and the *dynami*. "I don't know," she answered him. "But it ain't good, either way."

She couldn't believe the pillars were making such a move. For them to have gained enough strength to attack the king, their taint must have spread dramatically since she'd last seen them. Ebba didn't want to think about the taint spreading.

Caspian beckoned his sisters to the chaise, and Ebba focused on the Exosian ruler. King Montcroix sat on a hard-backed wooden chair situated beside a small side table, directly by the chamber door. With one hand, he gripped his sword, knuckles white. The other rested on the table, calm aside from the harsh tapping of his forefinger. A muscle in his jaw ticked. His white brows had drawn together. His mouth was pinched. Ebba couldn't decide if the king was angrier about the attack on his castle or that pirates were attacking his castle.

She shifted to look behind him. To his right, a massive painting covered the chamber wall from ceiling to floor, its width as wide as three Peg-legs standing on profile with their guts hanging out. The scene was of an armored knight astride a gleaming black horse, a picture-perfect Exosia at his back and a shining sword held high over his head. No crown sat upon the knight's head. That sword looked awfully familiar though. . .

Ebba wondered why the king kept the fancy sword locked in the treasury and settled for his current one, bland by comparison. Not that the sword in his belt was plain by normal standards.

The king lifted his head, and Ebba sucked in a breath, glancing away. . . .

. . . To the princesses on the couch opposite who were studying her just as hard as she'd been studying their father.

Honestly, the royal family had never held much interest for her, other than being her natural enemy, until Cosmo transformed into a prince. But Ebba could tell by looking at the princesses and Caspian that their mother must have been beautiful. Though they each had amber eyes, their faces were graceful lines and elegance in comparison to the king's harsh face.

Ebba stared at the two girls. "Ahoy," she greeted, absently wondering what the charm changed that to.

"You're very beautiful," the eldest said, clearly hearing the charmed version of Ebba's greeting.

She couldn't recall a thing about his sisters except that they wanted to grow up fast. "Cheers."

The younger of the girls tucked her hand into her elder sister's, peeking at Ebba through her thick chestnut lashes. Ebba wasn't fooled by that look for one second. Unless she was much mistaken, the younger girl was the one to watch out for—the surviving type.

Caspian hovered his mouth by Ebba's ear, and the princesses giggled. Ebba was certain he'd whispered in her ear before, but her body had never been so aware of his proximity.

"When does your charm wear off?" he asked.

Ebba froze. *Sink her.* "What be the time?"

He gestured at the clock on the wall, and Ebba rolled her eyes. Like she knew how to decipher that hunk of fancy. The sun was her watch.

"Uh, eleven. Just past eleven," he answered, a flush crawling over his jaw.

They exchanged a leaden look.

"Uh, I ain't sure. I'm guessin' after midnight. But I used it off and on afore comin' here to test it out, so that might've gobbled up some time." Ebba was stuck in a safety room indefinitely with a charm that had an expiry. "That be puttin' a different pressure on things," she stated.

His brows lifted. "Aye."

"What did you say, Caspian?" the king's cold voice was barely higher than a whisper.

Caspian glanced up, his expression mild. "High, Father. Mistress Fairisles was asking how likely it was that we would beat back the soulless *Malice* pirates."

The king held his eyes, and Ebba released a breath as he

blinked and returned his attention to the door, forefinger still tapping.

Verity said the charm would work until around midnight. Did around midnight mean half past eleven? Or half an hour into the next day? They still needed to get the *purgium* and make it past *Malice*, all the way back to *Felicity*.

Ebba stared at the sisters holding hands, and tilted her head to look at Caspian.

Nay, that couldn't be the plan. She wouldn't leave Caspian to face the darkness alone. And she'd never leave Caspian's family behind either. Except the king. The king could stay and face the shanty. Or if he had to come, they'd shove him in a barrel until her crew decided what to do with him.

"Any ideas?" she whispered to Caspian, ignoring the girls' giggles as she leaned in close.

He shook his head.

How to defend the castle against an evilness they'd both experienced and feared? Ebba could only think of evading the six pillars until they had this root of magic, so the sooner they got out of there, the better. Ebba assumed that eventually the pillars would be able to leave the ship. She didn't want to be here when they did.

A chattering sound echoed faintly throughout the quiet chamber, and everyone turned toward the huge painting on the wall. On the other side of the wall was the treasury. The sound was shifting and high-pitched as though—Ebba's mouth dried— as though coins slid over each other.

The king rose abruptly, and Caspian tensed at her side. In three strides, the monarch was at the front door of the safety chamber. He rapped out a pattern and then pushed a slotted grate aside at eye level to mutter something inaudible from where she sat.

He stood back, and ten soldiers entered, shutting the door behind them.

"There was a sound from my personal treasury," he told them. The king strode to the couch on Ebba's side and said, "Caspian. Go with them. Retrieve truth."

That seemed vague. Was he really sending his son in there instead of going himself? Not that Caspian wasn't capable and all.

Caspian didn't seem surprised. He stood, and Ebba leaned forward to follow suit, but was stopped by the king's heavy hand on her shoulder. "It is no place for ladies," he said curtly.

She'd been promoted from woman. Drat, she hadn't had time to tell Caspian where the *purgium* was. The treasury was still in a mess, but with the noise in there just now, maybe the king would assume someone else had caused it.

One of the soldiers pushed aside the painting, and the others fanned out. Ebba craned to see and was rewarded with the sight of a door behind the artwork. A secret entrance to the treasury. Impressive.

The soldiers opened the door and filed in, their pistols raised and ready to fire. After several minutes, one reappeared and waved Caspian inside. Ebba held her breath. If he found the *purgium,* at least that was a small step in the right direction.

"You know, Mistress Fairisles, I have not seen your face in my court before today."

Her breath hitched at the king's words. She tipped her head back to look at him, and watched as he rounded the back of the couch to sit where Caspian had been. *Uh-oh.* Ebba had the sinking feeling the king was about to interrogate her.

"What is your name?" he demanded, ignoring his silent daughters on the couch opposite.

"Ebba," she said, swallowing hard.

"Lady Ebba Fairisles," he said, eyes narrowing. "No doubt you're pretty enough to catch his eye, though I was surprised to hear of his sudden attachment." He leaned closer. "You know that despite the promises my son has made, your betrothal means nothing without my blessing."

He didn't wait for her reply. His rust-colored eyes were edged like a serrated knife and bore into hers. His breath held the sweet remnants of wine.

"My son has one arm, Lady Fairisles. What do you want with him?"

Ebba sucked in a breath, and a hot surge of anger flooded her chest. "So what if he only be havin' one arm? That don't make him any less, ye flamin' cruel bugger. Ye're meant to be his father. Why do ye say such things about yer son?"

The king sat back, quirking a brow. "Prettily said, mistress. I might even think that you loved him."

Her fingers twitched with the urge to rip off the charm and let him hear the ugly version, but she stayed her hand. Because of the likely death that would follow.

"Walk with me," he demanded.

Trembling with suppressed anger, she did as he bade, gritting her teeth as he linked arms with her. They strolled in the direction of the chamber entrance.

"My son is a prince," the king said plainly, breaking off his scrutiny of her to stare through the secret doorway. "He will be king one day, sooner rather than later, I imagine. I do not doubt he will be a great king. To be a great king, he needs a great woman by his side." He blinked several times. "All kings do. Without them, we wither."

What was he talking about?

"You are here claiming to love my son. Yet he's been back less than a fortnight, and I have never seen you in court. Tell me, Lady Fairisles, are you only here because of his title? If so, I will find out, and I will crush you. Consider the coming months your interview, and know this: I love my son. I love him too much to see him unhappy."

He sure had a cruel way of showing that love, but she found herself softening toward the ruler, simply because through his words, she did detect a real love for Caspian.

"Father," Caspian said, striding back through the door. "The men do not believe anyone has been in the treasury room. The shaking seems to have overset a great many things in there." His eyes flickered to Ebba for a scant second before returning to the king. "The soldiers are still checking the cabinets on the back wall, but if there was someone there, they would have left via the passage, and our soldiers would have spotted them."

The king hardly seemed to notice a word, his jaw slack as he focused on the sword in Caspian's hand. It was the vision sword she'd touched earlier. Ebba watched the prince closely, but he didn't seem bothered by the weapon. Was the weirdness that happened before all in her skull? She'd only hit her head *after* touching it.

"Here, Father. Truth." Caspian took a quick step forward and nearly managed to place the sword in the king's hand.

"No!" The king shied away, his eyes round. He whipped his hands behind his back as he whirled behind Ebba.

"No," he replied in a calmer voice.

The sword was named truth? That was what the king had sent Caspian in for?

She couldn't see the king's face and did not dare turn to satisfy her curiosity with the thick disappointment tightening the prince's face. Had the king had the same kind of vision as she had? He appeared fearful of the sword. Maybe it had shown him something he didn't like.

"No," the king said a third time. "You keep truth for now. I haven't touched it since your mother's passing."

When Ebba touched the sword, she'd been shown that her fathers loved her. She'd felt the truth of their devotion to her. Deep down, she'd known how deeply they loved her, but after the uproar at Pleo, the confirmation from the sword *had* settled a lingering discontent within her. Did this weapon really show you the truth?

Caspian clenched his jaw. "Nothing new then."

Ebba waited for the tongue-lashing retort from behind, but it never came. Instead, the king wearily replied. "Nothing new, son. But if it's of any consolation, I was never meant to hold truth. You will do a better job of it, I'm sure."

The soldiers filed back into the room and pulled the door closed, sliding the painting back into place.

"All clear, My Liege," the one at the front said with a bow as low as his armor allowed. "I believe the shaking upset the objects within."

The shaking. Ebba frowned at the thought. The shaking had stopped. The king and Caspian realized this at the same moment as she.

"What's—?" Caspian said.

The unmistakable ringing of two swords striking against each other rendered everyone inside the chamber mute. They listened to the muffled shouts in the hall outside. Caspian crossed to her, the gleaming sword in his hand.

The king crossed to the couch and sat heavily. "They are here."

Malice was here, she agreed. But were pirates about to burst in, or the pillars? If it was the pillars, surely as shadows they could already be in the room. Ebba's chest tightened at the yells and clanging on the other side of the door as the soldiers there fought for their lives and to protect their ruler.

"Who is here, Father?" the youngest princess asked, rushing to the king.

The king gripped her chin, and leaned forward to press a lingering kiss to her forehead. "My enemies. A darkness I was warned of long ago by a great friend whom I betrayed in a moment of weakness. I was meant to kill my enemy's spawn to ensure the line ended, but when your mother died. . . I have made many mistakes, my daughter, and they have chosen this moment to crash down around me."

He shook his head as though shaking off bad memories, and gestured to the elder princess. When she rushed to him, he pressed a kiss to her forehead also.

The clanging on the other side of the door had stopped, and no one spoke as the soldiers inside the chamber silently arranged themselves before the entrance. They, like Ebba, had likely assumed the soldiers out there were now dead. Which meant they were next.

Ebba stumbled back out of their way, Caspian at her side.

"What're we going to do?" she hissed at him. "The pillars can't get the cylinders."

He scanned the room. "They're coming for this room in particular. They're after my father."

That hardly mattered when the *dynami* was down her dress, and the *purgium* was rolling around on the ground next door.

"Prince Caspian." The lead soldier turned back as a banging began against the other side of the door. Ebba watched the hinges strain to keep the wooden door in place.

"We will hold them off here for as long as possible," the soldier continued. "Please take your father and the women into the treasury."

"And then what?" she asked. "They be pirates. There ain't no way they won't be ransackin' the place after."

The soldier nodded. "I know, fair lady, but there is nowhere else to go."

The landlubber had a point.

Caspian laid the gleaming sword on the small table, pushing the painting along its railing once more. He pressed an ear to the secret door and then swung the entrance open again. "Father, sisters, come. We must hide in here for now."

For how long? *Malice* had made it all the way inside. To be up here, they had to have taken over the entire castle. Were all of the king's soldiers dead? Had his court fled or been slain? They were to go into the treasury, and then what?

"I will remain," the king said, not glancing away from his daughters.

Caspian rushed to his father's side. "No, Father. Come with us. There is still hope."

"There is no hope for me, my son. No hope now. None for a long time." Rust-colored eyes peered into a softer and younger set. "But you and your sisters . . . ." His eyes shifted to Ebba. "And your betrothed. You stand a chance. If they do not kill me, they will scour the castle to find me. Until I am dead, I am a threat."

"No, Father," Caspian begged, dropping to his knees before his father and reaching for his hand. "Do not give up," he pleaded. "Exosia needs you."

Montcroix's mouth twisted. "That time is long gone. As is the time when you needed me." His amber gaze fell to Caspian's empty sleeve. "You may have lost an arm, but you returned a man. And now you must do what I did not: Kill Mutinous Cannon's bloodline, as I was meant to do. End their evil for good. Use truth to guide your rule, as I could not. I'm *certain* you'll be able to, my son; you must merely be strong enough to govern it," he hissed. "Kill the bloodline, heir. Kill the evil and restore our family's honor."

Ebba was missing something huge about all this truth stuff. Though Caspian appeared almost as confused as she was by his father's rambling.

King Montcroix's words did help to confirm one thing, however. The king was spouting words about Mutinous Cannon's bloodlines and evil. Ebba was now certain that the pillars *had* hidden within Mutinous, and that her fathers had been tainted while aboard *Eternal*. Ebba had no idea how the pillars had gone from Cannon to his son and then to Pockmark on *Malice*. But that the pillars had affected her loved ones for so long left her dumbfounded. They'd spread through her fathers since before her birth, in what felt like an entirely foreign time to her.

How could they compete with such sinister darkness?

Ebba focused on the king again, not having the heart to tell him that the evil he'd referred to no longer needed Pockmark's body. The king could have ended this all if he'd killed Pockmark's father all those years ago. He'd failed, and he knew it. But he wasn't the only one to have failed to do the right thing. In that, she was just like the sovereign.

Startled shouts from the soldiers by the door drew her gaze to the chamber entrance. The wood wasn't looking so solid now.

"Go, Prince Caspian. You must go," the soldier called back, sword clasped tight in both hands.

"Go, King Caspian," the king whispered, bringing his son's hand to his lips, kissing the back and inhaling deeply as though treasuring the scent of his child. "Go now."

A tear slid down Caspian's face. His breath came fast, but he jerked his head in a nod and took hold of his younger sister's hand. "Ebba, sisters, follow me."

Both princesses were sobbing, peering back at their father. The eldest was shaking like a leaf, but they obeyed their brother.

Ebba turned to follow but couldn't help asking, "Ye're really goin' to wait in here and die?"

The king's eyes flashed; however, the sight of the sword

gleaming on the table stole his attention. "The sword," he said hoarsely. "My son must take truth." He surged to his feet. "Take the sword with you."

Wood splintered behind her, and the pounding thundered through the chamber in a heavy beat.

The king lunged for the table and hovered his hands over the sword. "Take it," he said to her.

She wasn't saying no to a sharp sword with enemies beating down the door.

"Ebba," Caspian called from the door, his face white.

"Hold on," she called through the secret door. She reached for the sword, wrapping her fingers around the hilt. "I'm just—"

White light exploded, and then Ebba was soaring through the air for the second time that day. She had no idea where the walls were. No clue as to where the ceiling and floor were situated. Ebba wrapped her arms around her already-injured head and braced herself.

Her leg struck the edge of something, and Ebba landed flat on her back, the air forced from her lungs *again*.

Her eyes were wide. She'd been blasted into the treasury, thrown clean through the door—except for catching the doorway with her shin, or so the throbbing there told her.

She frowned at the ceiling, replaying what had happened. The white light only exploded when the *purgium* and the *dynami* were held by one person. But the *purgium* was nowhere near her.

Ebba groaned and lifted her head. She had no idea where Caspian was, but the king stood directly in front of her in the other chamber, staring down at the gleaming sword. A curious calm washed over his features as he crouched by the weapon, and the king smiled as he stretched his fingers to the hilt. "What does it matter at the end?" he asked, his words carrying to her.

He took hold of the hilt and hung his head. The muscles in

his neck bulged with tension, and the king threw back his head and screamed a guttural cry that made the hairs at the base of her neck stand on end.

Was he seeing the truth at last?

The king lowered his head, panting, and his gaze, no longer rusted with the serrated-like edge to them, but soft and amber like his son's, fell on her. He still held the sword, and his jaw dropped. *Pirate*, he mouthed.

The charm had worn off? *Shite*. Or was it because he held the sword? It didn't matter! Ebba rolled to the side and managed to get one knee bent to stand. She looked back at the doorway and tripped on the hem of her dress, falling back to the ground. She craned to see him, certain he'd be inches away from lopping off her head.

He stared at her from the doorway, his eyes flickering and blinking, his mouth opening and closing as he gripped the sword. It was as though he watched a rapidly changing scene, invisible to all but himself.

Montcroix blinked and focused on her, smiling once more. The strangest expression lit his face, as though he'd been simultaneously dealt a mortal blow and given the greatest gift in the world.

"Tell me. Does the silver-eyed pirate still live?" he asked.

Ebba couldn't utter a word, but she managed a shrug.

A shadow darkened his eyes, and his face firmed. "Take care of my family, pirate," he said.

Tossing the sword at her feet, King Montcroix stepped back, drawing the door closed.

TWENTY-ONE

"Caspian," Ebba whispered.

A moan was his only reply. The explosion when she'd touched the *dynami* and the sword must've hurt him. Ebba had a strong suspicion the sword was not what it seemed. She'd only ever seen the two magical cylinders cause such an explosion. Was the sword like the *dynami* and the *purgium*? Ebba left the sword where the king had tossed it. She wasn't eager for a third round of being thrown around. One of the princesses would have to carry the healing cylinder while Ebba took the *dynami*. Hopefully the princesses didn't have any terminal illnesses.

Caspian could take the sword.

Ebba hobbled through the destroyed treasury. Gone were the orderly rows and neatly arranged heirlooms. She'd wrecked the place earlier, but the second explosion had turned the room from a mess to chaos. She followed Caspian's groans to a cabinet. His arm and legs were sticking out from underneath. Here was something she could do. Ebba gripped the underside of the cabinet, feeling the *dynami*'s searing tickle against her chest. She heaved and pushed the cabinet off, wincing at the noise as it landed clear of the prince's body. Odds were, the sound would be missed over the muffled clanging of swords and shouts she could hear coming from the safety chamber.

Caspian groaned, but managed to gain his legs quicker than she had. "Sierra, Anya," he called.

"We are okay, brother," one called back from the direction of the door.

"The sword be at the secret door," Ebba said to the prince.

His face fell into a scowl. "Leave it," he withered. "I don't want it."

"We need it," she said over her shoulder. "I think it's one o' the magic tubes. Like the *dynami* and the *purgium*."

"What?" he said then gasped. "That can't be."

"Why not? I'm certain it showed me a vision or sumpin' earlier."

"*Veritas* has been in our family for centuries. I would have known," Caspian said, straightening. "Though the sword remained locked away in here, I suppose. And traditionally, the Colonel of the King's Army carried it, not the royal family. That was all before my time, however."

"The Colonel? Ye mean the knight in the paintin'?" she asked, despite the urgency of their situation.

Caspian nodded. "Yes, that was the last Colonel to bear the sword for my father. How did you guess?"

"He ain't wearin' a crown."

"Could the sword really be another magical object? Right under my nose this whole time," he said, bafflement coloring his voice. "When I was very young, my father spoke of the dreams the sword sent and of the truths it showed the bearer. I've always assumed his tales were designed to entertain a child, not that they were real. He never spoke of *veritas* after my mother's death, and I only have a handful of memories where he actually touched the sword."

"But ye touched it yerself," she said. "Didn't ye see anythin'?"

He lifted his hand, reminding her he wore a glove.

"Do ye think that be how yer father knew magic existed?" Ebba asked.

The prince stared at her, and she recalled they were about to die. "We'll discuss this later. Away with ye to get the sword. We need to move," she said. *If* that was even a possibility. They were at the dead end of the right wing.

Ebba clambered over an overturned chest, eyes scanning the stone ground for the *purgium*. It had been somewhere around here. Unless one of the soldiers moved it.

Where was the blasted thing?

She lowered into a crouch at a faint tapping noise. The staccato sound came from the inside of a cabinet to her left. Ebba crept forward, scanning the treasury for company, and then flung back the front of the toppled cabinet.

A glowing traitor with wings floated inside, the *purgium* clutched in her tiny arms.

"Sally," Ebba greeted coolly. In truth, her stomach unclenched at seeing her friend was safe even though she'd betrayed them for a champagne fountain. A closer look told her the sprite didn't look too hot.

Sally sighed in relief and flew up to Ebba's face, extending the *purgium* for her to take.

Ebba took a hasty step back. "Nay, I ain't takin' a third beatin' today. Ye'll need to carry it. That is, if ye plan to stick around." She glowered at the wind sprite. The reason behind the sprite's sagging appearance came to her. "Ha! The *purgium* cured ye. It cured ye o' yer grog addiction." Ebba laughed again. "Take that, ye shite," she said, adding, "It didn't hurt ye none, did it?"

Sally shook the *purgium* in Ebba's face, squeaking indignantly.

That meant the sprite was okay. Sally must've been the cause of the rattling coins they'd heard earlier. She'd been fishing around in here and had to hide from the soldiers. Ebba bet the sprite hadn't expected the *purgium* to heal her of alcoholism.

Ebba snorted, and Sally scowled darkly at her.

"Aye, well ye shouldn't have drunk so much. Don't be givin' me that look. And I'll tell ye right now, things will be changin' for ye when we're back on *Felicity*. No more drinkin'." She resumed her climb over the strewn furniture, heading toward the treasury door. The fighting in the next room still continued.

Caspian was already at the closed door.

"What're we goin' to do?" Ebba asked, ignoring the haggard Sally for the time being.

The princesses gaped at her.

"You're a pirate," the eldest said.

"Eh?" Ebba glanced down at the charm and then at the prince. "Gone?"

"Gone," he said. "I didn't notice."

His words soothed her frayed ego. Maybe the reverent way everyone had treated her tonight had affected her confidence.

"You *knew* she was a pirate?" the younger asked. "How do you know a pirate? Are you really marrying a pirate?"

Caspian interrupted her. "I'd love a chance to tell you, but not until we're out of this mess." He faced Ebba. "They'll come here next, won't they?"

"Aye, there ain't no way they'll rest until they've found what they came for," she said. "And I ain't convinced that's just yer father. We've got to get out o' the castle."

He nodded. "Sierra? You have any ideas on how to get out?

Strolling out of the grand entranceway won't be an option."

The youngest princess pursed her lips. "Yes, but we need to get to the third level. The servants have a narrow stairwell they use to do their chores. It goes all the way to the bottom, and the pirates probably won't know of it. Most people who live here don't."

They'd have to get to the grand stairway in the middle of this level to go down one floor. Ebba walked around the princesses and pressed her ear to the treasury door, listening hard. Discerning any sound from the hall outside with the sounds from the next chamber was impossible. "Now be our best chance to get past the room, while they're fightin'. Hopefully there be less o' them out in the passage. I don't like the odds o' us waitin' here. Treasure be mighty temptin' to a pirate, even if they ain't here for the cylinders."

"Yes, I agree. Anya, Sierra, get behind me," Caspian said to his sisters. "We need to sneak past the safety chamber. You'll need to be quick and very quiet. There are other pirates, bad pirates, in the room with Father. Ebba and I will be in front, but you don't worry about us, do you hear? If we're spotted, you run as fast as you can for the servant stairwell. You need to get out of the castle and hide in the building where mother used to get her dresses made. Do you remember?"

Both of his siblings nodded. The youngest kicked off her shoes, expression determined. The eldest glanced at her sibling, amber eyes huge, as though her sister had taken off every stitch of clothing and was frolicking naked through a meadow.

"Ye might want to do the same," Ebba said, wriggling her toes. "Yer shoes be too noisy to sneak well." And the only way they'd get out of this dead end was to sneak.

The eldest princess was clearly scandalized by the thought of taking off her shoes.

Caspian sighed. "Please just do it, Anya. Better bare feet

than a cold grave."

The princess blanched and hurried to obey.

"Ready, Sal?" the prince said to the wind sprite. The princesses dragged their eyes from him to the sprite but didn't voice their obvious questions.

Ebba exhaled and pulled the treasury key from the front of her dress, inserting it into the lock. She squeezed her eyes shut, holding her breath, and twisted. The clicks were like the boom of a drum to her ears, but Ebba didn't stop until the fourth click had sounded.

She only pulled the door open wide enough to get her head and shoulders through.

Ebba peered down the level passage, squinting through the haze of smoke. When had the guns gone off? Or was the smoke rising up the staircases from fires below? Bodies were strewn through the hall, but no one else was out in the passage. Most importantly, she couldn't see any shadows to suggest the pillars were around.

She pulled back. "It's empty." For now.

"The sounds next door have stopped," Caspian said.

Ebba opened the entrance completely. "Let's go. We have to move while they're in the chamber next door." If they waited, they risked that the pirates would come here next.

She and Caspian led the way toward the grand stairway, and Ebba cursed at the slight rustle of her dress. What point were quiet footsteps when your clothing announced your presence to the world? The elder princess sobbed softly as they encountered the first of the soldiers' bodies in the hall.

Caspian patted the air, and their group slowed as they neared the ajar door of the safety room.

Loud voices and sounds made by the shifting of many bodies moving about floated out of the chamber and toward them.

"Where is the *veritas*?" a familiar voice asked.

She inhaled sharply, and the prince threw her a look, not recognizing the voice. Unfortunately, she did. *Pockmark,* Ebba mouthed at him.

"I don't know what you're referring to," the king lied calmly.

Pockmark screamed, "Where is it?"

Caspian's eyes briefly closed, but when he opened them once more, they were hardened. He jerked his head, and their group crept forward, coming alongside the doorway.

Ebba, unable to resist, turned her head to stare into the chamber as they passed. The door was splintered and half closed. Ebba's breath hitched as she took in the familiar sight of *Malice*'s black uniform, the crimson sash about the pirates' hips. They were surrounding Caspian's father. She could only see the left half of the king's body. Pockmark held a sword to the king's neck, Swindles and Riot stood either side of their captain. Her heart thundered wildly, the muscles in her legs ready to bolt for her very life. She wasn't ever going back to that ship. She'd rather die than be there again.

She didn't dare pause, didn't even think to help the man at swordpoint. He'd chosen his fate, and deep down, Ebba knew he'd been right. They never stood a chance to escape unless he'd stayed as a distraction and a decoy. Even if the pillars were here for the *veritas* and not the two cylinders, Caspian now had the sword.

Her chest rose and fell rapidly as their group of five inched past the door. She glanced back to see Sally had hidden away in the folds of the younger princess' skirt to conceal her white glow.

Hurry, Caspian mouthed over his shoulder at them.

Once the safety chamber was twenty feet behind, they picked up their pace, and soon they were halfway to the stairs.

None of them spoke, and Ebba wondered if, like her, their

ears were straining to hear the loud conversation at their backs.

"Ye know," Pockmark taunted, "there be things worse than death."

The king's laughter echoed down the hall. She glanced at the prince and saw another tear rolling down his dust-streaked face.

"You think I have not suffered worse than death?" The king's laughter swelled.

They hurried on. Nearly at the stairs.

"Then die, o' great king," Pockmark called over his laughter. "Yer kingdom be mine. Yer people will be slaves to my masters, their will forfeit. But my masters wanted to thank ye kindly for not killin' my father when ye had the chance. That was a great help."

A sickening squelch rent the air, and Ebba stumbled, hearing Caspian's gasp and the soft moan of the eldest.

But the raw scream from the younger princess, Sierra, obliterated everything else.

Shouting ricocheted from the safety room, and Ebba grabbed the eldest princess, shoving her down the stairs, seeing Caspian was grabbing the still-screaming youngest. She'd announced their presence more effectively than a lighthouse beacon.

"Run!" Ebba hissed. "Run."

They tore down the grand stairway, the footsteps of *Malice* pounding after them.

Caspian managed to shake his sister from her panic as he hauled her down the stairs. Sierra began to run in earnest, yanking free of his grip.

"Where are the servants' stairs?" Caspian urged his sobbing sister as they reached the floor below. "We need to get off the main stairwell."

"End of this level. To the right," she choked out, ashen.

Shite, Ebba hoped they could make it. As instructed, they turned right, the footsteps of *Malice* now louder behind them. Their jeering calls bounced off the confines of the castle walls, and Ebba sprinted alongside the others, tearing toward the end of the hall as fast as the layers of fabric swirling around her knees would allow.

The group of pirates upstairs couldn't have stormed the castle alone. So where were the others?

Ebba's chest burned, and cold sweat trickled down the nape of her neck. "Sal," she panted. "Fly ahead, and open the stairwell door. Hurry."

The wind sprite didn't need to be asked twice. She surged ahead of them, the *purgium* still clasped tight in her tiny hands.

"There they are!" someone yelled behind them.

"Faster," Caspian urged his eldest sister.

Anya gasped for air, clutching her side. "I'm trying, brother."

A gun fired; the boom exploded at their backs. The bullet pinged into the stone walls behind them. "Get in a line," Ebba shouted. She didn't have the breath to explain it would make them a smaller target, but the prince understood.

He dropped back so the bullets would hit him first.

Ebba wiped her forehead, peering past Sierra, who led the way. "Sal has the door open."

"Quickly." The strain in Caspian's voice was clear, and she didn't dare look behind.

She reached the narrow stairway and didn't break her pace, all but throwing herself down the servants' narrow stairs. She stopped once inside and dragged Anya and Sierra in behind her before dodging the tip of the sword and clasping Caspian's wrist to drag him inside, too.

"Keep goin'," Ebba screamed as Sally flared a brilliant white back in the hall.

Agonized shrieks rose from outside the stairs, and Ebba reached for the door, shielding her eyes from the pure light glow.

The crewmembers had shied back from the perimeter of the sprite's light as though it was a flame burning their skin. Pockmark was stumbling back, arms thrown high. Swindles and Riot were doubled over just behind him.

"Inside, Sal," Ebba shouted.

The sprite dropped her glow and dove into the stairwell, and Ebba wrenched the door toward her, slamming the lock bar down. That wouldn't hold them for long.

Ebba took the steps two at a time, pelting after the others. The memories of her time on *Malice* breathed down her neck.

She caught up with them at the second level where they stood outside the servant stairwell in plain sight. Ebba didn't have time to dwell on their logic. The sound of smashing and cheering sounded from the top of the steps. They'd broken through the door.

She glanced over at the princesses. They were exhausted. And so was she. Sally's wings were fluttering limply after the *purgium* healing. Everyone was tired.

"Stand back," Ebba said, trying to sound confident. It was time to use these damn things.

Like water bursting from a dam, the searing tickle of the *dynami* exploded through her body. Ebba turned and placed her hand against the inner walls of the narrow stairwell she'd just exited.

And pushed.

A deep crack appeared in the stone of either wall. She heard one of the princesses gasp.

"Ebba," Caspian said tightly. "More."

More? Oh, she could do more. Ebba might not have known or particularly liked King Montcroix, but she considered

Caspian to be part of her crew. *Malice* had just taken the prince's father away. If someone had killed one of her fathers, there was no way she'd be holding it together right now. Ebba stood slightly in the stairwell and crossed her arms in front of her. Then, with a shout, the searing tingle mounting, she slapped her open palms against the stone walls.

The stone underneath her hands shattered like glass. Deep fissures split the walls of the accessway as fast as an earthquake split the ground. The walls groaned, and as Pockmark and his cronies appeared around the corner, directly in front of Ebba, large squares of stone began to cascade from the stairwell ceiling. More stone slabs fell. The tops of the stairs began to cave in.

Ebba was yanked out into the second level. She stumbled down the wide hall behind Caspian for a few steps before pumping her legs to race alongside him, eyes wide at the sound of stone crashing behind her.

It wasn't until the crashing stopped that they all paused to catch their breath, partway down the second level now. Sally hovered at the back of their group, and Ebba peered past the sprite at the damage she'd caused.

She'd probably brought down a fair bit of the right side of the castle. Hopefully, no innocents were hurt, but the pirates chasing them must have been crushed by the caving in of the stairwell. A twinge pulled under her ribs at the thought. She knew that the pirates aboard *Malice* were slaves to the pillars, but once they would have been everyday people. She'd nearly succumbed to the taint herself. Her heart twisted for the people they might have been if not for the pillars' evil. Just as she also felt relief that the pirates, even Pockmark, were now free of the nightmare.

"Caspian, I think I broke yer castle a scant bit." Ebba gasped, pressing a hand to the painful knot she'd gained at the back of her head in the treasury earlier. And then her side. When had she hurt her ribs?

His reply was dry. "Yes, I believe you might be right."

Ebba released her ribs and straightened, glancing either way. "We should move."

"Strolling down the grand stairway and out of the main entranceway isn't ideal, but it's the only plan left to us. Unless you know of another way," Caspian asked Sierra hopefully.

The younger princess shook her head. "There is only the main stairwell left, brother."

"Then that's where we'll go," he said heavily.

They set off, sticking close to the edges of the hall.

"I've seen you and your fathers use the *dynami* back in Selkie's Cove, but not since," the prince whispered, forehead shining with perspiration. "If the falling stonework didn't kill them, Pockmark and the others will be laid up for a while." He cast her a searching look. "Are you all right?"

She shrugged as they slowed to a jog. Killing wasn't her favorite thing, really, though she'd always do it to protect herself or her loved ones. Ebba had killed a pirate on Plco a couple of months ago, but never a group of people. Using a powerful object that gave her an unfair advantage wasn't sitting completely right with her, even if the pirates had been chasing her to either kill her or drag her to the pillars.

"Shh, I can hear people in the entranceway," Anya whispered from the front. She was fluttering her hand at them.

They trailed to a halt, and Ebba crouched to peer down around the corner.

The entranceway of the castle was right there, just at the bottom of the last flight of stairs. Beyond the entrance was the large rectangular courtyard, then the portcullis, and after that the open, cobbled trail down to the town. They'd need to make it back to Marigold's house and leave Exosia with all haste.

. . . Marigold's house seemed an awfully long way away.

Ebba didn't know who might be stationed outside of the castle or on the path to town, but at the base of the stairwell were around twenty *Malice* pirates. And . . . she squinted at their clothing. Hold on.

"Those aren't *Malice* pirates." Caspian beat her to the punch. "They aren't wearing black uniforms."

TWENTY-TWO

"That's how *Malice* were able to take the castle," Ebba said, retreating back around the corner of the grand stairwell. "There be other pirates helpin' them."

What pirate in their right mind would join such a quest?

She stilled, crouching to peer around the corner again. More specifically, at the eyes of the pirates not dressed in black uniforms. Ebba's tongue stuck to the top of her mouth, and she rolled back around the corner again. "They've been taken over." The pirates hadn't willingly joined the quest, she'd wager.

Caspian replied dully, "What?"

"Their eyes are black. It be the taint." That got his attention.

"You're sure?" he croaked.

Ebba nodded. "A pirate won't risk his gullet for much. There ain't no way these pirates are here o' their own accord. And I couldn't mistake the look now. The pillars have spread their taint to them. I'm sure."

Verity had said the pillars would have an exponential increase in power with regaining their shadow form and then again once they had their corporeal form. The tainted crew had to have left the ship and flooded Febribus and infected the other pirates. But that the pirates had lost their souls already was terrifying. She couldn't even fathom how strong the pillars must have become since she was on *Malice*. They'd claimed all of these pirates and taken over the kingdom. Even with the shadows regaining their actual bodies in the coming weeks, Ebba had thought her crew would have time to figure out how to destroy them before the pillars made their next move.

The pirates of *Felicity* had wasted so much time trying to decide if this was 'their' battle that they'd lost precious time.

Caspian tensed. "The pillars are the six shadows you saw manifest on *Malice*, yes?"

She nodded, peering around the corner again.

"I saw them when the taint had me," he said hoarsely. "In my head, as I got worse, six shadows used to stand around me."

She glanced back at him. He'd never spoken of his time while wounded before, other than to say the nightmares had showed him every failure and regret.

"Beautiful men but for the darkness seeping from their pores. The evil in them leant the air a handspan around their bodies a shimmering quality, like diamonds embedded in graphite. When I began slipping from this world from the tainted wound in my shoulder, they told me. . . ." He shuddered. "They told me horrible things. That I would fail my father, that I'd abandoned my family, that I best stay away from Exosia because I was unfit to rule."

Ebba stared at the prince, the *heir*. His sisters exchanged an anxious glance, and her heart went out to them because while Ebba had a small idea of what was going on, they knew nothing. Their brother had returned minus an arm. Their father was now dead. And they were learning a wave of horrible things they didn't have time to understand.

Caspian's shoulders hung heavy. Shadows masked his

expression, and his tone was leaden as he said, "They were right."

"Snap out o' it," Ebba said flatly.

Anya gasped. Caspian glared at Ebba, and she almost smiled, despite the situation. He'd never shown any animosity toward her at all; it would be funny in any other setting.

She tipped her head to the youngest. "We need to get yer sisters out. Have yer failure moment when we be safe."

A strangled noise worked up his throat, and Ebba blinked as she realized the prince was trying not to laugh.

"I'll do that," he said, shaking his head as he threw a look at her. "*Failure moment.*"

Maybe he'd been hit on the head somewhere, too. Actually, her head really wasn't feeling too flash. They'd been sitting here too long, and she'd begun to notice her numerous aches and pains.

"Any ideas?" the youngest said.

Anya drew herself up. "I'll go down as a sacrifice. When they're distracted, the rest of you run. Leave without me. I've chosen my fate."

Ebba winced, but Caspian cast her a warning glance.

"Sal," Ebba said slowly, instead of criticizing the princess' dramatic plan. "Can ye go down and glow a bit? The *Malice* pirates wouldn't enter the servants' stairs with ye glowin'. I don't think the taint inside the pirates likes yer goodness. Or whatever yer glow be made of." Probably made of brandy fumes.

The sprite's eyes narrowed.

Ebba sighed. "I ain't sacrificin' ye. Well, not much. Ye can just fly away."

Sally gestured rudely and then handed the *purgium* to the youngest princess.

"Don't be droppin' that," Ebba said to her.

Sierra studied the tarnished-silver tube. "Something is moving under the surface."

"Aye, and every one o' those pirates down there will seek to take that from ye. Best hide it in yer jerkin."

"You mean my corset?" she asked.

Ebba ignored her, saying, "If ye lose it, I'll maroon ye on the nearest island."

The young girl blanched and tucked it inside the top of her dress, patting the bulge it created on her flat chest.

Sally rolled her eyes and then dimmed her glow, flying up so she was as close to the stone ceiling of the second level as possible. Heart in her mouth, Ebba watched as the wind sprite hovered along the top of the cavernous entranceway, keeping close to the heavy purple and gold curtains as she could. Sally reached the opposite side. Peering back, the sprite held up a thumb. At least Ebba assumed she held up a thumb. Could be the other finger again.

"Get ready," Ebba said.

"Wait, where are we going?" Caspian said.

He'd wasted time telling his story, and now he wanted to discuss the plan? "I thought the courtyard was the only way out."

"There's a passage that exits from the gardens."

Sally was flying into position. "Make a choice, matey," she hissed.

"It depends what's down there," he managed to say.

Sally's white glow burst through the entrance and the four of them raised their arms in unison. Ebba was more prepared, having been close to the sprite in the servants' stairwell.

Arm raised, she urged them on. "Too late. Time to go." She kept low, rounding the corner and moving quickly down the steps.

The pirates were taking cover from the glowing light,

pressing themselves against the confines of the entrance. Some, those in black uniforms, writhed on the ground, while those in general pirate garb had hunched but remained upright.

She trusted that if the others had any sense whatsoever, they'd be behind her, but confirming this without glancing back was impossible.

A few pirates had spilled out of the entranceway to evade the sprite's light.

They'd have to fight their way out. Sally might be able to keep up her glow until they were clear of the castle, but Ebba had a strong suspicion the sprite's white light would be useless in stopping a bullet.

Sally's glare faltered, and Ebba picked up her pace, peering up. The sprite was shaking her head frantically. Huh? She wanted Ebba and the others to go back up? No way.

Ebba misjudged the width of the next step and nearly tripped face-first. Recovering, she shook her head at the sprite. Sally doubled her efforts, drawing a finger across her throat.

That . . . seemed more serious.

Sally dropped her glow, and Ebba cursed under her breath, halting to crouch beside the balusters that hopefully concealed most of their bodies from below.

"Why are we stopping?" Anya asked.

Ebba whispered over her shoulder. "Sal's ord—"

Orange and red exploded at the entrance, and the heavy wooden doors there blasted inward, collecting the recovering pirates in the middle. Thick black, acrid plumes of smoke billowed through, and all Ebba could see as she was flung back on the stairs were the flames that rose from the explosion in a mushroom, catching on the drapes and artwork in the huge castle lobby.

What was happening? She tried to sit, opening her jaw in a bid to pop her ears and be rid of the incessant ringing there.

Ebba propped onto her elbow, blinking in a stupor, and watched, still immobilized from the first blast, as a wooden barrel rolled through the castle doors.

A barrel. Filled with what?

The answer came to her.

"Cover!" she yelled. Or meant to. She couldn't hear her voice, only the faint hum underneath the whining in her ears.

Throwing her hands over her head, Ebba curled into a ball against the balustrade, shouting wordlessly as the barrel of gunpowder went off with a soul-shaking boom. The grand stairway they huddled upon lurched, and Ebba reached for the ankle of the person behind her. They had to get off the staircase. It was going to go.

Ebba slid down the steps, digging in her heels to help move her body downward. She didn't trust herself to stand when her head didn't know which way north was. She let go of the person's ankle once she was happy they were following her lead.

The high crackle of fire licking the decorated walls of the lobby was accompanied by pain-filled screams. Ebba turned to peek through the balustrade and swallowed at the pirate below, who was missing his body from the waist down. A burning corpse lay beside him, the pirate already dead.

The stairs lurched again, and Ebba dug her heels in, ignoring the stone scraping away the skin on her back. The bottom was in sight.

"Nearly there," she said thickly.

Someone answered her. A rich, deep voice, maybe Caspian's. Ebba glanced back and saw the others were all following. Blood trickled from a wound on Sierra's temple, but she was still moving.

Ebba stomach dropped with the stonework on the third lurch. The stairs were going. Ebba didn't waste a moment, throwing herself down the remaining steps. Her shoulder blade struck the edge of the last step, and she sucked in a harsh breath, rolling several times at the bottom before coming to a halt.

A body landed on top of her. A floral scent mixed with smoke. *Princess.*

Another body landed on top of the princess. Sandalwood and shoe polish. *Prince.* The final crack of the stone overrode even the roaring fire surrounding them.

"Oof," Ebba wheezed as a third body, another princess presumably, landed on top of her.

Her eyes watered from the smoke. Breathing was hard enough with the steadily building fire in here without two princesses and an heir suffocating her. Ebba whacked weakly at the closest leg, which turned out not to be a leg, but Caspian's stomach. A rather firm stomach. Interesting.

Ebba lay still, unable to do a thing about what might be around them. Her head lolled toward the entrance.

And a smile curved her lips.

"Where is she, ye spineless bastards?" roared Stubby from where he stood, one foot raised on the smoldering remains of a destroyed castle door.

He waved two pistols in the air, and the air lodged in her throat as Plank, Locks, and Grubby appeared on either side of him.

"Stubby." She coughed.

Caspian rolled off, and his sisters followed suit, lying beside Ebba. All four of them peered to the pirates in the doorway, two of them recognizing help had arrived, and two likely wondering if the pirates there would murder them in the next five seconds.

Ebba gathered her breath and bellowed over the anarchy. "Stubby!"

All four of her fathers' heads turned. And then Plank and Grubby were bearing down on them. They ignored the others and grabbed a wrist each to haul her from the rubble onto her feet. She wavered, leaning heavily against Grubby as dizziness assaulted her. Dragging in thin breaths, she pointed at the princesses. "Grab the others."

One of her fathers let off a pistol shot behind her, and she heard a muffled yell from the pirate it struck.

When she'd found her legs, she gently pushed Grubby toward the princesses, too.

"They be my fathers," she told the wide-eyed girls. "They're here to help." *And nearly killed us.*

Ebba patted her front. The *dynami* was still secure. She glanced at Sierra and saw the bulge of the healing cylinder still apparent.

The sword? Where was the sword? Caspian was a step ahead of her, picking his way across the rubble of the stairs to collect the *veritas,* which stuck upright from amidst the collapsed stairwell.

"We need to get out o' here," she shouted.

Caspian shook his head. "I need to free my people."

"Ye can't do that if ye're dead," she retorted angrily. They had *not* come this far for him to act the hero.

Plank gripped his arm as he returned from the rubble. "Yer people were marched down the hill an hour ago. We don't be knowin' where, but Ebba's right. Ye can't help them if yer dead, and by the looks o' it, ye be halfway there."

Caspian closed his eyes as if in physical pain, but allowed her father to tug him out of the destroyed entranceway.

Ebba coughed again, eyes streaming, though most of the smoke was escaping into the sky. She glanced farther into the castle, but if anyone had survived being so close to the explosion, then they were unconscious or making themselves scarce. She valued her own gullet more than theirs.

They reached Stubby and Locks outside. Sally drifted down to their level, her light flickering. Ebba held out her palm, and the sprite threw her a grateful look as she landed. Ebba tucked her at the back of her neck. Sally grabbed a dread in each hand, like they were bloody reins.

"There be other smoke about," Locks said, glancing up. "But we've made a mighty black signal to let everyone know all ain't well at the castle."

Aye, a signal that might bring any other tainted pirates running to check.

Stubby pulled Ebba into a tight hug, and she blinked, feeling the way he was trembling.

"Aye," he croaked, pulling away, eyes shining. "We best get away from here smart-like."

They moved in a pained, hobbling semblance of a run down the crumbling steps from the entrance and back through the long stretch of the rectangular courtyard, which was filled with small carriages similar to the one she'd arrived in.

Not a soul was in sight, and Ebba cast an inquiring look at Plank.

"Most o' the pirates escorted the court down the hill, but they left their gunpowder at the top." He shrugged. "Seemed a shame not to make use o' it. We rolled a barrel under the portcullis and took out the pirates they'd left as guards."

Make use of it, they had. The portcullis ahead was gone. In fact, the entire middle section of the wall had been blown to Davy Jones' and lay gaping wide open for anyone to enter and exit.

Ebba scolded them. "What if all the pirates inside had raced out here after hearin'? There only be four o' ye."

"We'd hoped they would. A mite annoyin' that they didn't. We'd set up a nice trap for when they raced out," Locks said smugly. "Ye ran through it halfway down the courtyard."

She frowned and glanced back, looking at the carriages they'd sprinted between. "Gunpowder in the carriages?" Ebba held her left arm stiff so as not to jostle the shoulder blade she'd landed on. The throbbing there was worsening.

"Aye," Locks said.

Impressive. She'd tuck that ploy away for another time.

"The pirates either didn't hear or didn't oblige," Stubby wheezed as they jogged. "We had to get creative-like."

Grubby grinned, showing his missing teeth.

They'd reached the cobbled gray path that led downhill. She'd taken it twice in shackles, once in a ballgown, and now a fourth time in what used to be a ballgown.

"I need to be out o' this dress," she said, stopping. "I can't stand it any longer. Cut it off."

Caspian immediately moved to the laces at the back of her dress but was shoved aside by Locks, who drew out a knife and sliced it upright through the tight confines of the dress.

"Ye already took her to a ball," Locks growled at the prince. "That's all ye'll be doin'."

Ebba groaned as she shoved off the dress and felt as though she'd lost twenty bags of sand in the doing. The corset would remain, and the billowing garment that covered her from the bottom of the corset to the knee. Marigold had called them underwear, but Ebba thought they looked almost like slops, if a little thinner and shorter than the pirate trousers she was accustomed to.

"That's better." She sighed and bent to retrieve the *dynami*. She cast a sidelong gaze at the younger princess.

"Got it," Sierra said, patting the *purgium*.

Ebba smiled tightly. "Good lass. Still there, Sal?"

The sprite squeaked, jerking on the dreadlocks she held.

They set off again, Ebba skimming the ground now that she was rid of her dress prison. She wasn't sure how the princesses ran so fast with enough fabric to clothe the Pleo tribe twisting about their ankles, but they somehow were. Had to respect that.

Grubby and Plank took the lead, setting a pace that the younger, albeit battered and bruised, members of their party struggled to keep up with.

"I used the *dynami* to collapse a stairwell," she puffed out. "We think it might've killed Pockmark and ten o' his crew, includin' Swindles and Riot. They were right behind him."

Caspian panted, hot on her heels. "They had plenty of time to get down to us on the first level, if they'd survived the collapse anyway. If they're not dead, they were certainly trapped."

"The lot o' them can rot," Locks said between gasping breaths. "What else happened? I assume these be yer sisters, Cosmo."

The younger glanced back. "Cosmo your servant?"

"I used his name when I was first picked up by *Felicity* to cover my identity."

"Caspian. Whatever," Locks replied.

"Yes, Locks, these are my sisters."

"Well, what happened in there?" Stubby interrupted.

What happened? Two daughters and a son lost their father. The king had found the courage to look at the truth—and hadn't killed Ebba when he could have. They'd escaped with Sally and the magical cylinders, maybe even a third. The pillars appeared to have overtaken the rest of piratekind and had overthrown the royal family. Their taint would now spread through the Exosian people. In mere weeks, if Verity was right, they'd have the power to transition from shadows to physical bodies and be almost unstoppable.

Ebba shuddered, looking ahead at the weary and pale faces of the princesses. "We'll tell ye back at the ship. Where be Barrels and Peg-leg?"

Plank whistled, the sound shaking with his jolting steps. "Ye should've seen Peg-leg when we told him he were too slow to join."

Ebba winced. "Ye were foolish to tell him straight like that. Yer supposed to go in sideways so his pride can accept the loss o' face."

Plank grunted. "Aye, but time were short. We had to make some hasty plans when the cannons started goin' off. *Malice* got through the town and up the hill with no one any the wiser. No bells were rung or alarms sounded. We had no idea Pockmark and his crew were here, and could only be assumin' until we saw them draggin' the court people down to wagons."

"Wagons?" the eldest princess said, clutching her side.

Plank glanced back. "Aye."

Caspian inhaled sharply. "They're taking them to the coal mines. They'll be slaves."

Stubby snorted. "If there be slaves already there, I say it'll be good for their character to get a taste."

"No." The heir was emphatic. "No slaves. The work is hard, but pays well. Many choose to work there of their own volition, but I doubt that is Pockmark's plan," he said, then corrected himself. "Or rather, the plan of the six pillars."

"Six pillars, aye," Locks mused. "They've been busy recruitin' from what we could tell. And I ain't likin' the look of the new recruits' eyes. They look fair-black to me."

"Ye haven't seen six shadows around, have ye?" Ebba asked, hoping she didn't tempt fate by asking the question.

"Nay, lass. I don't know if I'd recognize them, though, havin' never seen them. But we ain't seen nothin' like that," Plank said.

They'd recognize the shadows, all right. Or at least feel the malice emanating from them.

"Nearly at the bottom," Grubby called.

Ebba was so happy to hear it she could've kissed the damn siren in that moment.

"Perhaps we should count ourselves lucky the pirates took the court to the coal mines," Stubby said between breaths. "If the pirates weren't there, they'd surely be *here*. I was thinkin' we'd have to fight our way to the wharf."

The ground flattened, and soon the stone town houses rose on either side. Ebba focused on placing one foot before the other, welcoming the slight breeze their jogging pace created as it cooled the bare skin on her arms. Sally had to be boiling hot under her dreads, but the sprite didn't make a peep.

"Are the others stealing *Felicity*?" she asked.

"They were only to get Verity, Marigold, and her kin down to the wharf and wait for us to arrive," Plank answered.

"And did ye tell Peg-leg that was all he meant to do?" Ebba asked.

"Aye," Stubby said meekly.

So he would've gone to get the ship back. Ebba rolled her eyes. They'd shared a ship with the cook for how long and still didn't know how to manage his moods.

Plank took one look back at them and called for everyone to slow to a walk. "We're nearly there." He gulped in air.

"Jagger," Caspian said suddenly.

"What about him?" Ebba scowled.

"He was with you in the cages. Where is he?"

She shrugged, recalling the flaxen haired man's silver eyes staring down at her in the night. "He scampered up the chains from the cages and disappeared. Ain't seen him since."

"He brought *Malice* here," Caspian said angrily. "*He* did this. He knew the *dynami* and the *purgium* were up at the castle. He'd been in the courtyard before. He could've told Pockmark exactly what to do and how to get in."

Ebba frowned. She could still feel Jagger's arm about her waist as he heaved her through *Malice* to save her. Every moment where Jagger had appeared to do something bad, he'd had his reason. When he'd disappeared on Neos, it was to check on his tribe kin. He'd returned to Pockmark only to keep his family safe. He'd returned to *Malice* after saving the crew of *Felicity* on Pleo, knowing he'd be killed or that the taint might claim him. He'd done that to keep the magic cylinders from Pockmark, or so it seemed to her. When Jagger had disappeared up the chain instead of dropping into the crocodile-infested waters with them, Ebba hadn't taken it personally. He was a pirate, even if he'd been raised in a tribe, and she understood that way of thinking. She would've done the same if their positions were reversed.

Did she think Jagger would've gone back to *Malice* again? Not unless they had his family. But Caspian already had a reason to dislike Jagger—the pirate had been a breath away from killing him ever since they met. Or re-met. She still didn't know what Jagger's problem was.

"We don't be knowin' that. Pockmark was only askin' yer father about *veritas*." She broke the silence Caspian's vehement accusation had created.

"I thank you, Mistress Fairisles, but I know just fine."

Caspian had lost his father tonight. Then at a time when he should've been preparing to become king himself, he'd been forced to abandon his people and flee his home like a gutter rat. Ebba liked to think she knew the heir well by now, and she knew he held honor and responsibility in high regard, even if he'd yearned to be free of both when they'd first met. When he'd asked to return to Exosia, Ebba saw that was the moment he made his choice about who he wanted to be, or the person he felt he had to be. And now, despite resigning himself to that life, he was being flung away like trash by the same pirates who'd killed those on the navy ship he once sailed upon; the same people who'd caused the injury that took his arm.

Ebba kept her silence. He'd have time to sort things through once they were all safe. She'd help him.

The shine of water when they made it to the harbor nearly

brought a sob to her lips. The gentle lap of the waves against the shore was the call to come home. The jutting piers of the wharf were shadowed in the night and apparently abandoned with not a person in sight. By the looks, the navy docked their smaller ships here.

"Barrels," Stubby hissed into the night.

No answer.

"Where the flamin' hell are they?" Locks exploded. "I told him I was trustin' him to care for Verity. If they—"

A hand slid across his back, and Verity's blonde hair swung against her back as she came to face Locks. "I care for myself. Have you learned nothing in eighteen years?"

"Nothing," he replied, pulling her into his arms.

Gross.

Marigold and four middle-aged men who looked like younger versions of Barrels joined them, a small army of children in their wake. Marigold's children and grandchildren? Blimey, her sons had been drinking a whole heap of tea to make all those kids.

"Over here," a voice hissed.

Ebba squinted and made out the forms of Peg-leg and Barrels ahead. She walked as quickly as her body would allow and fell into their arms.

They were all together again.

Now they had to get out of here. She'd seen the stones fall down on Pockmark and his crew, but she didn't trust that meant he was dead. Not with the evil he'd carried within him for who knew how long. They had to leave before they were found. Ebba was more than ready to be away from this place. "Where is she?"

"*Felicity* ain't here," Peg-leg said grimly. "We've searched the whole place twice."

TWENTY-THREE

"*Felicity's* gone?" Ebba asked, scanning the wharf despite Peg-leg's surety. "That can't be."

"I'm afraid it is, my dear," Barrels said, rubbing his forehead. "And my cat with it."

Well, that was a win, in her eyes. And in the rest of the crew's, too, by the looks.

"Aye, that . . . be a right shame about yer cat. . . ," Stubby said dispassionately, and sighed. "We'll have to take another ship, lads."

Another ship? They couldn't leave *Felicity*. Ebba had never sailed another ship. *Felicity* was family.

Stubby wasn't looking at her, though; he was peering past her at Plank as the others caught up. Ebba half-listened to their conversation, reeling. It probably shouldn't mean so much to her. Except it did. It really did. In some ways, *Felicity* was her mother. The home of her heart. Still, she swallowed; her fathers were alive. Caspian and his sisters were here, and Barrels' family. They had what they'd come for and more. That would have to be enough.

"There be a sloop at the end o' the wharf up ahead,"

Peg-leg said.

He led the way, and their mismatched group of royalty, pirates, and rich Exosians trailed after him. Caspian had pulled his elder sister into his side, where she cried silently. Marigold and her family were staring at the royal family as though they had three heads. Stubby was limping after their dash down from the castle. Ebba hadn't even begun to think about what happened next. What happened now that the pillars ruled the realm, and pirates and Exosian landlubbers were slaves to the darkness?

Peg-leg led them down the third jutting wharf, his wooden pin tapping loudly. He stopped at the very end. "This one."

Ebba wrinkled her nose at the white ship.

"What sod in their right mind would be paintin' a ship white?" Grubby asked.

If he was thinking it, everyone was.

"It's all we've got," snapped Barrels, clearly at the end of his tether, like the rest of them. "Get on board, and we'll be away from this place. We have to find Pillage."

"Ahoy!" a voice boomed.

They turned as one, like puppets in some morbid show.

"I'll be damned," Locks whispered.

Felicity drifted through the water toward them, her curved cedar edges sleek and as beautiful as the day she'd been taken by the navy.

From the rigging hung . . . .

"Jagger," hissed Caspian.

"He's got *Felicity*!" Ebba said, waving a hand overhead at the pirate.

A furious *reeeeoow* echoed toward her.

"He's got Pillage." Barrels slumped in relief, pointing to where the ship cat prowled the bulwark.

"And Pillage. Yaaay," Ebba said weakly.

Peg-leg sagged. "I've never been happier to see someone I dislike."

"How did he get our ship?" Stubby asked, a wrinkle between his gray brows.

Ebba didn't care how or why Jagger was here, just that he was. She wanted her ship, her hammock, her rigging, her hold. Before she'd been happy enough to kiss a siren, but now Ebba was thinking she might even be able to kiss Jagger. And that just showed how messed up her head was after Caspian's romantic confession.

He left the rigging to furl the sails and then returned to spin the wheel, bringing *Felicity*'s portside against the wharf with confidence. A grudging respect churned within her. The man could work a ship, she'd give him that. He ran to the bulwark and threw two lines out. Grubby and Plank caught the ropes and moved away to secure the ship, just enough so they'd be able to climb aboard without *Felicity* drifting away.

"Where have ye been?" Locks called to the flaxen-haired pirate.

"Been hidin' here for days, waiting for a chance to steal *Felicity* for when ye got to shore."

That sounded like a pirate truth to her, but he *was* here, so maybe she was judging him too hasty-like.

"Did ye see me and Barrels fleecin' the wharf?" Peg-leg asked.

"Aye, I saw ye," Jagger replied. "No point comin' in until ye were all here."

"No point—?" Peg-leg's face turned a ruddy purple.

Barrels grimaced and rested a hand on the cook's arm. "Let's just be glad Jagger's here now and had the foresight to anticipate our movements."

Once the lines were secured, Ebba reached out for the ship's side and pulled *Felicity* closer. She prepared to spring into the ship, but Jagger leaned over and grabbed her around the waist, pulling her up.

"Uh," Ebba mumbled, meeting his silver gaze as he lowered her onto the deck. "Thanks?"

He scanned her from head to toe, and his gaze darkened as he reached his fingers to the back of her head and they came away bloodied. Shaking his head, he moved away to help the others. Weird.

Ebba stared at the deck, took two steps toward the mast, and then sank to her knees, a lump rising hard and fast up her throat. She lay down on her front on the deck and rested her cheek against *Felicity,* inhaling the smell of salt and cedar.

"My ship," she said, patting the deck.

Ebba lay there, listening to Pillage's harassed meowing and her fathers' calls as they brought in the two lines and unfurled the sails to get the ship moving again.

"Are you okay, my bird?" Marigold asked, resting a hand on Ebba's bare back. Barrels' sister gasped. "What happened to your shoulder?"

Ebba thought back. Was it one of the two times she was hurtled through the air by the magical objects? Or. . . . "When I threw myself down the stairs, I think."

". . . I see."

"Mmm," Ebba hummed in reply. She was staying right here to pat the ship.

"Is she okay?" Barrels dropped to her side, and Ebba groaned as the rest of her fathers came running.

They were going to fuss.

Ebba groaned and rolled onto her back, wincing at the new pressure on her head wound. She propped her arm under her skull to relieve the pain. "I be fine. I'm just happy to be away from that place and back on the ship."

Caspian was hugging both of his sisters close, stroking their hair. Marigold's children and their families stood quietly, though wide-eyed. They'd grown up with Marigold for a mother and grandmother, so Ebba was pretty sure they'd be made of stern stuff.

"Where are your clothes?" Marigold asked softly.

Ebba moved her eyes to look at the woman. "Got rid o' them. And I'm never wearin' a dress like that again."

Marigold's thin brows rose. "Like *that*?"

Aye, like *that*. Maybe she'd consider a different dress. She was saved from explaining the comment as Verity moved in front of her and hovered her hands over Ebba's body.

"I'm okay," she whined. Actually, each time *Felicity* slapped down into a trough, pain jolted through her entire body, but she'd take that with zero complaint.

Verity ignored her, muttering under her breath.

Caspian wobbled over to Barrels. "Is there a place I might show my sisters to rest?"

"Certainly. Marigold, would your family like to come down into the hold, too?" Barrels answered, the ship cat clutched to his chest.

Great. No hammock for her tonight, and the mainlanders probably wouldn't even appreciate it. Ebba guessed she'd live. Maybe.

She waited until their guests had disappeared through the bilge door to the sleeping quarters. "Hey, Verity? Just how powerful were ye afore the ship sucked it out o' ye?"

Verity fixed her periwinkle blue eyes on Ebba's face, her hovering hands stilling. "Mildly powerful compared to what's out there."

Ebba felt pinpricks on the side of her face and darted her eyes to Jagger. He glanced away when he saw she'd noticed his staring. He moved to check the sheets. Why was he acting so strangely?

245

"What about compared to a little ol' pirate?" she pressed.

Verity appeared to deliberate before admitting, "Extremely powerful."

"And when ye said the ship was drainin' yer powers. . . ."

The soothsayer's eyes shined brightly. "If you're asking if I'm the reason the pillars are back, then yes. It is the destiny I chose."

Locks knelt at Ebba's feet. "What do ye mean?"

"When you came to me with the injured prince, I had to make a decision."

Ebba recalled the soothsayer peering into the mirror for an awfully long time. Was that what she meant?

"I could let the prince die and let the world fall victim to the pillars. Or I could help you, help him, and become a victim myself, but be given a chance to love another. The pillars would rise sooner than they would have otherwise, but if I chose this path, darkness was not assured. In all other paths, the powers of the oblivion assured me it was so."

"Ye mean the Earth Mother?" Ebba asked.

"She is one of the three powers, yes."

Barrels rejoined them from the wheel, Pillage trotting in his wake. Peg-leg whispered to her father, no doubt bringing him up to speed.

"You couldn't have told us that afore?" Stubby asked, an edge entering his voice.

Verity shrugged. "A soothsayer is not an entity of his or her own. To be a soothsayer is to be a vessel for powers greater than yourself. They showed me, but a soothsayer cannot discuss what they have seen, what might be, or has been. That is the oath we bind ourselves to."

"And why can ye speak o' it now?" Plank asked from where he perched against the bulwark.

Verity looked around the circle of her six fathers, Jagger, and then back to Ebba. "I am no longer a soothsayer and am therefore freed from my oath. Now, I am nothing more than a healer with basic magic."

Jagger crouched beside Ebba, staring intently at Verity. "*Malice* wasn't the only ship to anchor down the shore. There were at least ten other ships. These pillars. Are they controllin' other pirates, too, now?"

Verity blinked furiously, and Ebba's heart squeezed for the woman who was clearly shouldering much of the blame, despite her otherwise calm demeanor.

"Yes, when the pillars regained their shadow forms, the souls of the crew succumbed to the taint. The pillars will not leave the strongest source of their power—the ship—until they regain their bodies, but through the crew, their taint can now spread unchecked. As their taint spreads, their power will continue to swell. In time, no facet of the realm will be free of their surveillance or taint. And not the seas beyond."

"Ye didn't think to warn us?" Jagger shot back.

"She did," Ebba said, glaring at him. "She told me."

Verity lifted her chin and regarded him with hard eyes. "Even I did not know it would happen so fast. I can feel the change in their power. Their power is. . . ." She shivered, and Locks moved to her side. "Unlike anything I've ever felt," she said. "I have already seen the future that awaits us if they should regain their bodies. Their minds will overpower everyone they come across. Exosia, Kentro, Maltu. The waters will darken to black. Pleo, Febribus, Neos, Zol. The creatures within will be powerless against them. Selkies, sprites, sirens, kraken. They will never stop feeding. Their taint will blanket the realm and suffocate all good. This time they will not fail." She trailed off and then blinked, shifting her eyes to Jagger, who had grown very still.

"Neos?" he asked.

She nodded. "Everything. The taint will claim all living souls. It will finish what it started within you and within Ebba's fathers. I know you feel the call of the dark now, just as I. The pillars haunt us, dog our steps, calling us back to their side so that their taint may finish what they started."

Jagger's chest rose and fell. His face was so stricken and lost that Ebba reached forward and touched her fingers to his hand, which rested on the deck.

He broke away from Verity's gaze to look at where she touched him. Aware of her fathers' scrutiny, Ebba drew back, and Jagger made no move to stop her. Or throw her off.

He scanned her fathers' faces and then sighed. "Do you know if my family on Neos still lives?"

"I do not," Verity answered him. "I have been shown snatches of the past, present, and future by the powers of the oblivion that connect with my path. And those snatches are not easily pieced together. I have felt the oppressiveness, the pain, the absence of light, the death of good."

Shite. There wasn't any mention of hammocks and palm trees in that.

"We need to find this root o' magic. It's past time we did," Plank said. From the beginning he'd been telling them they had to get to the bottom of all this.

Locks said, aghast, "If we'd killed Cannon, none o' this would be happenin'. If we'd started takin' this more serious-like, maybe Ebba wouldn't've been hurt."

They should have listened to Plank months ago, aye. They'd decided to fight too late. Now winning seemed impossible. But — "And if King Montcroix had killed Cannon's son, none o' this might be happenin' either," Ebba countered. "One person can't be shoulderin' the blame for what's goin' on."

Barrels hummed. "So how do we locate this root then?"

Ebba propped herself up. Sally crawled out from behind her

hair and perched on her collarbone. Jagger's black-rimmed eyes rested on the sprite, and then shifted to Ebba's pushed-up chest for a heartbeat too long before he blinked twice and moved his gaze away. Laughter bubbled up within her. Jagger was one of the males susceptible to dresses! That was bloody priceless. She bit back her grin.

"I was thinkin' we go back to the Earth Mother and make her tell us more. She'll have all o' her powers by now; she'll be able to really help," she said.

"You must assemble the weapon to fight the pillars," Verity said.

Stubby stared around their crouched circle. "Wait, is the root o' magic the weapon?"

"What?" Verity appeared confused.

Ebba held up the *dynami*. "Findin' the root o' magic has sumpin' to do with these." It had to. She straightened. "We found another one, too, a third; the king's sword. Afore he died, he was very ins'stent that Caspian get it from the treasury."

Verity was peering around the group, her eyes gradually widening.

"The king really be dead?" Jagger said. "I'd assumed so—with pirates swarmin' everywhere and Caspian fleein' back to this ship with ye. But the king really be dead?"

They all stared at the flaxen-haired pirate. He sounded excited about the king's death, like he so badly hoped the king was dead he feared believing it.

"Aye, lad. Killed by Pockmark," Stubby said. "What's it to ye?"

Jagger's glinting gaze shifted to the bulwark and stared at the sword left there by Caspian. His eyes were dark as he ambled closer to the weapon. "This was his sword?"

"Aye, when I picked up the sword while holdin' the *dynami*, it blasted me through the air, just like on Pleo when I touched two o' the cylinders. And Caspian's father kept referrin' to it as truth. *Veritas*."

Barrels stared at the sword. "It doesn't have the same pearly sheen as the other two cylinders. And I can't see the name etched anywhere on it, unlike the others." He paused. "Do you think there are more of these objects to find?" He spun toward Verity.

"I know of six," Verity said. "I—"

"One for each pillar?" Peg-leg cut her off.

Verity tilted her head, the action lending her a bird-like appearance. "Symmetry should never be discounted. But in this case—"

Ebba stilled. Davy Jones knew she'd learned not to discount symmetry—or parallels, as she'd coined the concept. "These six magic objects will help us find the root o' magic, won't they?"

The ex-soothsayer ignored her, still staring around the group. "None of you have any idea, do you?"

Her fathers exchanged looks.

Verity inhaled sharply. "The six parts *make* the root of magic. The six parts form the weapon that has the power to defeat the pillars."

What? Ebba said loudly, "I asked the Earth Mother outright if the *purgium* be the weapon, and she said nay."

"Well it's not. Not really. Immortals are literal beings," the woman answered. "The *purgium* is not the root of magic; it is just the *purgium* without the other five parts."

Locks exploded. "Ye're flamin' kiddin' me?" He seethed, hands clenched in fists. "I'll be havin' words with her if I ever see that bloody rabbit-killer again."

"Are you finished?" Verity asked him. Locks nodded meekly.

Ebba bit her lip to hold in her snigger.

Barrels was grim-faced. "Okay, so we have three of the six

parts already. That's good news. We're halfway there. Verity can help us locate the other parts."

She shook her head. "I was shown the *purgium*'s location because giving you the information was related to the path I had to take. Other than some grasp on magical history, I have no knowledge of where the other parts are hidden."

They'd found the *dynami* with the help of the magic fruit and Grubby's selkie nature, and the second cylinder with Verity's help. They'd only chanced upon the third. The remaining parts of the root of magic could be anywhere.

"This be truth, ye say?" Jagger turned to Ebba.

Was he still hooked on that? They'd moved on. She shrugged. "Aye." She'd jostled Sally, who fluttered off to where Pillage rested by Barrels' feet. The cat seemed unperturbed by the possible end of the realm. The sprite nestled into the cat's side and promptly started snoring.

"Mayhaps it can be helpin' us to the next part." Jagger bent down.

Right. She hadn't thought about that.

Jaw clenched, Jagger touched the sword.

As soon as he made contact, it was as though his hand couldn't let go of the sword. His head was flung back, and he extended in a backward arch before dropping to his knees. His breath sounded as though it was being physically pulled from his body.

Ebba burst to her feet, *dynami* in hand, one step behind her fathers.

By the time she reached Jagger, he was on his hands and knees. The sword rested flat underneath his palm, and his eyes were open, pupils darting side to side as though reading a book.

"Lad, are ye okay?"

That was nothing compared to being hurtled through the air by exploding parts. "What do ye see, Jagger?" she urged him.

The pirate's face was in shadow, but he was breathing hard. His knuckles were clenched, showing strained white beneath the skin.

The bilge door opened, and Jagger lifted his head.

Ebba glanced back and saw Caspian had reappeared, the *purgium* in his belt. Stubby plucked her out of the way as Jagger roared and ran at the prince, *veritas* in hand.

"I knew it," Jagger roared.

What had the sword shown him?

He swung the sword at the prince, and Caspian narrowly avoided it, dodging and stumbling into a barrel. His shocked expression morphed into fury.

"You led *Malice* to the castle," Caspian seethed. He waited until the pirate swung again and then rushed in, tackling Jagger to the deck. He rolled off, but threw himself back on top of Jagger, gripping the neck of the pirate's tunic with his hand.

"They're goin' to kill each other," Ebba cried, covering her mouth. "Stop them," she said to Stubby.

His mouth was grim. "Sumpin' else be goin' on here, lass."

Ebba stepped forward but Stubby stopped her.

"Stop fightin'. That wasn't Jagger's doin'," she shouted at them. Why were they doing this? They'd barely survived the night.

Jagger backhanded the prince, who went sprawling. He dragged the sword up to hold it in both hands. "I didn't lead them anywhere, Prince Caspian, but I would have if I'd known they'd kill yer scum father."

Fury contorted Caspian's face, and he shook as he faced the pirate. "Give me back my father's sword," he said through gritted teeth. "Give it back, or I swear that I will not rest until you are dead."

Jagger's eyes were murderous. "This sword be truth."

"Yes, and only someone who can be trusted to use it wisely may hold the sword."

"Like yer father, *Prince Caspian?*" Jagger asked. His eyes gained a steel glint, and Ebba shook free of Stubby's hold, not trusting the change. Hadn't Verity just said she still felt the call of darkness, and that Jagger did too? His soul may not be victim to the taint, but he wasn't free of it. Out of anyone here, he'd had the most exposure to the pillars' darkness.

Jagger circled the prince like a shark, not speaking again until he was in front of Caspian. "When I was a toddler, I lived on Exosia with my parents. My father was the Colonel o' yer father's army."

Ebba gasped. The man in the painting had been Jagger's father?

"You lie," Caspian said, watching the pirate closely.

"I hold truth in my hands," Jagger mocked. He scanned the weapon from hilt to gleaming point. "This be the sword that killed them, wielded by yer father's hands. When I touched the sword just now, I saw my parents' faces; I heard their screams as he drove this sword through their bodies. *Veritas* showed me how it felt to slice through their flesh." His voice trembled, and Jagger lowered his gaze from the sharp tip to stare at Caspian, whose eyes were now wide.

Something Jagger had said had pierced a hole in Caspian's anger.

Jagger continued flatly, "Yer father was on a tour o' the island more than sixteen years ago now. The tribe o' Neos were watchin' the ship pass by. They watched yer father kill mine, and then my mother. A servant placed me, a toddler o' only three years old, into a rowboat and pushed me out to sea. All I had o' my parents was my father's army medals that the servant pinned to my tunic. I had no notion what'd happened to my mother or to my father. I was a white mainlander, but the Neos tribe took me in, and when I was old enough to know the truth, I vowed to take away sumpin' the king loved." Jagger circled the prince again. "Early on, that was his life. But later on that sumpin' changed to his heir. I took particular pains to learn about ye, yer appearance, yer interests, and yer whereabouts."

"I didn't know," Caspian said at last, shoulders dropping. "He never breathed a word of it. Though after several goblets of wine, he would sometimes mention a great friend he'd once had."

Ebba had always noted the pirate's hatred toward Caspian. She'd first seen it in his eyes as they passed *Malice* in Selkie's Cove. And again when he'd so studiously ignored the prince's presence on their journey to Pleo. His comments about watching the taint claim the prince and that fate being far worse than any he'd planned. She doubted any of the crew had guessed at just how deep his loathing went.

He was going to kill Caspian. She could see it in the harsh lines of his face.

"Great friend?" Jagger asked, his voice deathly calm. "That's how yer father treated his *great friends*?"

"If it helps," Caspian uttered softly. "I believe whatever happened on that ship haunted him until his dying day."

Her eyes shifted to the prince. She noted the dejected hang of his shoulders; his empty sleeve and haunted eyes. And she remembered his words in the castle about the pillars being right. She recalled the bitter set to his mouth. The lackluster hue to his amber eyes. He'd lost his father today.

Creeping awareness itched the space between her shoulder blades, and Ebba couldn't shake the horrible, horrible thought that Caspian was going to let Jagger do his worst.

Jagger charged forward with a yell, and Ebba sprinted across the deck to launch herself between them.

The pirate's eyes widened as he saw her in the middle. He

tried to wrench the tip of the sword up. Her fathers were shouting, but Ebba made no move to evade the blade, flinging out her arms to place a palm on Caspian's chest, and one in the opposite direction to stop Jagger's charge.

The tip of the sword glanced past her side without cutting her, but Jagger couldn't stop his momentum.

Her palm pressed into his chest, her other still on the prince.

. . . And the world lit up.

The white light she'd seen exploding from Sally burst from their trio. Ebba stared at her glowing feet and then out to the far-flung perimeter of the orb surrounding them. Her very skin was alight; her hair was lifting around her like some invisible breeze was at work.

She lifted her eyes to Jagger's, and he returned her baffled look. The white glow had given the high-boned features of his face an ethereal appearance. His flaxen hair looked silver, like his eyes, which were blazing, no trace of the black ring in sight. Ebba blinked and glanced behind at Caspian. He was turning his hand over, studying his skin. But she gasped as he glanced up. His eyes were molten gold, his russet hair a deep bronze.

Her mouth moved wordlessly as she stared past him to the east.

A beam of the glowing light was shooting from where their trio touched off into the distance. A thin beam, no bigger than the flat side of a coin, but it shot straight. The point the light touched far in the distance seemed fixed, the angle of the light beam changing with *Felicity*'s forward movement.

For a second, she watched Pillage leaping up and trying to swat the beam of light. Then, shaking her shock away, Ebba dropped her hands, and the glow disappeared as though sucked into the oblivion.

She wavered, and Jagger dropped the sword, reaching for her elbow to steady her.

"What was that?" Barrels whispered.

Her mouth was dry. Her head was throbbing something fierce from the night's injuries and the revelations since. Her legs folded, and Caspian reached for her, helping Jagger to lower her to sit on the deck.

Ebba's gaze fell on the discarded sword. "Am I crazy for thinkin' what I be thinkin'?" she muttered.

Caspian crouched by her side. "You're crazy for running into the middle of a sword fight, but not for having that thought."

"That wasn't a sword fight," she said. "Ye didn't have a sword. He was going to run ye through."

Jagger lowered down, watching her. "He's right; that was foolish." He peered over at Caspian. "This ain't over. I have a debt to repay."

"Aye, it is." Ebba pounded a fist on the deck. "Don't ye see that Caspian doesn't want to live? He wanted ye to run him through."

Judging by Jagger's raised brows, he hadn't.

"That right?" he asked the prince.

Caspian didn't answer, his amber eyes on Ebba's face. His throat worked, but he didn't answer.

"Then it be a punishment for ye to live," Jagger said simply. "But if yer stance on death be changin', I'll be here to deliver yer end. Yer father killed my parents, and I will uphold my vow."

That was a win in Ebba's eyes. For now.

Her fathers had circled their trio and crouched in a ring around them, listening. Verity stood behind Locks, her eyes set on Ebba.

"That crazy thought ye were also havin'," Ebba said to Caspian. "What is it?"

The prince sighed, rubbing his temple, the *purgium* still in his belt. "That when we touched just now, a beaming light was pointing to the next object."

Ebba deflated. "Phew, that's what I was thinkin' too. It only happens when three people are holdin' a magical object each, though, do ye think?" It couldn't just be when she, Jagger, and Caspian touched, could it?

Jagger glanced at the discarded sword. "Why three?"

"Because the weapon wants to be whole again," Verity whispered. "The power when you were all touching right now was ten times than when the three objects were apart. When you touch, the objects fuel each other and have enough power to call to their other parts. To the next closest part, or so I assume."

"That solves the 'how' of locating the rest," Barrels said.

Plank added, "If this be the only thing that'll get rid o' these six pillars, we need to collect the rest o' the parts."

Ebba set her jaw as determination flooded her body. She saw it echoed on the faces of her fathers, Verity, Caspian, and even Jagger.

Caspian peered in the direction where the beam had shone moments before. "But what's in that direction? I can only recall the. . . ."

No one spoke, only the fluttering sails overhead and the slap of the ocean disturbed the dark night.

"There lies the part o' the sea that no sane pirate should enter," Stubby said finally.

Locks inhaled. "And if they do, no one be returnin'."

Ebba closed her eyes and said what they were all thinking. "The Dynami Sea," she said, a shiver working its way up her spine. "The next part o' the weapon be in the Dynami Sea."

ACKNOWLEDGMENTS

I've snuck away from my friends and husband while on holiday in Merimbula to write these acknowledgments. When I say 'snuck', I mean they simply told me to do what I needed to get done to meet my deadline. Anyone who has regular deadlines will understand just how much that unconditional support and acceptance of work pressures means.

A lot.

I have the greatest people around me, my husband being first and foremost. And each time I reach this point—after months of writing, edits, and all the other bits between—I'm always overwhelmed by how much my loved ones just *get me*.

To my beta readers, Lola and Courtney. A lot of hats must be worn, and each of you wear one or more for me. Not only does this prevent me from looking like the Mad Hatter; it stops me *acting* like the Mad Hatter. Thank you for your ongoing work and support

And to my manuscript team:

Editor One

Melissa Scott

Editor Two
Robin Schroffel

Proofreaders
Patti Geesey and Dawn Yacovetta

Map Illustrator
Laura Diehl

Cover Designer & Illustrator
Amalia Chitulescu

To my readers. There are millions of books in the world and you choose to pick up mine. A heartfelt thank you for being here.

Happy Reading,
Kelly

ABOUT KELLY ST. CLARE

When Kelly is not reading or writing, she is lost in her latest reverie. Books have always been magical and mysterious to her. One day she decided to unravel this mystery and began writing. *The Tainted Accords* was her debut series. Her other works include *The After Trilogy*, *The Darkest Drae*, and *Pirates of Felicity*.

A New Zealander in origin and in heart, Kelly currently resides in Australia with her ginger-haired husband, a great group of friends, and some huntsman spiders who love to come inside when it rains. Their love is not returned.

ALSO BY KELLY ST. CLARE

The Tainted Accords:
Fantasy of Frost
Fantasy of Flight
Fantasy of Fire
Fantasy of Freedom

The Tainted Accords Novellas:
Sin
Olandon
Rhone
Shard (2019)

The After Trilogy:
The Retreat
The Return
The Reprisal

The Darkest Drae (Trilogy) Co-written with Raye Wagner

Blood Oath
Shadow Wings
Black Crown

Pirates of Felicity:
Immortal Plunder
Stolen Princess
Pillars of Six
Dynami's Wrath

BONUS CHAPTER

DYNAMI'S WRATH

Ebba was about to do something drastic. Something huge. Something . . . unprecedented.

Face propped up on her hands where she lay across Verity's bed, Ebba watched Verity dress for the celebration. Her eyes tracked the way the woman brushed her long, blonde hair, the way she braided it, and how the ex-soothsayer twisted the shining mass atop her head.

Locks' one-and-only girlfriend usually wore plain dresses, and occasionally trousers and a shirt, but tonight she'd selected a lavender dress that highlighted her periwinkle-blue eyes. The dress perched on the tips of her shoulders, the neckline plunging. The bodice was tight and flared out at the hips, ending just below her knees.

The simple fact that there was a dress on Zol, let alone someone *wearing* it, was testament to how much Ebba's life had changed in the last three weeks. Their hidden sanctuary in the southern region of the Caspian Sea had never housed anything other than pirates—and Caspian.

Now it was filled with landlubbers and females. Females

265

who didn't behave the way Ebba had seen her only other woman friends behave. After her time in the Maltu brothel, she'd sworn to only ever be a pirate, both because of how much tea they drank, and because she'd thought her fathers might abandon her again. But the new women here . . . they were different.

"Hey, Verity?" Ebba asked, licking her dry lips.

The woman grunted.

That's why Ebba liked her: she made normal sounds and didn't waste too much time with politeness. Ebba didn't mind Barrels' sister, Marigold; the woman could get her six fathers to do chores with the snap of her fingers, and Ebba could respect that. But Verity was a survivor. She didn't take shite, she wasn't bothered by how people saw her, she was beautiful, and yet she was still willing to put on a dress to celebrate Ebba's eighteenth birthday.

Ebba sat up, swinging her legs over the end of the bed to face the woman who'd single-handedly brought Locks to heel. "Do ye think it'd be odd-like if I wore a dress tonight?"

Verity inspected her appearance in a mirror, swinging left and right. No one else had a mirror in their shack. The hut she shared with Locks contained many things that had simply appeared. Though no longer a soothsayer, Verity possessed what she referred to as 'simple healing magic,' which clearly included the ability to conjure mirrors out of thin air.

"No, you're a young woman," Verity answered without glancing back.

Ebba was glad the healer wasn't acting weird and badgering her with questions. Posing the question had been a test of how the others might react. "I'm not really a young woman, though," Ebba pressed, watching Verity closely. "I be a pirate."

Verity shrugged. "Why do you only have to be one thing? Seems to me you're a pirate and princess of a tribe. Just because you haven't wanted to be something else until now, doesn't mean you can't change your mind. When you're fifty, you may decide you're a man."

She contemplated this. "I do wear feathers in my hair sometimes now." She'd taken that away from her time on Pleo.

"Yes, and no one thought that was strange."

That was also true. Her fathers had commented on them, and Caspian, too, on the rare occasion he came out of his funk, and she'd caught Jagger's eyes on them a few times.

Ebba took a deep breath. "Well, I've been thinkin' of wearin' a dress tonight."

"Why? What's prompted this?" Verity asked.

She toyed with a loose stitch on the bedspread. "Nothing."

"Lie."

"It ain't—"

"Lie."

Ebba gritted her teeth and blew a dread out of her face. "Fine." She'd made the mistake of sitting down with the elder of Caspian's sisters, Princess Anya, last week. The *other* females, spawn of Barrels' sister Marigold, had flocked to join them, like moths to a flame, and soon they'd started talking about kissing, and fashion, and all sorts of girly things Ebba had no experience with.

"I'm eighteen today, and. . . ." Her face flamed. How to put her uncomfortable realization into words? All the women had talked about their first kiss. Ebba had sat and listened as the younger princess, Sierra, just thirteen, had shared hers. The girl was five years younger than Ebba. She swallowed. "Do ye think there be somethin' wrong with me that I haven't kissed a person my age?"

Verity snorted. "No, Ebba-Viva, I don't."

Ebba hadn't ever thought so either. In fact, only months ago her only urge had been to fill her black dreads with beads, go on a quest, and become a fearsome pirate. That was before the crews of *Felicity* and *Malice* had become embroiled in a war against each other, a war that had turned into something much darker. A battle against an evil force that would soon overtake the realm unless *Felicity* stopped it. The captain of *Malice* had taken her prisoner and cut her strands of beads away. And Ebba now felt she'd been on enough quests to last her until her thirties, when she probably wouldn't even want to do them anyway. Now that filling her dreads and embarking on a dangerous quest were no longer burning ambitions, Ebba had found her mind turning to other things.

"You don't feel pressured into dressing a certain way because of the other young women, do you?" Verity had turned from the mirror and stood with her hands on her hips.

"No." Ebba drew the word out, and then frowned. "I don't know." Ebba had been staying away from their Exosian guests where possible, and she'd be the first to admit that they brought a whole heap of new ideas and customs with them, most of which were very unsettling—including what a person should have done by a certain age and how they should behave.

The healer gestured to her lavender frock. "I'm wearing this because I like to dress up every now and again."

"It be a pretty dress," Ebba said.

The ex-soothsayer was the exact opposite to Ebba's looks. Ebba had the dark skin of a tribesperson, and moss-green eyes she'd inherited from her mother, chieftess of the Pleo tribe. She supposed Verity and she were both light-framed, but the ex-soothsayer was a head taller. And where Verity's hair usually hung in a rippling curtain of gleaming gold down her back, Ebba's fell in thick, ebony dreads that hung to just below her armpits, and was usually held back with a bandana over her forehead.

Verity sat next to her. "What I'm saying is that you

shouldn't wear clothing or change who you are for anyone but yourself. Do you want to wear a dress?"

"Aye, I do," Ebba confessed. She'd always liked accessories and clothing. She'd hated the dresses Sherry the brothel matron had put her in—the boning had dug in something wicked. And Ebba had mostly pretended not to like when Marigold dressed her back on Exosia. She wasn't mad-keen on how dresses restricted her movement and breathing, but for times like this, for a *celebration* when she didn't need to run for her life or dash up the rigging, she was beginning to think that maybe they were okay.

"Then wear one."

Ebba peeked up at the healer through her lashes. "Ye really don't think anyone will notice?"

The healer's face was completely smooth. "No. I assure you they won't."

A grin curved her lips, then faded. "Hey, Ver?"

"Don't call me that."

"Why not?" Ebba rolled her eyes. "Verity, do ye have another dress?"

The healer arched a brow. "No, but I might be able to rustle up a little something. Did you have anything in mind?"

Ebba spent a portion of every day deciding what she'd wear. For the last week, she'd been thinking up exactly what kind of dress she'd wear, *if* she ever wore one. "Aye, I do."

29413099R00170

Made in the USA
Lexington, KY
29 January 2019